I0748727

WHAT
Love
LEAVES BEHIND

Also by Marian L. Thomas

Saving Raine
Someone Like Me

MARIAN L. THOMAS

www.lbpublishingbooks.com

L.B Publishing
3343 Peachtree Rd NE
Ste. 145-712
Atlanta, GA 30326

Printed in the United States of America

Cover design by Yago Domingues
For information about special discounts for bulk purchases, please contact L.B Publishing

Library of Congress Control Number: 2025918408

What Love Leaves Behind / Marian L. Thomas - 1st. Ed.
ISBN- 979-8-9893979-3-8
First Trade Paperback Printing: March 2026
1. FICTION / Women. 2. FICTION / Family Life / General. 3. FICTION / Domestic Life. 4. FICTION / African American & Black / Women

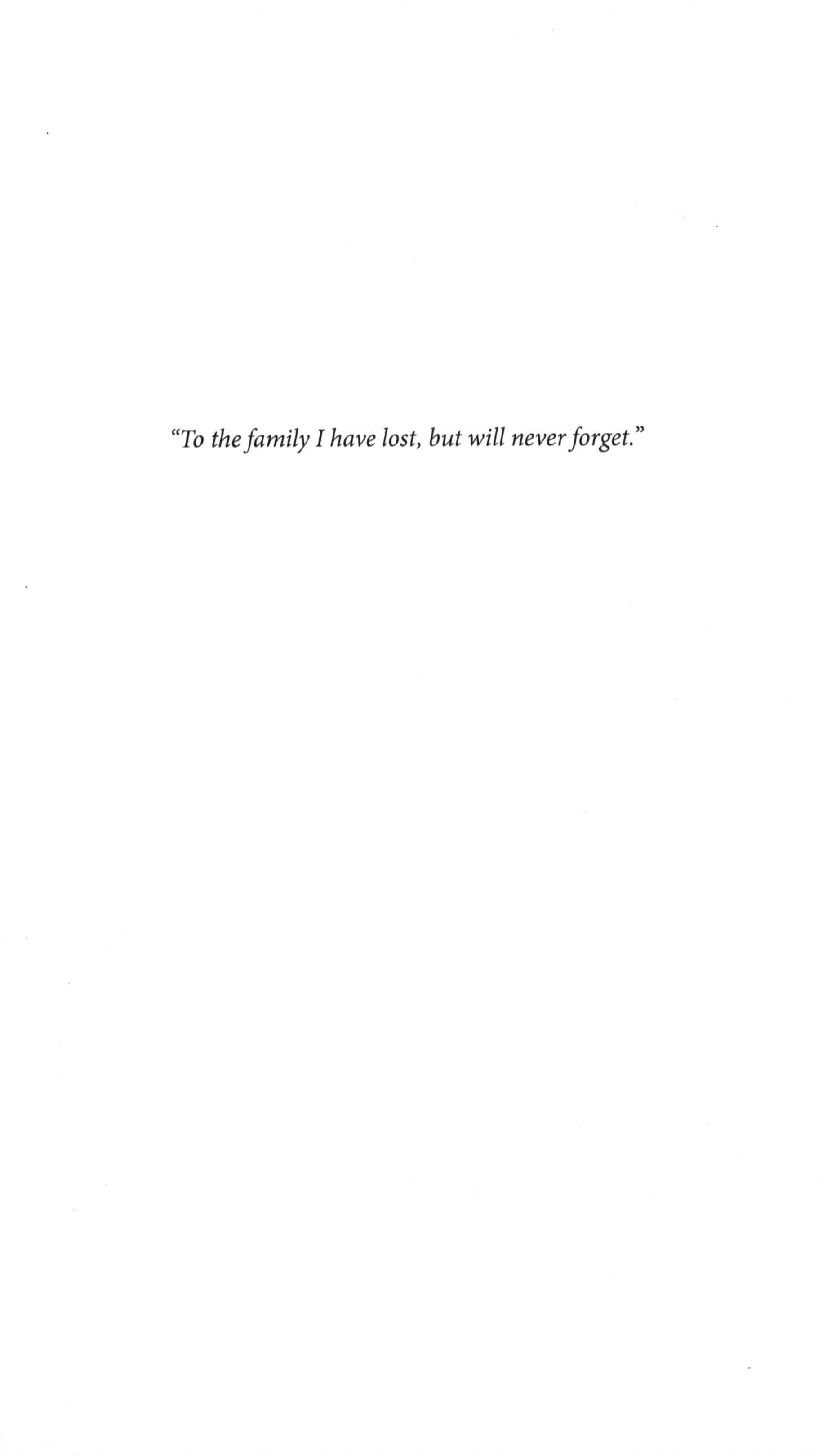

"To the family I have lost, but will never forget."

Acknowledgments

I am eternally grateful to my husband for the endless love and support you shower me with. Your encouragement, patience, and belief in me make this journey possible, and I couldn't ask for a greater partner in life.

To my mother—thank you for reminding me to keep going and for being my constant source of strength and inspiration.

To my mother-in-law—thank you for celebrating every milestone with such joy and enthusiasm.

To my sister—thank you for your unwavering support, even though I made you wait to read this book. Love you!

To my family, near and extended—thank you for carrying my dream as if it were your own. Your belief in me keeps me smiling.

And to my dear friends—thank you for walking beside me with laughter, encouragement, and love.

Finally, to every reader and book club who finds pieces of themselves in these pages—thank you for letting my words become part of your story.

"You can't rewrite the past, but you can choose the courage to shape tomorrow into something worth holding onto."

— Marian L. Thomas

WHAT *Love* LEAVES BEHIND

Prologue

THE CLOCK ON THE stark white wall read 10:05 p.m., its steady ticking muffled beneath the relentless storm outside.

Turning her head, the young woman caught sight of the rain streaking down the window, each droplet racing to meet the earth, as if mirroring the urgency inside her petite body.

The doctor's voice sliced through the haze, firm yet insistent, urging her to push.

The woman's insides burned, fire coursing through all her veins, every nerve alight as the moments dragged on, each one heavier than the last.

Tears began streaming down the sides of her face, soaking the pillow, mingling with the sweat that was pouring from her temples.

Then she screamed, her youthful voice primal and raw, a sound that seemed to erupt from somewhere deep and unrecognizable. And then, she did as she was told: she turned her gaze back to the clock and pushed with everything she had left.

Life.

The young woman was bringing life into the world.

That was all that mattered.

The sound of the baby's cry pierced the air like the lightning bolt outside, splitting open the night sky—fierce, defiant, and unapologetically alive.

It was as if the child had arrived with a purpose, demanding her voice be heard.

For one breathless moment, the chaos in the room stilled, everyone transfixed by the raw power of that sound, a declaration of life that silenced everything else.

"It's a girl," someone announced, their voice wavering with relief and awe. The words drifted to the mother, wrapping themselves around her heart like a warm blanket.

She longed to see her baby, to hold her, yet her body felt distant as if no longer belonging to her. The room blurred at the edges, the bright lights fading into something more transcendent.

"Bring her to me," her weak voice whispered at last, barely more than the merest huff of air. And then, the baby was there, cradled, a tiny, perfect human swaddled in a soft pink blanket.

Her hazel eyes locked onto those of the mother, the child's own wide and unblinking, as though already searching for answers, already knowing what her mother had done.

There was strength in the newborn's gaze, a raw intensity that held her mother captive even as she felt her grip on the world beginning to loosen and let go.

"My little Storm," she murmured, the name slipping out as naturally as the tears slipping down her reddened cheeks. "You are my strength, my reason. Everything …"

The newborn's tiny fingers curled around hers, and the weight of her felt like the most beautiful thing this mother had ever held.

The woman's heart swelled enough to shatter and rebuild a thousand times in the space of a single moment, the edges of the room fading further as her body gave way to exhaustion.

Her breaths were starting to come shallower, softer, barely audible.

But still she could hear the infant's cries, her fierce, wild cries that lit up the darkness closing in fast. "Life. I brought life into the world," she uttered, her voice wavering, rising above the pains now threatening to consume her.

He'd said the baby would never see the sun.

But the mother had won.

A slow and weary smile spread across her face.

Her child would be safe; she had made sure of it.

That was enough.

She could take that with her, could let go of her now.

Looking once more into her child's fresh eyes, the mother's lips moved ever so gingerly.

The words *forgive me* slipped off her tongue, soft and delicate as a whisper, carried away into the stillness of a night she would never see again.

They dissolved like smoky wisps into the air.

Chapter One

"ALL THAT CHILD DOES is cry," Etta muttered, her voice heavy with exhaustion as she pulled out the chair behind the nurse's station and sank heavily into it.

Her feet had been throbbing with each step, a relentless reminder of the ten long hours she'd been working without so much as a few minutes' break. Her stomach was growling in protest too, a sharp pang drawing her attention to the brown paper bag sitting untouched on the counter.

Her husband had packed her favorite, just as he always did.

Two peanut butter and jelly sandwiches, perfectly balanced on soft white bread, each slice lightly sprayed with Pam butter spread and toasted to golden perfection. She could almost taste the sweet and savory comfort of them, a small kindness from him to get her through another day.

But "almost" wasn't enough.

Her appetite had been buried beneath the relentless cries echoing through the ward, sharp and unyielding, piercing through every attempt at a moment of peace.

With a sigh, she extended her hand toward the bag and glanced down the hall. The baby's wail continued, fierce and mournful, refusing to be ignored.

"Poor thing," May said as she placed her clipboard on the counter, her voice softer, her eyes flicking toward the nursery. "It's not easy, coming into the world that way. She's going to have a hard time in life because of it."

Etta nodded, her fingers pausing just before they could dip into the bag for her sandwich. She knew all too well what May meant.

It seemed those cries were carrying more than the usual hunger or discomfort of a newborn; they already bore the weight of grief and loss, pain unable to be soothed with a bottle or lullaby.

And this child, this baby girl with her stormy hazel eyes, had already witnessed more darkness in her few days of life than most people would encounter in a lifetime.

"Where are you headed?" Etta asked, her voice quieter now.

"To check on our new father," May said with a sigh.

Etta finally pulled her sandwich out of the bag, but the thought of what that father was going through caused her to put it back. Her appetite was gone.

"Can't remember a time when we lost two moms like this," Etta murmured, shaking her head.

May nodded in agreement, the shadow of sadness crossing her face. "I know. And he won't even look at the child," she said.

"I'm sure it's just hard," Etta said gently. "He's just lost his wife."

"I know, but that baby boy needs his father regardless. You know what I mean?"

"Yes, I do, but give the father time. It's just that right now, he's in grief, and it's all way too raw. He'll come around, you'll see."

"I hope so. In the meantime, I'm going to put that beautiful baby boy next to yours. Maybe they can help each other."

"They're babies," Etta said with a faint laugh. "They have no idea what's really going on. Which is a very good thing in this case."

May's eyes were sad and thoughtful when she replied, "I don't agree, though I wish I did. I believe it's like my mama always told me growing up—that pain knows pain. And it's shown in the fact that when twins are born, they can't stand to be separated, right from birth. A lot of hospitals wrap twins together for that reason, you know."

Etta considered that, her expression turning pensive. She leaned back in her chair, the corners of her mouth lifting slightly despite the heaviness in her heart. "You've never spoken the truth more than just now."

Chapter Two

THE MOONLIGHT STREAMED INTO the room, casting a silver glow over the hospital bed, the one that only hours earlier had held the love of his life.

"Mr. Johnson, do you mind if I take your baby boy to the nursery?" May asked softly, stepping into the room with the bereaved man. Her voice was gentle, but it did little to mask the ache she felt as she looked at him. The depth of loss on his face was almost too much to bear.

Darren barely registered her presence. He couldn't take his eyes off the hospital bed, its emptiness a cruel reminder of what had been taken—stolen—from him.

His wife of only five years.

His mind kept replaying the moments: her laughter that morning; the way her hand had rested protectively on her belly; the way she'd smiled at him when they'd walked into the hospital together, hopeful, excited.

And then the screaming.

The endless blood, the frantic hands, the shouted orders.

The pallid stillness that had followed.

"Mr. Johnson?" May tried again, her voice firmer this time but still kind.

He blinked, slowly turning his head away from the bed, as if it cost him something.

It took a moment for her words to sink in.

"The baby," he said hoarsely. "You mean my … my son."

"Yes, your son," she replied, stepping closer, resting a warm hand on his shoulder. "It might help to get some rest. I'll bring him back to you later, whenever you're ready."

Darren nodded, the motion slow and mechanical, as if he hadn't managed to take in the words she had said. He simply watched, going through the motions as May moved toward the bassinet.

Every time he thought about his son, all he could see was his wife's face—how she had fought, how her eyes had glimmered with tenderness even through the pain, how she had left him alone to figure out the rest.

As May gently lifted the baby, Darren turned his eyes back to the bed, unable to stop himself. His chest felt hollow, his grief a weight pressing down on him, making it hard to breathe.

He wasn't aware of the door clicking shut behind her.

All he could hear was the echo of his wife's voice on replay.

"It's okay, Darren," she'd said just before everything had fallen silent. "He'll have you. You'll take care of him. I know you will.

"And I can take that with me.

"I can let go."

Her words lingered in the air, wrapping themselves around him in an embrace that was both comforting and suffocating. So he closed his eyes, letting the moonlight wash over him, a pale reflection of the warmth and joy that had filled this room not so long ago. But in its moonlit glow, he felt the weight of her absence more than ever.

He wasn't sure if he could live up to that promise.

He wasn't sure if he even wanted to.

Chapter Three

"MY HEART JUST BREAKS for that man," May said as she walked into the nursery, cradling the baby boy in her arms. "Mr. Johnson still hasn't moved, you know. He's just sitting in the dark, staring at that bed as if willing her to come back. It's the saddest thing I've ever seen."

Etta looked up from the rocking chair in which she was sitting, a soft sigh escaping her lips. "Tomorrow, the sun will shine, and I know that will give him a measure of strength," she said.

"Yes. My mama always said that tomorrow looks better than today," May said with a hopeful grin as she gently placed the baby into a nearby crib.

"Girl, your mama seems to have had a saying for everything," Etta replied, shaking her head with a small laugh. "Didn't she?"

They both let out a quiet frisson of laughter, a moment of shared levity in an otherwise heavy day. It was all they could do to keep the weight of it all from crushing them completely.

But as the baby boy stirred in his crib, their laughter quickly faded. The room grew still again, the only sound the faint hum of the fluorescent lights above. One of the lights relentlessly flickered as if about to give up and die any second now, just like that man's poor wife.

"I wonder what Mr. Johnson will name him?" May asked softly, her voice carrying a tremor of curiosity as she came over and took a seat.

"I'm sure they must have picked out a name before ..." Etta began. She did not like to complete the sentence, as if not speaking the words somehow made it less distressing.

"I hope so," May said, finishing the thought. Her eyes drifted across the room to the other crib. "I saw you talking to one of our social workers the other day. What are they going to do about your baby girl over there? Storm, right?"

"That certainly is a fitting name for her," Etta said. "She's been keeping up a fuss every day since she got here. In fact, this is the quietest I've seen her." She paused, letting out a weary exhale. "The father is dead."

May covered her mouth in disbelief, her eyes widening. "No ... do they know how he died?"

"I don't know all the details," Etta said, shaking her head slowly. "But they're trying to locate any other family members. If they don't find anyone in the next day or so, CPS is gonna put her in temporary foster care."

May shook her head, a deep sadness settling over her features. Her eyes seemed to drift somewhere far away, as though she was lost in a memory.

Etta glanced over at her, concern flickering across her face. "You okay?"

"Sometimes, the present just has a way of peeking into your past," May said, her voice tinged with an emotion Etta couldn't quite place.

She eyed May quizzically, studying her, her brow furrowing slightly. "What do you mean?"

"Nothing. Just getting lost in my thoughts," May replied, forcing a small, weary smile as her shoulders dropped and she exhaled slowly.

Her attention moved back to Etta, her tone quieter. "That poor child. No mother, and now, no father either. It isn't right. I just pray she's got some family out there."

Etta didn't answer right away.

Her thoughts drifted back to the letter.

She hadn't shared it with May — couldn't bring herself to. She had found it on the floor beside the hospital bed while gathering the young mother's belongings into a plastic bag. The folded paper had been easy to miss, nearly blending into the white tile.

But something about it had made her pause.

It was addressed simply:

To my daughter.

The handwriting had caught her breath — handwritten in a wavering script, the ink pressed hard in some places, faint in others. As if each word had taken effort. As if the woman had forced her hand to keep moving even when her strength was fading.

Etta had held the letter for a moment longer than she should have.

Protocol said not to look.

But something in her — something deeper than protocol — wouldn't let her simply hand it over without understanding the weight of what it carried.

She had read it.

Every word.

Each line had felt like a mother reaching through pain and fear to leave something behind — not just instructions, but love. Protection. Hope. A final act of devotion written in uneven ink.

The memory still pressed against Etta's chest.

She had slipped the letter back into the bag before giving it to the social worker, but its contents stayed with her. They always would.

"It's true, May, it isn't right," she finally said. "Every child deserves a mama and a father, if at all possible."

They sat in silence for a moment, watching the two infants — two tiny lives already shaped by loss and circumstance.

"I wonder," Etta said finally, almost to herself, "if they'll ever know just how much they've already survived."

May nodded, her eyes shining. "I hope the world is kind to them. They deserve that much."

And in the gentle hum of the nursery, hope and heartache lingered side by side — as delicate and fragile as the lives the two women were entrusted to nurture and protect.

Chapter Four

ETTA SAT IN HER car, the window still rolled down, letting in the crisp mid-April air. It carried the faint scent of freshly cut grass and damp earth, the kind of smell that usually made her think of spring, of new beginnings. Tonight, it only made her chest ache.

She stared at her four-bedroom, west suburban home in Maywood, Illinois, its red brick façade quietly nestled between two other houses. They were nearly identical, but the others seemed to be lacking the warmth she had worked so hard to cultivate in her own.

"This neighborhood is perfect for raising children," she remembered the real estate agent saying to her and James. "The schools are good and within walking distance, and there's a park just up the street."

The words had felt so hopeful back then, a promise of a future she was certain they'd have.

The thought didn't bring her its usual comfort. Instead, it reminded her of all the hours they had spent side by side, building a life that suddenly felt incomplete. A marriage full of love, yes—but also full of empty rooms and unasked questions.

Etta leaned her head back against the headrest, her fingers gripping the steering wheel loosely. She could see the faint glow from the kitchen window, the soft yellow light spilling onto the front lawn. James was still up. *Bakers never sleep*, she thought with a faint, tired smile.

She imagined him inside—scribbling notes for a new recipe that might or might not ever make it onto the menu. He poured himself into his work the way she poured herself into other people's children.

She rested her forehead briefly against the steering wheel.

Was this fair to him?

The question lingered, heavy and unwelcome.

Then she saw Storm's face in her mind—tiny, fragile, alone. A baby who had already lost everything before she'd even had a chance to begin.

Etta drew in a slow breath, letting the cool air fill her lungs, anchoring herself.

It's time, she told herself.

That little girl is worth the fight.

"Etta Harris, you can't be serious."

"James, you've always known that I wanted children," she replied, her tone calm but unshakable.

"We're too old for that now," he said, shaking his head. "We've built a life already, Etta. Changing everything now—" He stopped himself and rubbed his temples. "It sounds absurd."

"Actually, we're not that old," she countered. "The last time I checked, thirty-nine and forty-two wasn't ancient."

James reached for the remote and turned off the television, even though it had already been muted. The sudden quiet felt louder than the noise had. He leaned back in his chair, dragging a hand down his face.

"Etta, it's not just about our age," he said after a moment. "It's about time. Our time. Raising a child is a lot. And adopting?" He shook his head. "That's not something you just decide overnight. It's a lifelong commitment."

His words hung in the air, heavy and deliberate, but Etta's expression didn't waver.

She crossed her arms, her eyes narrowing slightly.

"I'm not saying it's a decision to take lightly, James. But I also know what I want. And I want to give a child—that child—a chance of a better life."

James looked at her, the weight of her words settling heavily over him. "You mean Storm."

"Yes," she said simply, her voice controlled. "Storm."

The name lingered in the air between them, a spark of possibility crackling amidst the tension. James let out another sigh, leaning forward to rest his elbows on his knees, his hands clasped.

"I knew there was a reason you'd been talking about her these last three nights," he said quietly, his eyes searching hers for an answer he wasn't sure he wanted to read in them. "Did you even realize you were doing it?"

Etta said nothing, meeting his eyes, her resolve evident in the silence between them. She was not intending to back down, not even slightly. This was too important to let it go.

"You really think we're the right people for this?" he asked at last, giving in to the oppressive silence and her sad, fixated look. His voice was laced with doubt, fear creeping in.

"Yes," she said without hesitation. "I do think so. I know so."

Her expression softened, and she reached out to place a hand on his, her fingers warm against his cool, calloused skin, roughened from years of kneading dough and working with flour.

His palms bore the faint texture of repetitive use, firm yet capable of surprising gentleness. He kept his nails trimmed short but never pristine, often marked by the faint shadows of dough or flour that persistently lingered no matter how much he scrubbed.

Etta looked down at the hands she had loved for over ten years by this time.

Hands that spoke of dedication, their movements always confident yet deliberate. Hands of someone who created not just food, but comfort, warmth, and stability for those around him.

She found herself studying his strong jawline and smooth, deep-brown complexion, a striking complement to his piercing, thoughtful eyes that always seemed to be quietly observing and understanding the world around him. She admired his neatly cropped hair and well-groomed appearance, a reflection of the attention to detail he carried into every corner of his life, whether he was perfecting a recipe at work or sharing a quiet moment at home.

"I know we are the right people for this, James," she said quietly. "And deep down, I think you do too. At least, I believe there's a reason why you haven't even said no to it yet."

James hesitated, his brow furrowing. "Etta, look … I don't know if—"

"We can do this," she interrupted, her voice rising despite her effort to stay calm. "They're going to put that sweet baby girl in a temporary foster home—if not tomorrow, then the next day. I can't just sit back and let that happen. I can't."

Her voice cracked.

"Calm down," he said gently, though his words carried weight. "I'm not saying no. I'm saying—" He exhaled. "I'm saying I'm scared of what this will do to us."

The honesty in his voice caught her off guard.

She drew in a shaky breath. "I'm scared too," she admitted softly. "But I'm more scared of doing nothing. Of letting her go and wondering for the rest of my life if we could've changed her story."

"But there are so many kids in foster care," he said carefully. "You surely don't think foster homes are all bad, do you? A lot of kids make it through just fine."

"Survive, yes," she replied. "Thrive? Not always. Some come out damaged. Feeling unwanted. Insecure. Struggling."

James met her eyes, and something flickered there—something he quickly tried to bury.

Her words scraped against truths he rarely allowed himself to touch.

How could he tell her that he had never truly wanted children? That part of him had been content with the life they had—predictable, quiet, safe? How could he admit that this conversation felt like the ground shifting beneath his feet?

Etta's passion, her unwavering conviction, pushed against him like a rising tide. And yet, the words he needed to say—desperate to say—were somehow still refusing to come.

Chapter Five

"THANK YOU FOR MY PB&J sandwiches, by the way," Etta said, changing the conversation to give James the time it was clear he needed.

He simply nodded, his attention fixed on the notepad and pen resting on the table. When he picked them up and began to write, she knew he wasn't jotting down bread recipes but instead making a list of pros and cons to help sort out his thoughts.

It was what he did when faced with a tough decision, and she respected him for it.

Without another word, Etta quietly walked out of the living room and into their bedroom.

Her reflection in the dresser mirror showed exhaustion in her expressive eyes—but beneath it all, there was a flicker of determination she couldn't hide.

The familiar creak of their bed greeted her as she sank onto it, a soft exhale leaving her lungs.

Carefully, she removed the gold pin she often wore and her small gold pendant earrings, placing them on the nightstand beside her.

Removing her shoes, she leaned back and began rubbing her tired feet, her graceful hands working at the ache in her heels—hands as familiar with offering comfort as they were with receiving it.

She'd been a nurse for over nineteen years by this time, ten of them spent caring for other mothers' babies, soothing their cries, and offering comfort with her calm, empathetic demeanor and sharp instincts.

Despite the weariness settling into her bones, there was an undeniable strength in her movements, a quiet resilience that had carried her through life's challenges time and again.

Finally, she thought, her smile widening as her hands worked at the ache in her heels. *It's finally going to be my turn.*

Her eyes drifted to the picture on her nightstand, a family photo taken when she was just a girl. Her parents, all smiles, held their arms wrapped protectively around her. They were the center of her world back then, and she couldn't help but wonder what her own life would have looked like if they hadn't adopted her. How would she ever have found her way?

They had never told her, not in so many words, but she had always known.

She had pieced it together from whispers and from mismatched dates, and from the curious fact that all her childhood photos seemed to start at the age of two. No baby photos.

She never told them that she knew.

And for her, it didn't really matter. She had never felt a pressing desire to find her birth parents. No, Robert and Jennifer Blackwell were all she had ever needed as parents.

They had given her comfort and security, and a home filled with warmth and love, and all good things. In her heart, they were unquestionably her parents, no qualifiers needed.

And she had never told James about it, either.

The secret felt fragile, threadlike, delicate but unbreakable, tying her past to her present.

And now, it also tethered her to a future she so desperately craved.

Maybe now's the time, she thought, lingering on the photo a moment longer. Her parents' faces stared back at her, filled with all the love and certainty that had shaped her life.

Maybe he needs to understand why this means so much to me.

Chapter Six

JAMES LOOKED DOWN AT the notepad. He had only written one thing in each column despite sitting He sat there for such a long time, staring at the lined white paper.

Under Pros, he had written: *It would make Etta happy. Give her what she needs.*

Under Cons, he had written: *It would make my life unpredictable. Take away what I need.*

The stark simplicity of the list—with its glaring contradiction—felt like a betrayal of the complexity swirling inside him.

This wasn't just about a decision. It was about the delicate balance of his marriage. Taking either route could threaten the life he and Etta had worked so hard to build.

Frustration welled up inside him as he stared at the page.

With a sudden burst of resolve, he ripped off the sheet of paper and tore it into tiny pieces, letting the fragments scatter onto the coffee table.

Sweeping the pieces into his hand, he walked into the kitchen and dumped them into the trash can. Leaning up against the counter, he crossed his arms and glanced at his watch.

It was already 11:00 p.m.

Tomorrow morning, he thought grimly. *She'll be expecting an answer.*

In a way, he was angry with her—angry that she had brought this dilemma into their otherwise peaceful life. But the deeper anger was reserved for himself.

He had seen the shift in her. Over the past three days or so, every sentence that had come out of her mouth had been about that child. Her obsession had grown, consuming her thoughts, her words, and even the quiet moments between them.

And he had said nothing at all about it.

Done nothing.

He had let the irritation simmer inside him and the longing bloom in her. And now, look what it had created.

Back in the living room, he looked around. A softly lit lamp illuminated the neatly arranged furniture. The coffee table was pristine. No clutter. No chaos.

He loved how Etta kept a clean, orderly home despite the long hours she worked at the hospital.

A child will change all that.

A child will change everything.

A child could ruin us.

Etta felt the covers being pulled back as James climbed into bed. She wanted to say something but knew it was best to keep quiet.

She turned over and wrapped her arm around her husband, pulling herself as close to him as she could. The faint trace of his cologne lingered, comforting and familiar.

He kissed the top of her hand, his lips warm and tender against her skin.

"I remember when we first met," James said, his voice just above a whisper.

Etta still kept quiet, listening.

"You were standing on the platform, waiting for the train, and I saw you the moment I hit the top step. You had on a brown trench coat over your nurse's uniform, and the wind was blowing through your hair like one of those scenes from the mushy movies you always watch."

Etta let out a small, quiet laugh, the sound muffled against his chest.

"I thought to myself," James continued, "there's no way someone like her is gonna give me the time of day. But then you looked at me and smiled, and I swear my heart just about stopped."

Etta tilted her head up slightly, catching his expression in the dim light filtering through the curtains. "You never told me that part," she whispered.

"Well," James said with a slight smirk, "figured I'd keep a few surprises up my sleeve for nights like this."

Etta gave a low laugh again, pressing herself even closer. Whatever tomorrow held, she let herself bask in the warmth of this moment, tucked safely in his arms.

"I love you, James."

"I love you too, Etta Harris," he said softly, his voice carrying so many unspoken emotions. He closed his eyes, but sleep didn't come easily because tomorrow, he knew, their lives—and their marriage—were going to change, in ways neither of them could fully predict.

Etta lay awake long after James's breathing had finally evened out beside her.

She stared at the ceiling, tracing invisible cracks in the darkness, listening to the familiar rhythm of his sleep. For years, that sound had meant safety. Tonight, it sounded like a countdown.

She turned onto her side, careful not to wake him.

If James says no ...

What happens to our marriage if I keep pushing?

The questions circled her mind like a slow, relentless tide.

She loved her husband. She loved their life. The quiet dinners. The shared routines. The comfort of knowing what tomorrow would look like.

But for the first time in years, comfort felt smaller than her longing.

Storm's tiny face filled her thoughts.

Not just a baby.

A beginning.

A chance to be brave in a way she had never had to be before.

Etta pressed her lips together, blinking back tears.

She reached out in the dark, resting her hand lightly against his arm. Solid. Warm. Real.

"I don't want to lose you," she whispered.

But as she turned over and closed her eyes, another truth rose just as clearly:

I don't want to lose Storm either.

Chapter Seven

MAY WALKED THROUGH THE doors of Providence Ridge Hospital at 7:00 a.m., thirty minutes before her shift started, with two cups of coffee in her hands. One for Etta. One for Mr. Johnson.

Her short, pixie-style hair was neatly styled, soft coils framing her face. Gold hoop earrings caught the morning light as she moved with purpose, her confident stride matched by the warmth in her deep brown eyes. A faint trace of her signature red lipstick added a bold note to her polished appearance—a quiet signal of the strength she carried into every room.

I'm going to give him this coffee, then I'm going to bring his son to him and put that little boy in his arms. As my mama would say, enough is enough. He's got to see how much his little boy needs him.

She tightened her grip on the cups, her resolve solidifying.

Tough love. That was exactly what Mr. Johnson needed.

This wouldn't be easy. Grief had a way of swallowing even the strongest hearts. But it was time—time for him to stop retreating into his insular pain and start becoming the father his son so desperately needed him to be.

And deserved him to be.

That was what she'd had to do ten years ago.

May placed both cups of coffee on the nurse's station and took a seat behind the counter.

Her thoughts traveled back to that day.

The day she had lost her husband.

She had been in labor for twelve long hours when they came and told her about the accident. The words had felt surreal, as though they were meant for someone else—spoken in a room she would never remember, by a voice she would never be able to describe.

An hour later, she was holding their baby girl in her arms, her heart breaking and swelling at the same time. Grief and love had collided in that moment, leaving her breathless and unsure how to move forward.

But she had done it.

Because she had to.

And even now, years later, there were mornings when the ache rose up without warning—not sharp like it used to be, but deep. A reminder. A quiet insistence that love didn't disappear just because someone did. That some losses never truly settled. They simply learned how to wait.

May blinked the memory away and reached for one of the cups, leveling herself.

And now, she was determined to help Mr. Johnson navigate the same road she had once walked alone.

With a deep breath, she headed toward the hospital room.

May opened the door quietly.

There he was, sound asleep on the small sofa pushed up against the window. The morning light filtered through the blinds, casting faint patterns on his face. Beside him, on the edge of the cushion, lay his wife's wedding ring, its gold band glinting faintly in the soft light.

"Mr. Johnson, it's Nurse Jones," she said softly, her voice gentle as she stepped closer, the aroma of coffee filling the room. "I brought you some coffee," she said, a little louder this time.

She was hoping the sound would rouse him.

He didn't move.

She hesitated briefly before reaching out and giving his shoulder a quick shake.

His red and swollen eyes opened slowly, blinking as he struggled to focus.

May took a couple of steps back, clutching the coffee cup, watching silently as he adjusted his tailored black suit, smoothing out the slight creases in his white collared shirt.

His fingers were trembling. He ran a hand over his clean-shaven head, his movements slow and deliberate, as if trying to pull himself back together.

His dark brown eyes carried a weight of thoughtfulness, but she could see the emotional journey he was navigating.

His jawline was sharp and defined, handsomely framed by a neatly trimmed goatee that added just the right touch of refinement to his appearance.

"I guess I should have gone home," he finally said, his voice hoarse.

She handed him the coffee cup.

"In the decade I've been a nurse, I've seen many fathers sleep on that sofa," she replied softly.

"Oh? Did they lose their wives too?" His tone was edged with grief and bitterness.

May's eyebrow lifted, then dropped just as quickly. Her silence and pursed lips spoke volumes, her eyes filled with a quiet understanding that words couldn't convey.

He cleared his throat and looked down at the cup in his hands.

"Look, I'm sorry," he muttered, his voice softening. "It was rude of me, and you didn't deserve me being unpleasant. Thank you for the coffee."

"I thought you might need it before I bring your son in this morning," May said matter-of-factly. "And I understand when you say things like that."

His eyes drifted to the bed, lingering on the emptiness as if it could somehow ease the pain he carried. May noticed the tears beginning to well. Usually, a man about to shed tears would turn away or move from the scene under some excuse or other, embarrassed by his perceived weakness.

And she would normally remove herself from the man's proximity. But not right now. There was something she needed to say to him first; otherwise, she might never utter the words.

"Mr. Johnson, I know this is a difficult time for you," she began carefully, "but you have a beautiful baby boy who really wants to be with his father."

"You know?" he asked, his voice unsteady. He placed the coffee cup down on the sofa and looked up at her, his expression filled with both confusion and pain.

May took a step back, giving him space. "Yes, I do."

"How?" His voice sharpened, edged with bitterness. "How do you know?"

She could hear the anger simmering beneath his words, but she refused to let it deter her. She met his reaction calmly.

"I'm not standing here, Mr. Johnson, acting like I can wear the same size shoe as you," she said. "But I can tell you this—ten years ago, I wore my own."

His expression shifted, the bitterness giving way to curiosity.

"I gave birth to my daughter only an hour after finding out that my husband had been killed in a tragic work-related accident. He worked in a warehouse. One of the machines malfunctioned."

May continued, her voice holding firm despite the burden of the memory.

"I know how it feels to hold life in your hands while you're mourning what you've lost. And I know how hard it is to take that first step forward. But you must. Not just for your son's sake, but for your own," she said firmly.

He glanced at the bed again, his shoulders sagging. "I don't think I can."

"You can," May replied, her tone reassuring.

"She told me to take care of him," his voice cracked. "Before she died. She said it with such confidence. But right now, I can't even take care of myself, let alone raise a child on my own."

May's expression softened as she stepped closer.

"You're stronger than you think, Mr. Johnson. And finding the strength doesn't mean doing it all perfectly, you know. It means taking one step at a time, even when it feels impossible, even when you're broken. Day by day. You can try to do that, can't you? For the boy … your boy."

"You don't understand!" His eyes were looking up, imploring. "I don't honestly think I can. All this feels impossible. Just breathing feels impossible. I don't see a way."

His voice was thick with fear and pain.

"That feeling isn't going to go away for a while," May said, her tone still gentle but truthful. "I'd be lying to both you and to myself if I said it would. Some days, it will feel like it's suffocating you. Like the impossible is pulling you under and drowning you."

She paused, her eyes softening again as she searched for the right words.

"But then, there will be days when you'll look into your son's eyes and see her—see pieces of her smile, her strength, her love—and that will give you what you need to get through. That will lift you out of the waters of the impossible. I promise."

She could see the doubt etched in the corners of his eyes.

"Do you mind if I sit down?" she asked.

He nodded and shifted closer to the wall, giving her space on the small sofa.

"My closest friend, Etta Harris, will tell you that I quote from my mama a lot. Probably too much." She smiled gently at him. "But that's because I didn't always listen to her when I should have. I came to appreciate all the things she used to say to me only after she was gone. That's my shame to bear. Don't let not being in your son's life be yours. Do you understand what I mean, Mr. Johnson?"

He nodded slowly, and she caught sight of it from the corner of her vision.

"Call me Darren," he said quietly. "And yeah, I do understand. But understanding and doing are two very different things." He hesitated, his hands gripping the coffee cup tightly. "Do you want to know what my shame is?"

"Not wanting to look at your son?" she asked softly.

A tear slipped down his cheek, and May felt a deep respect for him.

Few men would sit and cry in front of a woman, let alone a stranger. That's why she knew he would be a great father. He just had to see it in himself—and to believe it.

"That too, I suppose," he admitted, his voice cracking again. "But … the day my wife told me she was pregnant, I pretended to be excited because it was what she wanted. I knew she wouldn't be happy until we had a house full of children."

"You didn't want children?"

"It wasn't that," he said, shaking his head. "I really did want them. I wanted them with her. But the doctor had told us that because of her heart condition, there'd be serious risks. In my shame, I tried to convince her not to have the baby."

He paused, the memory visibly weighing on him.

"She didn't speak to me for a week. Worst week of my life. Not hearing her voice—it brought me to my senses. Then, I just had to pray the doctor would be wrong in our case, that my wife would make it through the delivery. Those things, the bad things … Well, they happened to other people, not to us. They were just numbers in statistics, and I couldn't see how they mattered."

He dropped his eyes to the floor, shoulders sagging. "We both know how it all turned out."

May nodded slowly, her own heart breaking even more for him.

"I'm so sorry, Darren. But you're still here. And your son needs you. That's how you honor her. That's how you pass on the love she left behind for you, and for your son."

She paused.

"Let your son see her through your memories. It's the only way he'll ever know the woman who loved him so much she was willing to give her life to bring him into this world."

She let her words linger for a moment before adding softly, "I'll go get him, shall I?"

Darren nodded in agreement, his sad expression shifting ever so slightly, as if a small piece of hope had begun to find its way through the grief.

Chapter Eight

DARREN SAT ON THE faux leather sofa, his focus fixed on the bassinet in the corner of the room. The quiet hum of the fan above seemed to amplify the silence, filling it with memories he couldn't escape. He thought back to the hours it had taken to assemble a similar crib at home.

It wasn't the work that had taken so long—it was getting started.

He rubbed his head and let out a long, regretful sigh, his chest tightening as his eyes drifted to the pale-yellow walls. They reminded him of the time he and Michelle had argued over the color for the baby's room. She had wanted something bright and cheerful, while he had pushed for more earth tones. In the end, they'd settled on yellow, a quiet compromise that felt like the best of both worlds. Only it had taken him months to finally paint it.

Then there'd been the two-month project to put the baby's dresser together.

Michelle had always demanded to know why everything she asked of him took so long. She had once asked him—directly, pointedly—why it always took her persistence or her tears to spur him into action. Hadn't he also wanted the best for their baby?

The question still echoed.

A lump formed in his throat.

He'd give anything for another chance.

Another chance to get it right, he thought, as sadness overwhelmed him.

Still, even now, he wanted to delay.

"You ready?" May's voice broke through his thoughts, firm but soft. She stepped into the room, cradling the baby in her arms, her expression warm and encouraging.

Darren stood up, his movements slow, hesitant. His eyes fixed on his son. "I have to be, right? I mean, that's the point of all this."

May smiled gently as she crossed the room. "Sometimes, being ready isn't about knowing what to do. It's just about taking the next step." She gave him a wink. "And for the record, that's a quote by me, not my mama. But what I mean is take it one moment at a time."

A small smirk formed at the corners of Darren's mouth, a flicker of warmth breaking through his grief. May carefully handed the baby to him, her movements deliberate but kind, then stepped back, clasping her hands lightly in front of her.

She watched silently, her eyes filled with quiet encouragement.

"Did you and your wife give him a name?"

Darren looked up at her, his eyes heavy with emotion.

There was such a struggle etched in the corners, the internal battle he was fighting. He shifted slightly, wanting to hand the baby back to her.

May felt her own heart pounding.

Tomorrow, he would have to take his son home.

Hospital policy.

Unavoidable.

She slowly placed her hands behind her back, her warm smile softly encouraging him to find the strength she knew he had buried beneath the agony.

This was his moment, and she wouldn't let him walk away from it.

Darren let out a weary smile, but he noticed the subtle gesture. "His name is Isaiah," he finally said.

May's shoulders relaxed. "Hi there, Isaiah," she said, stepping close enough to touch the baby's tiny hand. "What a strong name for such a little boy. It's the perfect name for you, little man."

Darren also looked down at his son. "It's amazing how he looks like he's been on this earth for months, not just two days." He paused, the weight of the moment slipping into his tone. "I wish Michelle could have gotten a chance to hold him."

"He's a handsome little thing," May said, her eyes warm as she watched the connection forming between father and son. Darren took a deep breath, his eyes lingering on Isaiah.

"You know, when I took the bar, I thought that was a defining moment in my life. When I made partner at thirty, the youngest to ever do so at my firm, then I thought that was a defining moment. When I married my wife, that seemed to be a defining moment for both of us."

He paused, his voice growing quieter. "But this moment—this moment isn't defining. It's becoming."

May understood.

Darren wasn't just holding his son—he was becoming a father.

Chapter Nine

MAY GLANCED AT THE clock hanging above the nurse's station.

It was 7:45, and she still hadn't seen Etta yet.

Etta was never late.

Just as she extended her hand toward the phone to call her, the hospital doors slid open, and Etta strode in.

"You okay, Etta? I was about to put out an APB on you," May said with a slight smile and a hint of laughter, setting the phone back down.

Etta didn't return the smile. She looked more serious than May had ever seen her.

"Girl, what's going on? You and James have a fight or something?" May paused. "I don't even know why I asked that. You and James never fight."

"There's always a first for everything," Etta said quietly. "Isn't that one of your mama's quotes?"

"Something like that," May said, her brow furrowing. "You want to talk about it?"

Etta took a deep breath, then slowly exhaled. Her focus drifted somewhere far away.

"Not now. I need to go check on Storm."

"Storm isn't here," May said carefully, watching Etta's face.

"What do you mean she isn't here?" Etta's voice rose, panic flashing in her eyes.

May stepped closer. "The social worker came about ten minutes ago with CPS. I think they found a temporary foster home for her."

Etta's expression tightened as she gripped the edge of the counter. "I was supposed to be here for her," she whispered, her voice barely audible.

"If it's any consolation, the couple seemed real nice," May offered gently.

"That child needs love, not nice," Etta said firmly, her voice shaking as she turned and made her way toward the nursery.

May stood up and quickly followed her, closing the door behind them.

She watched silently as Etta stood frozen, her eyes fixed on the empty crib.

"I wanted to adopt her."

Etta gripped the sides of the crib, her breath hitching as tears silently fell.

"I'm so sorry, Etta," May said softly, moving closer.

"Hey. It's still possible. You know how these things work. There's a process, but if anyone can give her what she needs, it's you and James."

Etta shook her head. "I waited too long."

May shook her head. "No, Etta, this isn't over. That little girl still has a chance to be with someone who truly loves her."

Etta didn't respond, her attention still fixed on the empty crib.

"Is that what you and James had a fight about?" May asked carefully, her tone gentle but probing. "He doesn't want to adopt her?"

"He didn't say no, but didn't say yes, either," Etta admitted. "I wanted him to be excited."

May could hear the frustration layered in Etta's tone.

She glanced at Isaiah's empty crib, her expression thoughtful. "James just needs time. You can't expect him to jump into a decision that big that fast. Men aren't like us. They need time to process things. We go with what feels right in our hearts. They tend to get stuck in what's logical and practical."

Etta let out a deep sigh, her shoulders dropping. "I just don't know if I have the time to wait for him to figure it out. That little girl needs someone now."

"And maybe," May said gently, "he just needs to see how much this means to you. Sometimes, they just need a little nudge to see what we already know in our hearts."

Etta let out a weary smile. "That you talking or your mama again?"

May laughed softly. "Girl, it's a little bit of both of us."

Etta glanced at the other empty crib. "I guess his father has him now?"

May nodded, her tone reflective. "Isaiah—that's what they named him. Yeah, both of our babies are gone, but not forgotten, right?" She smiled slightly.

Etta placed her hand gently on top of the blanket inside Storm's crib. "I will not forget you. I promise," she whispered. "I will apply to take you. To take you…to your forever home. You'll see."

May stepped closer and gave Etta's hand a gentle squeeze.

"I brought you a coffee from your favorite café. It's waiting for you at the nurse's station—I don't know why, but I figured you might need it this morning."

"I do. Thanks." Etta lingered a moment longer, her hand still resting on the blanket. "I'll keep fighting for her, May. I can't give up."

May gave her hand another squeeze, silently promising she'd fight too.

Later, as May walked past Darren's old room, she thought she heard a baby crying. She stopped, her heart skipping a beat, and turned back around.

Please don't tell me Darren left without his son. Please, don't let that be the case.

She opened the door slowly, the faint squeak of the hinges breaking the stillness of the hallway. The dim overhead light cast long shadows across the room, accentuating the pale-yellow walls and the faint scent of antiseptic that lingered in the air.

Her hand hovered near her chest, bracing herself as if to shield against what she might find.

The soft cries grew louder, tugging at her heart as she moved cautiously toward the bassinet. Her shoes tapped lightly against the tiled floor, the sound echoing faintly throughout the room.

Her hand instinctively went to her heart.

She leaned down, preparing to pick up baby Isaiah, to comfort him—and to explain how much torment his poor daddy was going through, that he didn't have the mental strength to take him home just yet... but he'd be back. The blanket inside the bassinet was slightly askew, and the faint warmth of the baby's presence still lingered.

The sudden creak of the bathroom door made her freeze mid-motion. Darren stepped into the room, his sleeves rolled up and a towel draped over his shoulder.

May's eyes went wide. Startled, she grabbed the side of the bassinet to brace herself. "I thought you two were already gone," she said, her voice betraying relief as she exhaled.

Darren glanced at his son, a glimmer of a smile touching his lips. "No! I'm waiting for my mother," he said. "She's coming to help me take care of this little guy for a while."

A smile spread across May's face, the tension in her chest easing as she straightened.

Darren noticed and murmured a laugh, the sound breaking through the heaviness of the moment. "You thought I'd left him, didn't you?"

"I..." May started, but Darren waved her off, his laugh deepening.

He stepped toward the bassinet, something tender softening his features as he looked down at his son. "Me and this little guy, we're walking out of this hospital together. I can promise you that. Now, what happens afterward, I don't know. But thank goodness for my mother."

May smiled again, her heart welcoming the quiet determination she heard in his voice.

"I'm so pleased—so happy! You've got this, Darren."

"That's what you keep telling me," Darren said, a faint smile at the corners of his mouth.

"Nurses never lie," May replied with a playful smirk.

They both smiled then, the quiet levity briefly lifting the heaviness in the room.

Darren glanced back at Isaiah. "How did you do it? How did you raise your daughter on your own? She's what, ten years old now?"

May felt the tears welling up before she could stop them. A lump formed in her throat as she carefully chose her words. "She would have been ten this year," she said quietly.

A crease formed between Darren's brows, confusion crossing his face at *would have been.* His expression showed he was sorry to have asked.

May exhaled slowly, quieting the tremor in her chest.

"A week after I brought her home, I found out she had congestive heart failure. She was such a sweet child. Quiet, unlike most babies her age. I loved her something fierce."

She caught the hint of panic on Darren's face.

She knew what he was thinking—his wife had died from the same condition.

May reached out, her hand resting lightly on his arm, her tone gentle but firm, grounding him.

"I'm sure your son will grow up to be an amazing lawyer, just like his father. You'll give him a good life, Darren. I know it."

The quiet beeping of a monitor in the hallway filled the silence as Darren nodded slowly, turning his eyes back to his son.

"I'll try," he whispered.

Chapter Ten

JAMES STARED OUT THE window, his hands gripping the armrests of his chair as though they might anchor him in the swirling tide of his thoughts.

The silence of the house pressed on him, broken only by the rhythmic ticking of the wall clock. Time marched on, indifferent to the chaos within him.

The memory of Etta's tears was unbearable. It was the way her voice had trembled when she spoke, the pleading in her eyes, the anguish etched into every line of her face.

He couldn't forget the distraught look she'd given him as she turned away from him that morning.

He replayed the argument in his head for the hundredth time. Her words had been heavy with longing, a yearning he couldn't quite comprehend.

"We could give this child a life, James. A home. Love. Isn't that worth the risk?" she had said, her voice cracking as she held his eyes.

But he hadn't answered her then. He couldn't.

Instead, he had turned away, his silence speaking louder than any words could.

He had thought he was protecting her, protecting them both.

But now, sitting alone, he felt the weight of his choice crushing inward.

"Why can't I see what she sees?" he whispered into the empty room, chastising himself. He ran a hand through his hair, frustration mounting. Was it fear that held him back? Selfishness? Or had wanting to keep life simple made him blind to the kind of hope she carried so fiercely?

James leaned back, closing his eyes as a fresh wave of guilt crashed over him.

How do you mend a heart you've so carelessly broken? He didn't know. But one thing was certain—if he couldn't find the answer soon, he feared he might lose her altogether.

A woman's maternal instincts could sometimes override everything. He should have considered that. But then again, this was not about conceiving their own baby, was it?

It was about a stranger's baby. The two were not the same. So he gave himself a little slack. This wasn't a moment's whim—it was a major, life-changing decision.

He walked into the kitchen and pulled the cabinet open, his eyes scanning the neatly arranged shelves. The familiar sight of his baking supplies greeted him: flour, sugar, spices.

His hand hovered over the flour container, but his thoughts were far from recipes or kneading dough.

He just needed something to do—anything to escape the guilt raging in his chest.

He set the flour on the counter and grabbed the mixing bowl. The act of gathering ingredients felt mechanical, almost comforting in its simplicity. Eggs, butter, vanilla extract—all lined up in a row, as if their quiet order might restore some sense to his chaos.

He thought about his wife and the moments they shared in this kitchen together.

Etta loved baking almost as much as he did. It was their way of showing love, of filling their home with warmth even on the coldest days.

He could picture her standing beside him, humming softly as she watched him work, her face lighting up when he offered her the first bite of whatever he had made.

He cracked an egg into the bowl, watching the yolk spill out.

For a moment, he paused, staring at it. "I don't get it. Why does she want this so badly?" he muttered under his breath.

He couldn't shake the question.

Was he blind to something that was so clear to her?

Or was she asking for too much?

James sighed and reached for the whisk, gripping it tightly as if it might somehow whip clarity into his tangled thoughts.

The rhythmic motion of mixing gave his hands something to do, but it did little to quiet the voice in his head—the one that kept whispering, *what if you're wrong?*

The whisk paused mid-motion, his breath catching as another thought hit him with unexpected force.

But what if she's right?

He set the whisk down slowly, his fingers brushing the edge of the mixing bowl as if grounding himself in its solidity. The kitchen, usually his sanctuary, felt heavier now, laden with unspoken words and unresolved fears.

Yet, amidst the weight, there was a flicker of something else—a small, fragile hope trying to take root.

He thought of Etta again, her face alight with joy whenever she talked about the possibility of adopting Storm.

There. He'd acknowledged her name.

Storm.

It wasn't just a word anymore. It wasn't an abstract idea or a whirlwind of fears he couldn't quite grasp. It was a name, a person—an innocent little girl who had already begun to weave herself into their lives through Etta's love and longing.

The name settled into him, quiet but persistent, like the first drops of rain before the sky opened up.

Had he been so caught up in protecting their current life that he hadn't seen the beauty in what having her in their home could bring? Had he been so blinded by the risks that he'd missed the possibility of something extraordinary?

James leaned against the counter, staring at the half-finished batter in the bowl.

It struck him then that life itself was messy, imperfect—a mix of ingredients that didn't always seem to fit, but could somehow be brought together to create something remarkable.

Maybe Storm wasn't a disruption to their life.

Maybe she was the piece he'd never known was missing.

He took a deep breath, the tension in his chest easing just enough to let the possibility settle in.

Maybe Etta had been right all along.

And maybe, just maybe, it was time to let himself believe in the future his wife had been fighting.

Chapter Eleven

ETTA SAT BEHIND THE computer at the nurse's station, the untouched cup of coffee May had brought sitting next to her. The faint buzz of monitors filled the quiet space, occasionally interrupted by the echo of footsteps or a muffled overhead announcement.

Her fingers rested lightly on the mouse, her eyes fixed on the screen.

With a click, she opened the globe icon, waiting for the familiar chime.

"Welcome to AOL," the computer screen greeted her.

Etta glanced at the coffee, then over her shoulder to ensure no one was watching. Her heart thudded a little harder as she typed her first search.

The Adoption Process.

The words stared back at her, bold and definitive on the screen.

For a moment, her hand hovered over the keyboard, doubt creeping in.

What if James never comes around?

The image of Storm's empty crib flashed through her mind, and with a resolute breath, she clicked Enter.

The search results loaded—lines of text that seemed to hold both answers and more questions.

"Why do you look like you're up to no good?"

Etta jumped slightly, turning to see May pulling up a chair beside her.

"I'm just doing some research," Etta replied, her voice a little too casual as she tightened her grip on the mouse.

May leaned over, her curious eyes darting to the screen.

She reached over and squeezed Etta's hand, her touch warm and reassuring.

"Why don't you just go talk to the social worker? I'm sure they could tell you what steps you need to take to at least get guardianship."

Etta fidgeted with the edge of the keyboard, letting out a slow breath.

Her eyes lingered on the search results.

"It's not that simple, May. What if they say no? What if they don't think James and I are good enough? What if they find family out there and decide Storm belongs with them instead?"

May tilted her head. "If my mama were here, she'd say it sounds like you're inviting the 'what-ifs' and all their cousins to your party before you've even stepped foot into the social worker's office. The worst they can do is give you answers, Etta. And if there's anyone who can fight for that little girl, it's you. You can get the ball rolling... see if this even looks possible."

Etta hesitated, staring down at the coffee cup.

"I don't want to start something James isn't going to let me finish," she said, her voice tight with frustration. "And I'm also so scared that I just won't be considered. Maybe it's easier to think I let the chance get away than to be told I'm not good enough—not at all what they're looking for. So I just won't start anything."

May let out a light laugh, then settled into her chair.

"Why are you laughing?" Etta asked.

"Looks like you're already starting something to me."

They both turned their eyes to the screen, the words **The Adoption Process** glowing back.

"And besides," May said, "why wouldn't they think you could be the perfect mom, the perfect couple? You're young, healthy, and you are deeply committed to Storm."

Etta sighed, her fingers brushing the keyboard. "Yes, I am, but there's James—don't forget. But I feel like if I can just present my case better to him, he'd understand."

Her voice lowered, a whisper slipping out. "May, I was adopted."

May blinked, her expression shifting from curiosity to quiet understanding.

"Oh, Etta…" she began gently, a tear coming to her eye. "Now I understand."

"It's not something I ever talk about," Etta continued. She kept her eyes on the screen, unable to look at May. "But maybe it's why this feels so personal. I know what it's like to have someone step in and change your whole life for the better. And I also know what it feels like to be alone. Not physically on your own, but surrounded by people who aren't yours."

May stayed silent for a moment, letting Etta's words settle.

"If anyone will understand why this is so important to you, it's your James," May said, her tone confident.

Etta lowered her head, her fingers now fidgeting with the edge of the desk.

"No, he doesn't know."

May leaned back in surprise. "What do you mean, he doesn't know? He doesn't know why this is so important to you?"

Etta shook her head slowly. "He doesn't know that I was adopted."

May reeled in surprise. This was one big secret Etta had been keeping.

The overhead speaker crackled to life, announcing a patient's name.

But neither woman moved. Their conversation needed closure.

May exhaled slowly, leaning forward. "I see," she said thoughtfully. She reached out and squeezed Etta's hand again, her touch gentle but insistent. "Well, it sounds like you and he are going to have a major heart-to-heart tonight, right? Promise me you will open up to him?"

Etta hesitated, her lips pressing into a thin line.

May gave her a reassuring look. "Etta, if you want him to see what this means to you, you've got to show him where it's all coming from. He loves you. Let him in. He deserves it."

Etta glanced back at the screen, the weight of her fears still heavy on her chest. But May's words hung in the air, offering her something she hadn't let herself feel yet.

Hope.

"I'll think about it," Etta said softly.

May smiled, the kind of smile that offered no judgment, only encouragement. "That's a start."

In the distance, the faint sound of a baby crying reached their ears. Both women turned toward its source, their attention holding there for a moment before returning to each other.

"Step by step, Etta," May said quietly as they both stood. "You'll get there."

Etta nodded, a flicker of tenacity crossing her face. "I have to."

Chapter Twelve

THE NURSERY DOOR CREAKED open, drawing both Etta's and May's attention.

James stood in the doorway with a bouquet in his hands, his presence filling the frame like a question no one had asked out loud. His eyes swept the room—past the cribs, the shelves lined with neatly folded blankets, the soft animal decals climbing the white walls—before finally landing on Etta.

For a moment, he didn't move.

May did.

She rose with the calm efficiency of someone who had done this a hundred times before and reached for the baby in Etta's arms, murmuring something soothing as she lifted her. The baby's cries didn't stop, but they softened, as if the sound itself had found a gentler place to land.

"I'll take this sweet little thing to her mother," May said, offering Etta a warm smile. Then, with a brief glance at James—polite, knowing—she slipped out.

The door clicked softly behind her.

The room felt suddenly smaller.

Etta sat up straighter in the rocking chair. "What are you doing here?" she asked, surprised but curious. "Why aren't you at work?"

"I took the day off," James replied.

His tone tried to be even, but something in it wavered. He shifted his grip on the flowers, the stems creaking faintly beneath his fingers, and glanced around the nursery again.

"Can I sit?" he finally asked. "Or… maybe go somewhere else to talk?"

"We can talk here," Etta said, watching him cross the room.

He moved carefully, like someone trying not to disturb more than the air. When he sat in the chair across from her, she noticed the slight tremble in his hands as he rested the bouquet on his lap.

"Those for me?" she asked.

James stared down at the flowers, his thumb brushing the edge of a petal as if he needed proof they were real.

"Yeah," he said. "I didn't want to come empty-handed after…"

"After our fight this morning," Etta finished, her voice softening despite herself.

He exhaled, long and controlled, and nodded. "I wouldn't call it a fight exactly. More a difference of—"

"I'm adopted," Etta blurted out.

The words landed between them with the weight of something that had been waiting far too long.

James went still. Not stiff—just… arrested. As if his mind needed a second to catch up to his heart.

"You're… adopted?" he said quietly.

Etta nodded once, the movement small but sure.

James leaned back, eyes fixed on her, breathing slow and measured. "Why didn't you tell me that?"

"I honestly don't know," she admitted, shaking her head. "I was going to. I tried to. But this morning… the conversation took a turn I didn't expect. And the timing didn't feel right." Her throat tightened. "We've never fought like that before. It scared me."

"I know," he said, softer now. He rubbed a hand over his jaw, then let it drop to his lap. "It scared me too."

He looked up, and there was something naked in his gaze—something he rarely allowed anyone to see.

"That's probably why I downplayed it," he continued. "Called it a disagreement." His voice thickened. "I hate fighting with you. You're the person I love more than anything else in this world. I don't want to lose you, Etta."

"There was never a chance of that," she said firmly. "I love you, James."

She paused, letting the silence stretch just long enough for him to hear the truth of it.

"But I need you to understand why this matters to me," she added. "Why I'm not just… chasing a feeling."

James's grip tightened around the bouquet. "Okay."

Etta drew a careful breath, as if stepping onto a bridge she couldn't see the end of.

"I admit, I never had to experience what I can only imagine children who live out their entire lives in foster care have to go through," she began. "But I do know what it's like to have parents who make you feel chosen. Wanted. Fought for."

James watched her intently, his expression shifting—not resistant, not yet softened—just focused.

Etta's eyes stung, but she didn't look away.

"That's what I want for Storm," she said, her voice steadier than she felt. "Not just a home. Not just stability. I want her to grow up with what I had." She touched her chest. "I want her to know she belongs. That she isn't temporary. That she's ours."

James's throat bobbed as he swallowed.

The nursery was quiet except for the distant shuffle of footsteps down the hall and the faint breathing of babies in their cribs.

James's voice was quiet. "I like the way our life fits. The way it… works."

Etta nodded, careful. "I know."

"It's like baking bread," she said gently. "You knead the dough a certain way because you know how it's going to turn out. There's comfort in that predictability."

A small, sad smile touched her lips.

"But raising a child isn't predictable," she added. "It's messy. Uncertain. It will change us. And I believe it will change us for the better." Her voice softened. "I just wish I could help you see that."

James stood up, bouquet in his hands, his knuckles pale around the stems.

"Change has never been easy for me," he said. "But I want you to be happy, Etta. That's what I promised you when I asked you to marry me."

Etta rose, the movement slow and deliberate. She crossed to him, stopping just close enough that he could feel her warmth.

"James, I'm not trying to take away your happiness," she said softly. "I'm trying to share our happiness with a child I believe is worth sharing it with. I hope you can understand that."

"Well…" he said quietly. "Maybe I'm just starting to."

A smile of hope etched across Etta's face as she took the flowers from his hands.

A baby's cry broke the moment.

James glanced toward the sound and smiled softly. "I think that's my cue to let you get back to work. We can talk more about it tonight."

He leaned over and placed a gentle kiss on Etta's cheek. "I'm open to talking it through."

Etta closed her eyes, letting the warmth of his kiss settle into her heart—quiet and hopeful.

"I just saw James walking down the hallway with a smile on his face. You two work things out?" May asked, stepping into the nursery with a stack of papers in her hand.

Etta glanced up from the baby she was rocking, her expression reflective. "I wouldn't say we've worked it all out, but I think he's starting to warm up to the idea of adopting Storm."

"That's good to hear," May said, her tone encouraging. She paused, her eyes shifting to the sleeping baby. A brief silence filled the room before she spoke again, her voice quieter now.

"Can I ask you something?"

"Sure."

May hesitated, glancing down at the papers she was holding. "I can't help but wonder why—"

Etta cut her off, sensing where the question was headed. "Why James and I don't just have children of our own?"

"Something like that," May admitted.

Etta carefully placed the baby back into her crib, smoothing the blanket over her with deliberate care. She lingered a moment, watching the baby's chest rise and fall.

Then she turned back to May.

"I don't know why exactly," Etta said thoughtfully. "James has always known that I wanted children, but we've never really talked about starting a family. We just fell into our routine—our lives. Things were good, so I guess we didn't feel the need to stop and have that conversation. It would happen when the time was right. And the time wasn't right."

"But adopting Storm is something else—something that feels different?" May asked.

Etta looked back at the crib, her expression wistful. "Yes. Now it's different. Maybe I just realized I don't just want biological children—I want to adopt. And I want to adopt Storm. She's here, right now, in front of my eyes—well, you know what I mean."

"I do," May said gently. "And she is a beautiful little girl." She set the papers into the empty crib beside her and met Etta's eyes. "And I could see from the way you held her that you've formed an attachment—no doubt about that. But, Etta, I've seen you hold a hundred babies. Maybe even thousands, if I'm being honest. Why her? Why Storm?"

Etta's voice dropped to a near whisper, her expression clouded with a painful reality.

"Because I think her mother killed her father."

May pressed a hand to her chest. She gasped. "What makes you think that?"

Etta hesitated, her fingers tracing the edge of the crib. "I was gathering the mother's belongings for the social worker when I noticed a letter on the floor. It was addressed, 'To my daughter.' I shouldn't have read it, but I couldn't stop myself."

May's expression tightened with shock. "What did it say? She just… came out and admitted it?"

"In a way, yes," Etta said, her voice quivering. "She wrote, 'His blows landed harder than ever before. He was trying to take you away from me, but I stopped him this time. I stopped him for good. He can't hurt either of us anymore.'"

May took a step back, a crease forming between her brows as she processed the revelation.

"Well, I guess that explains the bruises we saw on the mom," she murmured, almost to herself. "But when would she have had the time to write a letter? When she came through those doors, that poor thing was already in advanced labor."

"I don't know," Etta said softly. "But the day will come when Storm reads that letter, and I can't let her face that alone, May. I just can't."

May reached into the empty crib and picked up the papers she had placed there earlier. She handed them to Etta with a determined look.

"Then you're going to need these."

Etta glanced down, her fingers brushing the top sheet as she read the header.

"I stopped by and spoke to the social worker," May explained. "I hope you'll forgive me for doing it, but I wanted to get the information for you. You and James need to contact Child Protective Services immediately and fill out these forms to start the process for legal guardianship."

Etta's grip tightened around the papers as she looked back at the crib.

"Then I'll do whatever it takes. And… thank you!" She clapped, almost bouncing in place.

She looked overwhelmed with excitement, relieved that the daunting step of asking the question had been taken out of her hands. "I'll give it my all!"

May nodded, placing a hand on Etta's shoulder. "I know you will. But, Etta, I do think you need to tell James about the letter—like, right away. Do you agree?"

Etta sighed, her shoulders sinking slightly. "You're right. I'll tell him tonight."

A sly smile crept across May's face. "Maybe tell him after he's had a good dinner. My mama always said the best way to get a man to see things your way is to fix his favorite meal."

Etta let out a small laugh, shaking her head. "I guess I need to stop by the store then."

"And don't forget the wine," May added with a mischievous grin. "A good meal and a glass of his favorite wine? He won't stand a chance."

Etta smiled, her mood lifted by May's playful encouragement. "You should write a book about all this advice from your mama."

May smirked. "Maybe one day. But for now, let's focus on getting Storm to her family."

Chapter Thirteen

ETTA COULDN'T TAKE HER eyes off the stack of papers sitting on the passenger seat.

The sheer number of pages—at least ten—seemed to mock her. Each one represented a hurdle, a step in a process that felt monumental.

She drummed her fingers on the steering wheel, the sound filling the quiet car. "One step at a time," she murmured, repeating May's mantra as if it were a lifeline.

But as she looked down at the top sheet, the bold title—**Application for Legal Guardianship**—seemed to glare back at her, its legal jargon tightening a knot in her chest.

If this was overwhelming for me, how would James react?

With a deep breath, she scooped up the papers and grabbed the grocery bag from the back seat. The evening air carried a slight chill, wrapping around her like the weight of the decisions ahead. Etta squared her shoulders and headed for the house.

Stepping inside, she instinctively glanced toward the living room, expecting to see James in his chair, a notepad and pen in hand, jotting down ideas or half-watching the news.

Instead, a soft light drew her attention from the kitchen.

She paused in the doorway, her breath catching.

Candles flickered on the table, their soft light illuminating neatly set plates—their best ones, reserved for special occasions.

A basket of fresh bread sat at the center, its aroma mingling with the rich scents of roasted garlic and herbs. Glasses of wine were already poured, the ruby liquid glinting in the candlelight.

And there was James, standing beside the table, his sleeves rolled up and the faintest trace of flour dusting his shirt cuffs. He looked up, a small, hesitant smile softening his features.

"Oh, James," she said, her voice tender as she set the groceries and papers on the counter.

"I thought we could have dinner together—something nice," he said, stepping toward her.

Etta's grip on the counter loosened, her heart tugging in a way she hadn't anticipated. "You made all this?" she asked, a light laugh escaping as she gestured toward the table.

"Of course," he replied, pulling out a chair for her. "You've been talking about making big decisions, and I thought a nice meal might help us work through them. Isn't that how you and May think you can get me to see things your way?"

Etta blinked, her cheeks warming. "She told you, didn't she?"

James let out a quiet laugh, low and warm.

"Not directly. But I've been married to you long enough to know when a plan's in motion." His eyes flicked toward the papers on the counter. "What's all that?"

Etta hesitated, her fingers brushing the edge of the counter.

Then she shook her head, a bright smile breaking across her face. "Nothing for now. Let's eat," she said, settling into the chair he'd pulled out for her.

As she looked around, the care James had put into each detail filled her with quiet awe. "It's all so beautiful," she said sincerely, meeting his eyes. "I can't believe you did all this."

James sat across from her, his expression caught between pride and humility.

"You know," she teased, "if this is your way of convincing me to keep you, you didn't have to go all out. You're stuck with me."

James smirked, settling back in his chair. "Oh, I know. But maybe I'm trying to make sure you *want* to stay stuck with me."

Etta laughed and reached for the breadbasket. For the first time in days, the knot in her chest began to unravel.

This... this was what she wanted to fight for.

A family that could grow, change, and weather the unexpected—together.

One step at a time.

Chapter Fourteen

JAMES RAN HIS FINGERS down Etta's arm, the soft rhythm of his touch matching the quiet of their living room. She leaned into him, her back pressing against his chest.

His warmth was a comforting anchor.

"I want you to be happy, Etta," he said, his voice dropping into something softer, laden with a vulnerability he rarely allowed himself to show.

She shifted slightly, turning to face him.

Her eyes searched his. "I already am happy," she replied with conviction, her eyes alight.

"Right now, yes," he admitted, his hand lingering on her arm. "I can see that. But I don't want us to ever fight like we did this morning. If we're going to do this, we can't let that happen again."

Etta studied his face, tracing the lines of concern etched across it.

Reaching up, she rested her hand gently against his cheek. "We won't, James," she said with tender certainty. "We'll figure it out. Together."

James hesitated, his eyes faltering as if searching for courage.

"I want to tell you something," he began. "Something I should have told you a long time ago. But… know this: it's not entirely how I feel now."

Etta stilled, her hands folding in her lap as she waited, her heart bracing for what was to come.

James exhaled deeply, his stare distant, as if he were looking into a part of his past.

"I never really wanted children," he confessed. "Growing up, I always felt like my parents only stayed together because of me. Everything about our house was chaotic. Loud arguments. Slamming doors. There was no love between them—just obligation. Somehow, I blamed myself for it." His lips pressed into a thin line. "When my mom finally walked out, I was eighteen. She didn't even look back at me. Not once. No glance to see the love she was leaving behind. I didn't even matter."

Etta's heart ached for him, but she stayed quiet, letting him share his truth.

"A few years later, after the divorce, my father told me something I've never forgotten. He said, 'Don't have children. They'll only ruin everything.'"

James's words hung heavily in the air.

"I went through life believing that," he continued. "I convinced myself that children would bring more pain than joy. That it was better to focus on what I could control—my work, my routines, the life my wife and I would build together. But now…"

As he looked at her again, she saw something new in his eyes—a tiny glimmer of possibility breaking through.

"Now, I'm starting to wonder if I was wrong. Watching you, seeing the way you're fighting for Storm, the way you're opening my eyes to what family could mean—it's made me realize that maybe, just maybe, I've been holding on to someone else's fear for too long."

Etta reached for his hand, threading her fingers through his.

"James," she said gently, her voice filled with warmth, "I'm so glad you told me this. Like you said to me when you found out I was adopted, I wish I'd known sooner. But I understand why you kept it to yourself. And I want you to know—you're not your father. You don't have to carry his hurt anymore. Those are his wounds, not yours to bear."

James nodded slowly, smiling slightly. He pulled her close, his arms wrapping around her with quiet intensity. When his lips met hers, Etta felt it—a shift, a release.

It was as though the shadows of his past had finally let him go.

After a moment, Etta pulled back, adjusting her posture. "Since we're sharing truths right now," she began, "there's something I need to tell you too."

James tilted his head, concern flickering across his face. "What is it?"

Etta exhaled, her hands resting in her lap. "The day Storm's mother died, I found a letter on the floor. It was addressed to Storm." She paused. "In the letter, she wrote about how her husband abused her… and how she stopped him."

A crease formed between his brows. "You mean she…"

Etta nodded. "Killed him? I believe so."

James leaned back slightly, his expression contemplative. "It sounds like self-defense."

Etta nodded again, her fingers fidgeting with the edge of her shirt. "As brutal as it was to read, I gathered that from the letter too. But still… it was hard to take in."

James lowered his eyes to the coffee table, the weight of his thoughts written across his face.

"Why would someone write a letter like that to their child?"

Etta shook her head slowly. "I don't know. Maybe it was the only way to tell her side of the truth." She paused. "But I do know this—Storm's going to need us. People who love her. To help her make sense of it."

James pulled her close again. "Then we'll be there for her. Together."

He glanced toward the counter where the stack of papers sat. "You want to tell me about those now?"

Etta sighed, her heart swelling with hope. "They're for the guardianship process."

James smiled softly. "Okay," he said. "Then let's take a look."

Chapter Fifteen

ETTA STOOD BEFORE THE wall, her eyes moving over the photographs and plaques chronicling the history of Providence Ridge Hospital.

Above them, bold letters read: **A Legacy of Care Since 1919.**

The display told the story of a modest beginning—just sixty beds in a small building—and its transformation into a bustling urban hospital with over 319 beds. Nestled beside Douglass Park on Chicago's West Side, it had become a beacon of hope and healing for the community.

Her eyes lingered on a row of black-and-white photos from the nursery's opening in 1950. Nurses stood poised in crisp white dresses that fell just below their knees, their starched aprons spotless and folded caps perfectly aligned. Behind them, rows of bassinets stretched out, a promise of new beginnings. The polished white shoes and serene expressions of the nurses seemed to echo a quieter era, one in which care had been simpler, yet no less meaningful.

The sight stirred something deep within Etta. The gradual evolution of the hospital mirrored her own journey—a reminder that transformation, though often uncertain, was vital.

Her thoughts shifted to James and the change she'd seen in him last night. It hadn't been inevitable, nor was it necessary. But it had been real. And she'd embraced it, wholeheartedly.

A small smile formed as the memory warmed her heart.

"What you grinning at?" May's voice broke through her thoughts.

She stepped up beside Etta, her tone light, though her curiosity was clear.

Etta reached into her purse, her fingers brushing against the edges of a yellow envelope. She pulled it out, folded neatly in half, and held it up for May to see.

May raised an eyebrow, her curiosity deepening.

"Are those the papers? Did James sign them?"

Etta nodded, her smile growing as she carefully unfolded the envelope.

She slid out the last page and handed it to May, her hands calm despite the hint of nervous excitement in her chest. "I woke up this morning and found them filled out, sitting on the kitchen table," Etta said, her voice tinged with disbelief and gratitude.

May scanned the page quickly, her eyes widening slightly before meeting Etta's.

"He really did it… and by himself?"

"He really did it," Etta replied, her words brimming with awe.

"That must have been one heck of a dinner last night," May teased, a sly grin creeping across her face.

Etta laughed softly, rolling her eyes as she gave May a playful nudge. "You're impossible."

May laughed, but her attention stayed on the signed paper. "Etta, this is just the beginning, you know."

Etta turned back to the wall, drawn again to the rows of photographs and plaques.

Each image spoke of transformation, resilience, and progress. They reminded her of what could be achieved with determination and hope.

"I know," Etta said finally. "But it's a start. It's an amazing day for me."

Her gaze settled on one particular photograph of the nursery's early days—smiling nurses, tiny bassinets, the promise of caring for something precious.

Change is necessary.

For Storm.

For James.

For herself.

And with that thought, Etta felt it in her core.

She was ready.

Ready to become a mother.

Chapter Sixteen

ETTA STEPPED CAUTIOUSLY INTO the office of Jackie Dean, the hospital's social worker.

The room exuded practicality and warmth in equal measure, with bright white walls adorned by framed certificates and inspirational quotes, their edges slightly faded.

A neatly organized desk dominated the space, its surface holding two gold picture frames. Etta couldn't help but notice the photographs inside. One showed Jackie and her husband with two young children, their bright smiles radiating joy, while the other featured Jackie shaking hands with an older woman, likely during some kind of recognition or ceremony. The familiar yellow folder in Etta's hands felt heavier as she took it all in, her nerves on edge.

"Etta," Jackie said, glancing up from her desk, her olive skin tone contrasting with the tired lines framing her almond-shaped eyes. "Come in. What can I do for you?"

Etta hesitated for a moment before stepping forward, holding up the folder.

"My husband and I filled out the papers to start the legal guardianship process for Storm," she began with a bit of apprehension. "I was hoping you could help me understand how to file them and who I need to contact to move forward."

Jackie's expression softened, but there was a hint of hesitation in her eyes.

She set her pen down and folded her hands on the desk. "Etta, I need to be honest with you," she began carefully. "This morning, the couple currently fostering Storm also submitted their paperwork for legal guardianship. CPS informed me they're also pushing for adoption. Not legal guardianship, Etta. An adoption is the pot of gold at the end of the rainbow as far as what the system wants for any baby. Legal guardianship just isn't the same."

The words hit Etta hard, a real punch to the gut. Her heart plummeted. She wanted to weep.

"Adoption?" she echoed, her voice barely above a whisper.

Jackie nodded. "CPS prioritizes what they believe is in the best interest of the child. Continuity of care is a big factor, and since Storm is already in their home, they see this couple as a stable option. So if they want to go ahead and adopt, they will be considered first."

Etta sank into the chair across from Jackie's desk, clutching the folder as if her life depended on it. "But they've only had her for a couple of days," she protested. "They're no further along than I am." She sounded like a petulant child complaining that another kid got all the candy.

Jackie shifted closer, her tone firm but compassionate. "I know it feels unfair, but it only took a couple of days for you to form a bond with Storm too. And this baby is a newborn, in their home. In those two days, they will have done so much for her already. This isn't a reflection of your love or commitment, Etta. It's about how the system weighs stability for the child. And bear in mind that they want her just as much as you do. That's good, isn't it?"

Etta's lips pressed into a thin line, but she nodded, signaling Jackie to continue.

"Let me explain what lies ahead," Jackie said, leaning back in her chair. "Like I said before, legal guardianship and adoption are different, and that does put them further ahead. It would even if they didn't already have Storm in their care, because legal guardianship is temporary. You'd be responsible for Storm's daily care and decisions, but her biological family, if any exists, would retain some rights, and we would still be looking at adoption as the best path for her future. In Storm's case, with her parents deceased and no next of kin stepping forward, CPS' ultimate goal has to be permanent adoption as easily as possible."

Etta listened intently, her heart racing.

"For now, guardianship is but a brief steppingstone. If CPS and the courts do grant you guardianship, it gives you a path toward adoption. But it's not guaranteed," Jackie continued. "The courts will evaluate both your case and the other couple's. They'll look at home studies, references, and each family's ability to provide stability and opportunity for Storm, as well as examining in great depth what each of you is prepared to offer her."

Jackie paused, letting the weight of her words settle.

"CPS will conduct a home study for you and James. They'll visit your home to assess its safety and suitability, interview both of you, and gather input from people in your lives—friends, coworkers, neighbors, and ex-partners. In other words, they will take many references. They'll also run legal background checks and evaluate your finances and parenting philosophies."

Etta looked down, her fingers tightening slightly. "What else?"

"You'll need an attorney experienced in family law," Jackie said, reaching for a small Rolodex on the corner of her desk. She flipped through the cards with practiced precision before pulling one out and handing it to Etta. "This attorney is a real go-getter. She'll help you navigate the legal side of this and ensure your case is presented as strongly as possible."

Jackie's tone softened as she shifted slightly.

"But Etta, remember, this process is about more than just your love for Storm. It's about demonstrating, without a shadow of a doubt, that your home is where she'll thrive best. That's what everyone involved in this process will be looking for."

Etta straightened, her grip on the folder tightening. "We'll do whatever it takes."

Jackie smiled, her expression warm and encouraging.

"All right then. I'll help you prepare for the home study and gather everything you need for court. Just know it's a marathon, not a sprint."

Etta nodded, her determination evident in the firm set of her jaw. "I already know Storm's best future is with us."

Jackie offered a small, encouraging nod. "I don't doubt you think that for a second, Etta. But so will the other couple. And remember, I'm not the one you and James have to convince." She straightened in her chair, pulling a folder closer. "So, let's get started, shall we?"

Chapter Seventeen

JAMES WAS AT THE kitchen sink, sleeves rolled up, drying a plate when Etta walked in.

He looked up at the sound of the door, his expression shifting instantly when he saw her face.

"What happened?" he asked, setting the towel down. "You're home early."

Etta didn't answer right away. She set her purse on the counter, then the yellow folder beside it. The familiar sight of it between them felt heavier here, in their kitchen, than it ever had in the hospital hallway.

James's eyes went to it immediately.

"Talk to me," he said, more quietly now.

She took a breath. "The foster parents filed for adoption this morning."

The words landed hard.

James went still. Not frozen—just braced. As if something he'd feared hearing had finally found its way into the room.

"Adoption," he repeated.

Etta nodded. "They'll be prioritized. Jackie said continuity of care carries a lot of weight."

For a moment, he stared at the counter. Then he turned away, gripping the edge of the sink.

"So that's it?" he asked, his voice tight. "We're already behind?"

"No," Etta said quickly. "Not out. But it just got harder. A lot harder."

James dragged a hand down his face. He didn't speak right away. When he finally did, his voice was low.

"I knew this wouldn't be simple," he said. "But I didn't think we'd be competing with people who already have her."

Neither did I, Etta thought. But she didn't say it.

"They'll do home studies," she continued. "Court evaluations. Lawyers. It's... a process."

James let out a breath that sounded almost like a laugh, but held no humor. "Of course it is."

He turned back to her, and for a split second, she saw it—the old reflex. The instinct to retreat. To decide it was safer not to hope.

"I don't want you to get hurt," he said. "I don't want us to build our lives around the idea of her and then have someone else take her away."

Etta stepped closer. "That's exactly why I have to try."

His jaw tightened. "And what if trying is what breaks us?"

The question hung there—raw and unguarded.

Etta didn't flinch. "James, loving her won't break us. Losing her might hurt. A lot. But not trying?" Her voice softened. "That would hurt in a way I don't think I could ever forgive myself for."

He looked at her then—really looked at her.

"You're already her mother in your heart," he said quietly.

"Yes," she replied without hesitation. "And I think you are too. Even if you're scared."

James exhaled slowly, the fight draining from his shoulders.

"I am scared," he admitted. "Because if I let myself believe she could be ours… then it means I can lose her. And I've spent most of my life building walls so I wouldn't have to feel that again."

Etta reached for his hands, still cool from the sink water, and wrapped her fingers around them.

"But you already broke those walls," she said gently. "You did that the moment you signed those papers. You did it the moment you said yes to even trying."

James swallowed.

"I didn't think I was capable of this," he said. "Of wanting something this much."

Etta squeezed his hands. "Neither did I."

He was quiet for a long moment.

"Okay," he said. "Then we fight for her."

Etta's breath caught.

"We get the lawyer. We do the home study. We let them talk to whoever they want, open up every drawer and closet of our lives if that's what it takes." His voice steadied as he spoke. "Not because I'm not afraid. But because Storm deserves people who don't walk away just because it's hard."

Etta's eyes filled.

James pulled her into his arms, holding her tightly.

"I can't promise this won't hurt," he said into her hair. "But I can promise I'm not running. Not this time."

Etta pressed her face against his chest, tears finally slipping free.

"Thank you," she whispered.

James closed his eyes.

For Storm.

For us.

Chapter Eighteen

MAY GLANCED AT HER watch—6 p.m. She let out a long, tired sigh, relieved that her shift was finally over. Thursdays had a knack for being chaotic, with admissions piling up and unexpected challenges at every turn. Without Etta by her side, the day had felt even more overwhelming.

Etta had taken the day off to prepare for the next critical step in her journey toward guardianship, now that the CPS home study was underway and the inspection was happening tomorrow. Meanwhile, May couldn't shake the worry growing in the pit of her stomach.

The attorney recommended by Jackie Dean hadn't been encouraging, strongly cautioning Etta and James about the steep challenges ahead.

The way she put things, Etta and James were up against a fight that was almost impossible for them to win.

It really burned May up to her core.

Yet if anyone could rise to meet the odds, May knew it would be Etta and James.

She only wished she could do more to help.

"Ms. Jones."

May turned toward the voice, finding Darren approaching.

His tailored black suit was slightly rumpled, his tie loosened just enough to hint at a long day. He carried himself with his usual composure, but something lingered in his eyes.

A crease formed slightly between his brows as her concern surfaced. "Isaiah is doing really well," he said quickly, as though he'd noticed her unease.

Relief softened her expression.

"That's so good to hear," she said, a genuine smile lighting her face.

Darren offered a hesitant smile in return. "I actually came to see if anyone had found a brown teddy bear. I must've left it here, but things have been so hectic, I couldn't get back until now."

May tilted her head thoughtfully.

"I'll check the lost and found for you, but since it's been a few weeks, I can't promise they would still even have it. That bear must hold a lot of meaning."

"It does," Darren admitted, glancing down before meeting her eyes again. "Michelle picked it out before Isaiah was born. I can't believe I left it behind."

May studied him. "It happens all the time," she said gently. "And just wait till he's throwing things around; then you'll be picking up after him all day long. Anyway, how have you been?"

Darren paused, his hands brushing his coat pockets as though searching for the right words. "Every day, I miss my wife, and things at home… well, they are a work in progress," he finally admitted. "But we're finding our way."

"One day at a time," they said in unison, and May gave a low laugh at the shared sentiment.

"Is your mother still able to help out?" she asked, steering the conversation toward lighter territory.

Darren nodded. "She's been a rock for me and Isaiah. I don't know what I'd do without her. She's been such a constant presence for both of us."

"That's good to hear," May said warmly. "A strong support system makes all the difference."

"It really does," Darren agreed, his smile holding.

May's stomach let out a loud growl, and she laughed, slightly embarrassed.

"I'm so sorry. I didn't get lunch today."

Darren smiled with a hint of laughter, some of the tension easing from his frame. "Sounds like you need to take your own advice about self-care."

"Touché," May replied playfully. "Says the guy juggling a newborn and a demanding job."

"Guilty," Darren admitted with a laugh. "But I'm working on it—one day at a time, right?"

"Right," May echoed, smiling.

There was a brief pause before Darren spoke again, his tone lighter.

"We could grab some dinner together if you like? My treat. I figure it's the least I can do; you've helped me through far more than you probably realize."

May hesitated, touched by his sincerity.

"That's kind of you, Darren, but you don't owe me anything."

"I know," he said earnestly. "But I'd still like to. You were there for me and Isaiah when I didn't know how to move forward. That's not something I'll forget. You are the one who saw me when I was at my lowest ebb and made me see what was possible."

"All right, in that case, dinner sounds nice. But only if you promise not to call me Ms. Jones the whole time. It's May."

"Deal," Darren said with a slight cackle. "Let me call my mother and let her know I'm grabbing dinner. She's been cooking up a storm lately."

May grinned knowingly. "Bet you're loving that. Mom's food is always the best!"

Darren's smile faltered briefly. "Well, Michelle always had dinner ready when I got home. She loved to cook, too. I guess my mother is trying to ease the loss of that somehow."

May could see the creases of pain circling his eyes.

She knew that look all too well.

Pain recognizes pain. "Your wife must have been amazing," she finally said after a few moments of silence filled the air.

"She was," Darren replied, a bittersweet smile forming. "To Michelle, dinner wasn't just a meal—it was her way of showing love. I guess I appreciate that more now than ever."

"She left so much love behind, Darren," May said. "You and Isaiah are living proof of it."

"Thanks, May. You say all the right things. I mean that. Since my wife died…"

Her stomach growled again, louder this time. It was also time to change the subject before he became too melancholy.

"Speaking of food!" she said enthusiastically, seeking to shift the mood.

He chuckled. "All right. Let's get you something to eat. There's a great little Chinese restaurant nearby. That work for you?"

"That's perfect," May replied with a grin. "My mother always said, when you're not paying, anywhere is perfect!"

Darren laughed as they headed for the door. "I like that."

The restaurant buzzed with lively energy as May and Darren stepped inside.

The clinking of glasses, bursts of laughter, and the savory aroma of soy sauce filled the air. Tables were packed with diners, their faces illuminated by lantern-style lights hanging overhead.

"You know the food's good when you can't even get a table," May remarked, scanning the crowded room.

"This place is always packed," Darren replied with a knowing smile. "Good thing I know the owner. Give me a second. I'll see if he can squeeze us in."

As Darren moved through the restaurant with practiced ease, weaving past servers balancing trays of steaming dishes, May waited near the entrance.

She took in the room, noting the cheerful chaos. The sight of egg rolls and fried rice only heightened her growing hunger, and she sighed softly. It was a good thing the place was buzzing with chatter and background noise, as her stomach was gurgling even louder.

A few minutes later, Darren returned, waving her over with a triumphant grin. "Come on, we've got a spot," he said, gesturing toward the back of the restaurant.

May followed him, weaving through the tightly packed tables. Her white nurse's uniform stood out against the sea of casual diners clad in straight-leg Levi's, graphic T-shirts, and well-worn Converses. *At least I remembered my red lipstick,* she thought, the small pop of color giving her a measure of confidence in the bustling space.

Darren gestured to a small table tucked neatly into the corner and pulled out a chair for her. "Here you go," he said warmly. "Not exactly the best seat, but at least we didn't have to wait."

"Works for me," May said, sliding into the chair. "How do you know the owner?" she asked after their order had been taken.

"Ming—he's an old client of mine," Darren replied, settling into his chair. "I helped him and his wife adopt their little girl."

May's eyes lit up with interest. "So, you're a family law attorney?"

"I am indeed," Darren said. "Mostly, I focus on guardianship disputes."

"You mentioned you're a partner at your firm. Does that mean you only handle big cases?"

Darren tilted his head, studying her for a moment. "Not necessarily. Being a partner gives me the flexibility to choose my cases. I handle a mix. Some are high-stakes, others more straightforward and day-to-day stuff. It really depends on the circumstances."

May nodded, her fingers tracing the edge of her water glass. "It just seems like you'd have to be really good to focus on something so complex."

Darren smiled faintly, leaning forward.

"It's a lot of navigating emotions, relationships, and the law. But most cases, big or small, boil down to one thing: what's in the best interest of the child or person involved. That's the core of everything. But to answer your question directly—yeah, I'm good at what I do."

May responded with a smirk, but Darren caught the subtle pause in her expression.

Picking up his glass, he took a slow sip of water before setting it back down. "Is there something specific you're wondering about, May? Let's just say I get a certain vibe."

Her eyes lowered for a beat, then rose to meet his. "Actually, yes," she said softly. "But let's eat first," she added quickly as the waitress arrived with their food.

Darren managed a small smile as he picked up his fork, though the weight of her unspoken thoughts lingered between them.

Chapter Nineteen

THE WAITRESS CLEARED DARREN'S plate just as May was finishing the last bite of her egg roll. She wiped her hands with a napkin as their wine glasses were quietly refilled.

"You're right—the food was amazing. I'm surprised Etta and I haven't been here before, seeing how close it is to the hospital."

Darren took a sip of his wine. "Well, now you have somewhere to come back to, right?"

"Absolutely," May said, glancing around the restaurant again.

"So, are you looking to adopt a child, May?" Darren asked, his tone curious but gentle as he set his glass down.

May shook her head. "It's not me," she said quickly. "It's my best friend, Etta, and her husband, James. They're trying to adopt a baby girl named Storm. Her mother passed away shortly after bringing that sweet little thing into the world. It happened a few days before..."

"My wife died after giving birth to Isaiah," Darren finished for her.

May hesitated, her hand resting on the table. "Yeah. I didn't want to bring it up, but... the timing felt significant."

Darren reached for his glass, pausing before taking a measured sip of wine. "It's okay," he said finally, his tone reflective. "Life has a way of weaving these moments together, doesn't it?"

"It seems so," May agreed, lifting her glass.

She took a small sip, her eyes meeting his briefly over the rim.

Darren shifted in his chair, his expression thoughtful. "Tell me about their situation."

May took a deep breath, setting her glass down gently. "It's a much longer story than our dinner will allow, but here's the short version: Storm was placed in foster care because both her parents are deceased, and CPS hasn't been able to locate any other family members. Etta and James are trying to get legal guardianship, but the process hasn't been easy."

Darren's brows furrowed. "If there's no family, what's the hold-up?"

May paused, her fingers tracing the edge of her napkin. "Storm's foster parents have filed for adoption as well. Etta and James are doing everything they can to show they can provide Storm with the loving, stable home she deserves. The home inspection is tomorrow."

Darren leaned back, his fingers brushing the edge of his glass. "That sounds like an uphill battle. They have a good attorney, right?"

"They do. Her name is Carter Mills," May said, her frustration evident in the tension in her shoulders. "Carter came highly recommended, but she's not what they need. In my opinion, she's too passive, and this situation requires someone willing to stand up and fight."

Darren nodded, his brow furrowing deeper. "Carter Mills… I know the name. She's effective in simpler cases, but if this is shaping up to be a battle, they'll need someone more assertive."

"Exactly," May said, leaning forward slightly. "My mother always said you don't go into battle with a hound dog—you bring the pit bull!"

Darren laughed, his grin breaking through his thoughtful expression. “And she was right. This kind of fight requires someone who won’t back down. Someone like me.”

May nodded in agreement. “Wait, what?”

Darren’s fingers tapped lightly against the edge of his glass. “I can help them,” he said confidently. “I have a few contacts at CPS. Let me see who is handling the case.”

Disbelief and gratitude spread across May’s face. “You’d do that for them?”

“Of course,” Darren said firmly. “Sometimes it’s about who you know, not just what you know. If I can help tip the scales in their favor, I will.”

May exhaled deeply, the tension easing from her posture.

“You don’t know what this means to me. Etta and James are my family. I just want to see them happy—and to see that child grow up and call me Auntie May, or something similar.”

“Storm’s fortunate to have all of you in her corner,” Darren said warmly. “And with everything you’ve shared, I can tell Etta and James aren’t just fighting for her. They’re building a future for her.”

“They’ve met,” May said, climbing out of Darren’s Mercedes and closing the door behind her.

He glanced at her, a crease forming between his brows. “Sorry, I’m not following.”

“Isaiah and Storm,” she clarified, walking around to join him. “She was crying something awful one day, and Etta and I didn’t know what else to do, so I went and got him. I don’t know why, but I felt like they could help each other.”

Curiosity flickered in Darren's eyes as he followed her words.

"The moment I placed him in the crib next to her, she stopped crying," May continued, her voice softening. "This might sound crazy, but the way he looked at her… it was as though he understood. Like he could feel her pain, her loss."

Darren's eyes softened. "I wish I had been there to see that."

May smiled faintly, warmth filling her at the memory.

"It was something I won't forget. It was like they just… belonged together, even if only for that one moment."

Chapter Twenty

ETTA AND JAMES SAT in Darren's office, the weight of anticipation pressing down on them as they waited for his arrival. The room, bathed in natural light from a large rectangular window, felt both inviting and professional. Outside, the May breeze carried the mild scent of spring, a refreshing 65°F day in Chicago. The sunlight bounced between drifting clouds, a calm contrast to the uncertainty swirling in their minds.

The office exuded timeless charm.

A large oak desk dominated the space, flanked by matching beige-upholstered chairs. Shelves filled with thick legal tomes lined the walls, their spines embossed in gold. Interspersed among the books were glimpses of Darren's personal life: an antique clock, a neatly placed globe, and framed photographs that spoke of the man beyond his title.

Etta's eyes rested on one particular photo on the desk, a picture of Darren's late wife, Michelle. The warmth in her radiant smile and the graceful way her slightly wavy hair framed her face caught Etta's attention. She shifted closer, drawn in by the quiet beauty of the image. It was clear why Darren had spoken of her to May with such love and reverence. The photo seemed to hold its own light amid the books and files, a reminder of a life that had left an indelible mark.

Straightening in her chair, Etta glanced at James, who was studying a black-and-white courthouse photograph hanging on the wall. The framed image stood as a silent testament to the many legal battles Darren had fought and won in his career.

"You can tell he takes pride in his work," she said softly.

James gave a small nod, his eyes still fixed on the photograph.

The sound of approaching footsteps broke the quiet, and both of them shifted slightly in their seats, bracing themselves for the conversation that would surely come to shape their future.

The door opened, and Darren entered with a slim folder tucked under his arm.

His warm, inviting smile instantly eased the tension in the room. Etta felt her shoulders relax. May was right—Darren exuded the perfect mix of confidence and calm.

"Thank you for coming in today," Darren began as he stepped behind the desk, setting the folder down. "I know you were scheduled for your home inspection today, but I had it postponed so we could strategize. This isn't just about preparing for the process—it's about setting you up to bring Storm home to where she belongs."

His eyes moved between them before settling on Etta.

"This isn't just about paperwork or hearings. It's about showing the system that Storm belongs with you. That's my job—to make that clear to everyone involved."

Etta's lips curved into a small smile, gratitude tightening her chest. James nodded in silent agreement, brushing his hand against hers.

Darren took a seat behind the desk, adjusting the brass lamp with its green glass shade. Leaning forward, he folded his hands.

"Let's dive in. This will be a team effort, but I'm here to take the lead. Together, we'll make sure there's no doubt where Storm's future lies."

"Before we start," Etta said, her hands clasped tightly in her lap, "I was wondering if it would be possible to arrange a visitation with Storm. My husband hasn't had the chance to meet her yet. Ms. Mills told us it wasn't possible because Storm's foster parents aren't in agreement, but I was hoping there'd be something you could do."

Darren leaned back slightly, his brow furrowing in thought.

"I understand how important that is," he said after a moment. "Visitation can be tricky when foster parents push back, but it's not impossible. The law prioritizes the best interest of the child, and if we can present a case that meeting James is in Storm's best interest, we have a strong argument."

Etta's shoulders relaxed slightly, though her hands remained clasped. "So, there's a chance?" she asked, her voice laced with cautious hope.

Darren nodded. "There's more than a chance. It's all about presenting it correctly. I'll file a motion for visitation with the court. We'll need to demonstrate that this meeting benefits Storm emotionally, especially since you're seeking guardianship—and potentially, adoption."

James finally spoke, doubt in his voice.

"What if the foster parents oppose it?"

Darren looked over at him, confidence grounded in experience.

"Their opinions will be considered, but they don't have the final say—the judge does. If we build a compelling case that this visitation is in Storm's best interest, the court will take that seriously. There's no reason to believe the judge won't approve it."

Etta let out a sigh of relief. "Thank you," she said softly. "This means so much to us."

Darren smiled, leaning forward.

"You're not alone in this. I'll handle the legal side and make sure everything is airtight. For now, let's focus on preparing for the next steps. The CPS home inspection is going to be pivotal. That's why I postponed it to next week—so we have time to get everything in place."

He opened the folder on his desk and slid a blank sheet of paper toward them.

"Let's start with this. Write down a list of people who can vouch for you. Neighbors, coworkers, friends—anyone who can speak to your character and readiness to provide Storm with a stable, loving home."

Etta nodded, determination replacing some of the anxiety in her expression. "Absolutely. We've got plenty of people who can vouch for us."

James leaned in slightly, his expression focused.

"What else can we do to strengthen our case?"

Darren tapped his pen lightly against the desk. "I'll push for visitation with Storm. That'll help show the judge that you're starting to build a connection with her as well. Beyond that, I'll personally visit your home tomorrow evening to ensure every detail is in place. We need to demonstrate that your environment is not only safe but also nurturing."

James gave a small nod, though his lips pressed into a thin line as Darren's words sank in.

While he was eager to meet Storm, the thought of holding her filled him with quiet uncertainty. His face seemed to say, *What if I don't do it right?*

Etta noticed the slight change in his expression.

She reached over and rested her hand on his. Her touch was warm and grounding. "In your arms, she'll feel it, James," she said, faith in her voice. "She'll know exactly how much we love her."

James turned to her, gratitude in his eyes. "You're right. We got this."

Darren watched the exchange, a faint smile forming. "I like hearing that," he said. "Now let's get to work."

Chapter Twenty-One

IT WAS LATE, AND exhaustion clung to them, but as Etta and James stepped through their front door, a trace of optimism burned brightly for the first time in weeks.

Darren had rekindled that optimism with his unflinching confidence.

Etta slipped off her jacket and hung it on the coat rack, her movements slow but deliberate. Her footsteps carried her down the hall, stopping at the threshold of the room she had dreamed of transforming into Storm's nursery. The hallway light spilled softly into the space, casting a warm glow on the rocking chair in the corner and the bare walls waiting to tell a story.

James came up behind her, his presence a silent comfort, his arms wrapping gently around her waist. She closed her eyes, leaning into him as the scent of his cologne enveloped her.

"I can almost see her in here, James," Etta murmured, her gaze fixed on the corner where she imagined the crib would stand. "I never let myself picture it before, not completely. But after tonight..."

James tightened his embrace, his voice an anchoring calm.

"After tonight, we have someone in our corner who wants this just as much as we do."

Etta turned in his arms, her smile teasing.

"Darren is definitely a step up from Ms. Carter Mills," she said.

They both laughed, the sound light and unguarded, a welcome reprieve from weeks of tension.

James' laughter faded into thoughtful quiet. "What if we're not good at this?"

Etta tilted her head, her eyes meeting his. "Oh, I'm not worried about me. It's you I'm concerned about," she teased.

James smirked, but his eyes searched her face for reassurance.

Her expression softened. "You're going to be the most amazing father, James. You're kind, compassionate, and, most of all, you love me. That's how I know you'll love her—with everything you have. And remember, every new father has the same concerns. Even men whose partners are about to give birth for the first time have these periods of self-doubt."

His eyes met hers, brimming with emotion.

Slowly, he leaned in, his lips brushing against hers in a kiss that was tender and unhurried, carrying the depth of their shared dreams and the quiet promise of their future.

When they parted, Etta rested her forehead against his, her hands lightly gripping his arms for balance.

"You're the best thing that ever happened to me," she whispered.

James smiled, his thumb drawing slow circles along her back.

"And you're mine," he said, his voice rich with certainty.

For a moment, the world around them seemed to fall away, leaving just the two of them, connected by the strength of their love and the hope they held for what was to come.

Chapter Twenty-Two

OUTSIDE, THE STREETLIGHTS STREAMED a muted glow through the living room window as Etta bustled around, fluffing pillows and straightening details until every corner of the room felt perfectly arranged. Her eyes shifted to the clock above the fireplace.

Darren would be there in ten minutes.

Calm down.

She inhaled deeply, smoothing her cream skirt and taking one last sweep of the room.

James entered quietly, his navy-blue dress pants and crisp white shirt catching her attention. The steadiness of his smile eased her nerves.

"Well, don't you clean up nicely, Mr. Harris," Etta teased, her hands finding her hips.

James' amusement spread across his face as he stepped closer. "I could say the same about you, Mrs. Harris. That blouse and gold pin… regal."

Etta laughed, smoothing the fabric of her blouse. "Regal, huh? I'll take it. Let's just hope our home makes the right impression on Darren," she said, casting a quick glance around the room.

James gently touched her cheek, a playful grin on his face. "Trust me, he'll be impressed the moment he tries those cookies I baked."

Etta arched an eyebrow, her tension easing with a laugh. "They do smell delicious."

James' grin widened. "Consider it a little extra charm in our arsenal."

The doorbell rang, cutting through their banter. Etta pressed a hand to her chest, feeling her heartbeat quicken. James leaned over, pressing a kiss to her cheek before moving to the door.

"Welcome, Darren," he said as he opened it.

Darren stepped inside, his eyes scanning the room with a warm smile. "You have a lovely home," he remarked, setting his briefcase on the sofa. "Mind giving me a quick tour?"

James glanced at Etta. "I'll follow, as my wife takes the lead."

Etta exhaled, offering Darren a smile as she motioned down the hallway. "Right this way."

As they moved through the house, Etta mentally scanned each room, trying to remember if she'd taken care of every last detail.

"When CPS visits," Darren said, sensing her nerves, "they're not looking for perfection. What matters most is that they see a home that's safe, stable, and filled with love. And from what I've seen so far, you're already creating exactly that."

Etta repeated the words to herself—*safe, stable, loving*—as they stepped into the nursery.

"This would be Storm's bedroom," she said, gesturing to the empty space where the crib would go. "We haven't set everything up yet. We're waiting for... well, for her, obviously."

Darren nodded, taking in the room. His eyes lingered on a framed photo of Etta and James on the wall, their smiles filled with determination. He took in the rocking chair in the corner, a folded blanket draped neatly over its arm, and the small basket of baby essentials nearby.

"I like this space," he said. "It feels welcoming. Peaceful."

Etta folded her hands. "It's a work in progress, but we'll make it perfect for her."

"Life is a work in progress, Etta," Darren said.

Etta stole a quick glance at James before clearing her throat.

"It is," she began, her voice steadying. "That's why this is so important to us. I was adopted."

Her posture straightened, and she lifted her chin with quiet pride.

"My parents gave me everything—love, stability, a sense of belonging. They made me feel wanted. And now, we want to give that same gift to Storm."

Respect gleamed in Darren's eyes as he watched James place a supportive arm around Etta's shoulders. The moment tugged at something deep within him, reminding him of his late wife, Michelle. She, too, had been adopted.

Darren's thoughts drifted to the countless nights they'd spent talking about her gratitude for her adoptive parents—the stability, love, and opportunities they'd given her. It had been one of the driving forces behind his shift from criminal law to family law. To him, justice wasn't just about righting wrongs; it was about placing children in homes where they would be loved unconditionally.

"That's an incredible story, Etta," Darren finally said, his tone warm and sincere. "Sharing that with CPS next week will be a powerful part of your case. It shows that this isn't just about what you want—it's about what Storm truly needs. No one could know that better than a woman who has been through the adoption process herself. Thank you for sharing that."

"We also want her to know she's wanted. That she belongs," James said, his arm still resting on Etta's shoulder.

Darren looked thoughtfully around the room.

"Every effort you've made, James, reflects the love you both have for her. That's what CPS will notice—and it's what will make all the difference."

As they left the nursery, Etta glanced back at James, catching his eye. A warm smile spread across his face, as if to say, *That went well.* She couldn't help but return the expression.

Chapter Twenty-Three

THE KNOCK CAME EXACTLY on time.

Three sharp raps on the door—polite, professional, unavoidable.

Etta barely moved, afraid that any small adjustment would reveal how nervous she felt. Her eyes flicked to James. He looked ready—calm, composed, braced.

"You ready?" he asked softly.

"As I'll ever be," she replied, though her voice betrayed her nerves.

James reached for her hand and gave it a reassuring squeeze. "I've got you."

She nodded, drew a deep breath, and opened the door.

A woman in her early forties stood on the porch, clipboard tucked under one arm, tablet in the other. Her brown hair was pulled into a low, practical bun, and her eyes held the kind of measured kindness that came from years of seeing too much.

"Mrs. and Mr. Harris?" she asked.

"Yes," Etta said. "I'm Etta. This is my husband, James."

"I'm Linda Carter with Child Protective Services," the woman said, offering a professional smile. "Thank you for having me. I'll be conducting your home study today."

"Of course," James said, stepping aside. "Please, come in."

Linda stepped into the living room, her gaze already moving—cataloging, noting, assessing. Etta suddenly became acutely aware of every pillow, every throw blanket, every framed photograph on the walls.

The house was clean. Safe. Warm.

But now it had to be evaluated.

They settled into the living room. Linda took a seat on the edge of the sofa while Etta and James sat across from her, their hands clasped tightly together.

"This visit will include a walkthrough of your home and a series of questions," Linda explained. "Some of them may feel personal. That's part of the process. My role is to assess whether this environment is safe, stable, and appropriate for a child."

Etta nodded. "We understand."

"Good," Linda said gently. "Let's start with some basics."

She tapped her tablet.

"How long have you been married?"

"Ten years," James answered.

"And what made you decide to pursue guardianship now?"

Etta inhaled slowly. "Storm."

Linda looked up. "Tell me more."

"She came into my care at the hospital," Etta said. "I held her. Fed her. Comforted her when she cried. And I realized—she wasn't just another baby. She was a child who needed someone to fight for her. We both did."

Linda's gaze shifted to James. "How did you feel about this decision initially?"

James hesitated for half a second.

Then he told the truth.

"I was scared," he said. "Not of Storm. Of failing her. Of repeating the patterns I grew up around. But I realized fear isn't a reason to walk away. It's a reason to do better."

Linda studied him carefully, then typed something into her tablet.

"Tell me about your childhood, Mr. Harris."

James swallowed. "It wasn't stable. A lot of conflict. Not much warmth. That's exactly why I want something different for Storm."

Etta felt his hand tighten around hers.

"And you, Mrs. Harris?" Linda asked. "Your background?"

"I was adopted," Etta said, her voice steady. "My parents chose me. They made me feel wanted every single day of my life. I grew up knowing I belonged." She paused. "That's what I want for Storm."

Linda's expression softened—just slightly.

"Thank you for sharing that," she said. "That perspective matters."

They moved through the house next.

The kitchen.

The guest room.

The bathroom.

Linda opened cabinets. Checked smoke detectors. Noted outlet covers and stair rails. Etta followed her, answering questions, pointing out the safety features they had already installed.

And then they reached the nursery.

Linda paused in the doorway.

"This will be Storm's room?" she asked.

"Yes," Etta said quietly.

Linda stepped inside slowly.

"It's peaceful," she said. "You've left space."

"We wanted to," James said. "For her."

Linda turned to him. "Some people rush to fill every corner before a child arrives."

"We wanted her to be part of choosing what this room becomes as she grows," Etta said softly. "Not just placing her into something that feels… already decided without her."

Linda made another note.

They returned to the living room for final questions.

"Who will provide childcare?"

"What are your work schedules?"

"How will you handle discipline?"

"What support system do you have?"

They answered everything.

Honestly. Carefully. Together.

At one point, Linda looked directly at them.

"There is another family pursuing adoption," she said plainly. "Are you aware of that?"

"Yes," Etta said.

"And how does that make you feel?"

James answered before Etta could.

"It makes me determined," he said. "Not to compete. But to be very clear about what we can offer Storm. Stability. Love. Commitment. For the long haul."

Linda held his gaze for a long moment.

Then she nodded.

"I've seen homes that look perfect on paper," she said. "And families that look messy but love fiercely. The system values structure. But children thrive on connection."

She stood and gathered her things.

"I can't make promises," she said. "But I can say this—you've given me a lot to document in your favor."

Etta's breath caught. "Thank you."

Linda offered a small, genuine smile.

"Storm is lucky," she said. "No matter where she lands, she has people willing to fight for her. That matters more than you may realize."

After the door closed behind her, the house felt impossibly quiet.

Etta turned to James, emotion flooding her face.

"How do you think it went?"

James pulled her into his arms.

"I think we told the truth," he said. "And I think that's all we can do."

Etta rested her head against his chest, listening to his heartbeat.

"Whatever happens," she whispered, "I'm glad we fought for her."

James kissed the top of her head.

"Me too."

In those words, hope had made a home.

Chapter Twenty-Four

MAY SAT AT THE nurse's station, staring at the phone in front of her.

She tapped her fingers lightly on the counter, debating whether to make the call.

Her thoughts were interrupted by Etta's cheerful voice.

"What a cute bear," Etta said, leaning across the counter and pointing to the plush toy sitting beside May.

May gave a small smile, picking up the bear and turning it in her hands. "I had to dig through the lost and found to find it."

"That was nice of you."

May shrugged, though a hint of a smile hovered on her face. "It belongs to Darren's son, Isaiah."

Etta watched May carefully, noticing the subtle tension in her posture. "Are you okay? You've been staring at that phone like it's going to bite you."

May smirked. "I don't want to overstep. Calling him seems so personal."

Etta shook her head. "May, you broke bread with the man a couple of weeks ago."

May hesitated, her thumb brushing over the edge of the bear's ear. She let out a slow breath before looking at Etta. "That was different."

Etta leaned in closer. "How so?"

May shrugged. "I don't know. It just was."

Etta raised an eyebrow. "May, is there something you want to tell me?"

"Stop looking at me like you're trying to find something out, Etta. I know what you're thinking."

"What am I thinking?"

"Whatever it is, remember that man just lost his wife," May retorted.

"Obviously, but I'm not the one who needs to remember that." Etta gave May a wink.

May shook her head, rolling her eyes with a faint smirk. "You're impossible, Etta."

"I'm just saying—you're putting a lot of thought into this call. Just do it and keep it casual."

May sighed, still holding the bear, her fingers absently brushing its soft fur. "I don't want him to think I'm crossing some line. He's dealing with so much already."

"May, you're not crossing any lines by letting him know you found something important to him. You're being thoughtful. That's one of the things you're best at."

May glanced at Etta, her eyes betraying the tiniest hint of uncertainty. "You really think so?"

"I know so," Etta said with a reassuring nod. "You're the reason Darren stepped up for us—why he's fighting so hard for Storm. Because of him, the CPS inspection went amazingly well. If he knows anything about you—and I think he does—he'll see this for what it is: a kind gesture."

May bit her lip, still debating. "I just don't want to make this weird."

"Showing someone kindness is never weird. Now, pick up the phone. You'll feel better once you've done it."

May stared at the phone for a long moment before finally reaching for the receiver. "If this gets awkward, I'm blaming you."

Etta grinned. "I'll happily take full responsibility."

May dialed the number, her heart racing slightly as the line began to ring. Etta gave her an encouraging thumbs-up, though she also knew there was more to this than May was letting on.

Darren's receptionist answered on the third ring.

"Hi, I'd like to speak with Mr. Johnson, please. It's May Jones, the nurse from—"

Before May could finish, the receptionist interrupted. "One moment, please."

The line clicked, and a familiar voice greeted her. "Hi, May."

May swallowed, willing her voice to remain casual. *Why am I so nervous?* She glanced at Etta, who was watching with barely concealed amusement.

"Hi, Darren. I hope I'm not catching you at a bad time."

"Not at all. I'm just wrapping up for the day."

May glanced at her watch. It was nearly 7 p.m. "Right. I forgot how late it is."

"What can I do for you?"

She hesitated, her fingers tapping lightly against the counter. "I, um, found Isaiah's teddy bear. The one you mentioned."

"You found it?" Darren's tone brightened with genuine surprise. "I didn't even think that was possible. I can't thank you enough."

"No need to thank me. It was the least I could do."

"You didn't have to do it at all. But I know you—you go out of your way for people. Especially for people you care about. It's clear you care about Isaiah."

May cleared her throat, feeling a sudden warmth rise in her cheeks. "I do. He's a handsome little boy."

"He is. He's looking more and more like his mother every day."

"That's amazing," May replied, her voice softer now, resisting the urge to add, *and he's growing more like his father too.*

Darren paused for a moment. "Why don't I come over to pick it up? Or better yet, how about we meet at the restaurant if your shift is over? Have you eaten?"

May hesitated, glancing over at Etta, who raised an eyebrow in silent encouragement. "My shift is over. I could eat," May said, trying to sound nonchalant.

"Great. I'll leave now."

May smiled despite herself. "Don't forget to call your mother."

Darren laughed. "Right. I'll call her now. See you soon, May."

As May hung up, she exhaled deeply and placed the receiver down before glancing up to see Etta grinning mischievously.

"Don't say a word," May warned, narrowing her eyes.

Etta raised her hands, feigning innocence. "Wouldn't dare."

Laughter filled the air as May picked up the bear and pressed it to her chest.

Chapter Twenty-Five

MAY ADJUSTED THE STRAP of her purse as she stepped into the lively hum of the restaurant, the comforting weight of Isaiah's teddy bear tucked securely inside.

Her eyes scanned the room, her heart quickening when she spotted Darren standing near a small table by the window, his phone in hand.

The warmth of the lantern-style lights overhead softened the room's energy but sharpened the clean lines of Darren's black suit. An approachable ease about him settled her nerves just a little.

When Darren looked up and caught her eye, May wove her way through the crowded restaurant, her thoughts momentarily drowning out the clinking of glasses and quiet hum of conversations.

"Hey there."

"Hi, May," Darren said, slipping his phone into his pocket. He stepped forward and pulled out her chair. "Thanks for agreeing to meet me. And for finding my little guy's toy."

Sliding into her seat, May offered a small smile, her fingers tightening briefly on the strap of her purse. "I'm glad we could meet. And it was the least I could do to look for the bear."

As they settled, she opened her purse, her hand brushing against the bear's familiar plush fabric. Gently, she pulled it out and set it on the table.

"It's been through the lost and found, but at least it's still in one piece."

Darren stared at the bear, sadness gathering at the corners of his eyes. He extended a hand toward the small toy, turning it in his hands as if absorbing the memories it carried.

"I didn't think I'd ever see this again," he murmured. "This… means a lot."

May hesitated, her stomach tightening as she watched the pain of loss flicker across Darren's face. *This is too close. Too personal.*

"I'm glad I could find it for you both."

Darren glanced up, his eyes meeting hers. "Thank you again." He reached across the table and laid a hand on her forearm in thanks.

May gave a small nod, searching for the right words, but none came. For a moment, the bear sat between them on the table, a silent presence bridging the space—until the waitress appeared, her cheerful voice breaking through the stillness.

"Are you ready to order? I see it's become a table for three!" She giggled, and Darren and May joined in.

"It sure has," Darren said, grinning. Then he gestured to May. "Ladies first."

May picked up the menu, grateful for the distraction, and scanned the options. The brief pause allowed her to collect herself.

"I'll have the pepper steak in black bean sauce, and a diet coke with lime," she finally said.

Darren ordered the spicy fried rice and a glass of red wine.

Unable to let the silence linger after the waitress left, May said, "Etta told me that her CPS inspection went well."

"It did," Darren said, his posture relaxing as he unwound. "Etta and James are amazing. That little girl doesn't know how fortunate she is to have them fighting for her."

May grinned. "Auntie May is fighting for her too."

Darren laughed lightly. "And doing a great job of it."

"I appreciate that! When do you think this will go to court?"

"We still have quite a few hurdles to overcome before that happens."

As their drinks arrived, Darren took a sip of his wine before asking, "How did you do it, May? How did you move forward after… everything?"

May's smile faltered. She glanced down at her glass and let out a heavy sigh.

"In all honesty, after my baby girl died, I crawled into a hole until it got so dark and so deep that I couldn't see the next day. That's when I knew."

"Knew what?"

"That there was no choice. I couldn't let the grief swallow me whole."

She paused, forcing back tears as his eyes widened with quiet admiration.

"It wasn't easy, Darren. But I told myself that every step forward, no matter how small, was still a step."

Darren nodded, watching her closely, his expression reflective.

"It takes incredible strength to come back from something like that. More than me getting over my wife's death… because she was your baby. Your flesh and blood."

"It's not about being strong," May said gently, shaking her head. "It's about having people who refuse to let you fall apart. People like Etta. When I was brand new at the hospital, Etta barely knew me, but she wrapped her arms around me and showed me love."

May paused, her attention drifting to the bear on the seat beside Darren.

"I got through it because of her. She was the friend I needed, and she didn't hesitate. You want to know why I dug through the lost and found for that bear?"

Warmth crept into her tone.

"Because I saw that you needed a friend."

Darren leaned back, letting her words settle. A thoughtful smile played at the corners of his lips.

"Thank you for paying it forward. You're an incredible woman, May."

She murmured a light laugh, a hint of playfulness returning. "That's what my mama used to tell me. I guess she was right about some things," she said, giving Darren a quick wink—just as the waitress arrived with their food.

They both chuckled when the young server set down the tiniest plate as well.

"For Mister Bear," she said. "Rice and honey."

She smiled before walking away.

Chapter Twenty-Six

THERE ARE DAYS THAT etch themselves into a person's soul—moments so profound they remain forever. Under the gentle glisten of the May moon, as its light spilled across the night sky, Storm's wide, curious eyes met James'. In that instant, he felt it—a deep, unshakable certainty that he was holding his baby daughter.

This was the moment he would carry in his heart for the rest of his life.

Her skin was soft, delicate as a whisper, while her perfect, tiny fingers curled tightly around his, anchoring him to the present as he cradled her close.

The weight of her in his arms felt both fragile and extraordinary, and he loved how she fit there, as if the formation of his arms had been created to cradle her that way.

"So, you're the precious little girl we've been battling the world for," James murmured.

He glanced over at Etta, who sat on the sofa across from him, her eyes fixed on the man she loved as he gently held the child who had already captured her heart.

The soft radiance of the table lamp cast a tender light across her serene expression, and for a fleeting moment, all the challenges she and James had faced seemed to melt away.

In that beautiful, captivating moment, her world felt perfect.

"Etta, I need a towel… She just threw up."

James' voice, laced with both humor and mild panic, fractured the quiet.

Etta turned toward him, her smile widening as she laughed softly.

Reaching into the baby bag the caseworker had provided, she pulled out a wet wipe. "Welcome to my world," she teased, handing it over. "I can't tell you how many times a week that happens to me in the nursery at work."

James glanced down in amusement. "You owe me a new shirt," he said, directing the comment to Storm, who looked up at him with innocent eyes. "It's going on a long list of things you'll need to give me when you're all grown up."

Etta laughed again. "By the time she's a year old, she'll owe you a whole new wardrobe."

James couldn't help but grin as he wiped at the mess.

"Then it's a good thing I'm not too attached to this one."

Storm let out a soft coo, as if attempting to apologize.

Both James and Etta looked at her, their smiles growing.

"Well, let's say I'm attached just a little bit," he added playfully.

In the joy of the moment, they realized that these small, imperfect instances were the threads that would weave together their new family.

"I still can't believe Darren convinced the judge to let us have her this weekend," Etta said, pulling a clean onesie from the baby bag. She held it up and turned toward James. "Here, let me take her. I'll clean her up and slip this on."

"Give her to me," James said, reaching out. "I can do it."

Etta raised an eyebrow, her expression halfway between doubt and amusement. "You sure?"

James nodded with a small smile. "Might as well get used to it, I suppose..."

He feigned reluctance and cast a wink at Etta.

Etta watched as James carefully cleaned Storm and slipped the onesie over her tiny arms, head, and legs with surprising ease.

"You're great at that," she said, her tone laced with playful amazement. "Made to be a dad!"

James glanced up with a smirk. "Why do you sound surprised?"

"I'm not a bit surprised," Etta replied, her lips curving into a smile. "I'm... impressed."

"Which is just a fancy way of saying you're surprised," James teased, raising an eyebrow.

Etta leaned closer, placing a soft kiss on his cheek.

"That's not going to help me forget that you doubted my skills," he said, his voice mock serious.

"Well then," Etta replied with a sly grin, "let me do it again."

James gently placed his hand over Storm's eyes. "Not in front of our child."

"She might as well get used to it."

"Used to what?"

"Seeing love in this house," Etta said playfully. "That's all she'll ever see."

James leaned closer. "And feel," he added before kissing Etta softly.

The Sunday morning sun slipped gently through the curtains, casting soft patterns of light across James' face and stirring him awake. He blinked a few times, stretching lazily before noticing the empty space beside him. Etta wasn't there.

Swinging his legs over the edge of the bed, James let his feet rest on the cool floorboards. Just as he was about to stand, a sound reached his ears—soft, melodic, and unmistakable.

Etta was singing.

James paused, a smile framing his lips. He leaned back, grabbed the baby monitor from the nightstand, and brought it close. Etta's voice flowed through, light and soothing, wrapping around him like a warm embrace.

Closing his eyes, he pictured her in the nursery, cradling Storm in her arms, the gentle rhythm of her rocking matching the lullaby's cadence.

I could get used to this.

Her singing stirred a memory long buried but never forgotten.

As a boy, his mother had sung to him every night before tucking him into bed, her voice a blanket of comfort. It had been years since he'd felt that kind of peace—until now.

Etta's voice reminded him of what he'd always wanted from his parents: warmth, security, and love. Storm would never have to worry with Etta.

With her, the music he'd cherished would never stop.

Holding the monitor tightly, James settled back against the pillows, letting the melody wash over him. He wasn't in a hurry to start the day—not when this moment was so perfect.

Chapter Twenty-Seven

A DOCTOR'S NAME CRACKLED over the hospital intercom as Etta and May made their way to the nurse's station, their steps slower than usual. Tired but thankful, it was finally time to clock out.

"I won't ask what you and James are doing this weekend," May said, reaching into the bottom locked drawer for her purse.

Etta leaned against the counter, still holding the flip chart from her last set of rounds. "Can you hand me mine?" she asked, her voice heavy with fatigue. "We've got Storm again this weekend."

May handed her the purse with a small smile. "Four weekends in a row now, right?"

Etta's face lit up. "Can you believe it? James and I are loving it. But it hurts every time she has to go back."

"I'm sure it must."

"I just can't wait for this to be over," Etta said, her shoulders slumping slightly. "You should see James with her, May. It's beautiful. I didn't think it was possible, but I love him even more."

"With the heart, all things are possible."

"Ain't that the truth. That little girl has expanded both of our hearts."

"Has Darren said anything new about your case?" May asked casually.

Etta raised an eyebrow. "You should know."

May smirked. "What's that supposed to mean?"

"Well, while James and I have been seeing Storm for the past four weeks, you've been…"

"I have not been seeing Darren, if that's what you're hinting at! And even if I had, it would not be like that," May interrupted, defensive but playful. "He needs a friend. And honestly, so do I."

Etta set the flip chart down and leaned over the counter. "So, what am I then?"

May reached out, resting her hand over Etta's. "You know what I mean."

Etta's shoulders relaxed as a teasing smile crept onto her face. "Yeah, I do. I think."

"Stop it, Etta Harris. Stop it right this minute."

Before Etta could respond, the phone at the nurse's station rang. May picked it up, her expression shifting slightly before holding it out to Etta.

"It's James."

"Hey there."

"Etta, Darren called," James said, his tone urgent. "He needs us to meet him at his office right away."

Panic rose in Etta's chest. "Why?"

"He didn't say, but he made it sound important."

Etta's grip on the phone tightened. "I'll meet you there."

"Whatever it is, we'll handle it together. Remember that," James said firmly.

Etta exhaled, gathering herself. "I will."

"I love you."

"I love you too," Etta said before placing the phone back on the receiver. She turned to May, her eyes betraying her worry.

"What's going on?" May asked, concern flashing across her face.

"I don't know," Etta replied, grabbing her purse. "But something tells me everything is about to change."

Chapter Twenty-Eight

THE MOMENT JAMES SAW Etta step out of her car, he knew. The tightness around her eyes, the way she clutched her purse—she was worried. But so was he.

Without a word, he extended a hand toward hers, his touch comforting as they walked toward the building's entrance. The familiar hum of the lobby buzzed around them, but Etta barely noticed, her thoughts consumed by the possibilities waiting on the twentieth floor.

"It could be good news," James said softly as they stepped into the elevator. "We really don't need to go thinking the worst." He pressed the button, glancing at her.

His voice was calm, but she caught the faintest flicker of uncertainty in his eyes.

Etta tried to smile, but it felt more like a grimace. "Maybe," she murmured, her heart pounding in her chest. *Breathe, Etta. Just breathe.*

The movement of the elevator filled the silence as they ascended, and she found herself staring at the floor numbers above the door, willing them to move slower. Then faster.

She wasn't sure which she wanted.

When the doors opened, Etta hesitated just outside the elevator.

"What if we go in there and he tells us the judge has denied our petition for legal guardianship or—"

"No 'what ifs,'" James interrupted. He turned to face her, his eyes anchored on hers. "No speculation. Let's just go in and hear what Darren has to say. Whatever it is, I know he already has a plan. We have to trust that, right? And besides, whatever it is, you and I can't change it."

Etta stared at him, letting his confidence wrap around her like the warmth she needed.

She nodded slowly, taking a deep breath. "Right."

James gave her hand a reassuring squeeze. "We've made it this far. We'll handle whatever comes next. Together."

Her grip tightened in his, drawing strength from his certainty.

As they walked toward Darren's office, the knot in her stomach loosened just enough for her to take another deep, calming breath.

Darren's desk wasn't as meticulously kept as usual. Files lay scattered across the surface, some teetering precariously near the edge. Balled-up pieces of paper dotted the floor—a stark contrast to the precision they'd come to expect. The sight alone sent a chill down Etta's spine.

When they stepped into the room, Darren stood by the window, his back to them, staring out at the Chicago skyline. The subtle stream of city lights reflected off the glass, spilling long shadows across the disarray.

"Come in," he said without turning. His voice was quiet. Weighted.

As Etta and James stepped further into the office, Darren finally turned to face them. His expression was guarded, but his eyes betrayed a sadness that made Etta's stomach twist.

He motioned toward the chairs in front of his desk. "Have a seat," he said, moving behind it. He shifted a few files from one side to the other, as though organizing his thoughts rather than the papers.

Etta glanced at James, her heart already sinking. She reached for his hand as they sat, gripping it tightly, interlacing their fingers and needing the reassurance of his presence.

Darren settled into his chair, his shoulders slumping.

"There's no easy way to say this," he began, his tone uncharacteristically hesitant. "I got a call from CPS today."

The room seemed to hold its breath.

"They found a relative."

The words landed like a gut punch. Etta's hand slipped from James' as she leaned back in her chair, her breath catching in her throat. The air felt too thick. Too heavy.

Her mind raced, each thought more overwhelming than the last.

James shifted in his seat, his jaw tightening. "A relative?" he repeated. "Where have they been all this time? Why has it taken them so long to show up if they're interested?"

Darren sighed, running a hand over his face.

"It's the sister of Storm's biological mother," he said. "Child Protective Services is legally required to consider all biological family connections before finalizing any guardianship or adoption."

Etta stared at the desk, her fingers gripping the armrests as her chest tightened with every word. "What does that mean for us? For Storm?"

"It means there's going to be a hearing. The court will evaluate whether this relative is a viable option for placement." Darren leaned forward, locking eyes with Etta. "But this doesn't mean it's over. Far from it. Please—let's keep looking forward."

Etta shook her head, trying to process.

"How can she just… step in now? After everything? I mean, like James says, it's been so long already. She had to have known her sister was expecting and…"

She trailed off, throwing up her hands, defeated.

Darren's expression softened, though the strain around his eyes remained. "She's been out of the country. She only recently learned about Storm's situation and came forward as soon as she could. I'm scheduled to meet with her and her attorney tomorrow."

Etta shook her head in disbelief. "And the foster parents? How are they reacting to this?"

"They're not going to challenge her," Darren said, frustration threading through his voice. "They've decided to step back from the fight. They believe a child belongs with family first and foremost."

Etta drew in a sharp breath, anger rising.

"But that's ridiculous. Just because someone's family doesn't mean they have their life sorted or that they'd even want to be responsible for a child. It's ridiculous."

James nodded. Darren did too.

"I know," Darren said quietly.

"So how much did they even want her?" Etta pressed. "They're leaving us to fight an even bigger battle!"

Darren nodded slowly, his expression apologetic. "It seems that way."

James reached for Etta's hand, but she felt the slight tremble in his grip.

"I don't care if it's Goliath we have to go up against," he said, his voice filled with unshakable resolve. "We love that little girl. She's our daughter."

Darren leaned back slightly, giving them both a measured look.

"I know," he said. "And we'll make sure the court sees that. I know this feels like a setback, but it's not the end. We're going to fight this, and I won't let Storm end up anywhere that isn't in her best interest."

Etta swallowed hard, clearing the lump in her throat.

"If the foster parents aren't in this fight anymore, could we... could we become Storm's foster parents until this goes to court?"

Darren pressed his lips together in thought.

"It's possible. If we can demonstrate that staying with you would provide continuity and stability, the judge might approve temporary placement with you and James."

James turned to Darren, urgency sharpening his voice.

"Can you try to get the judge to agree to that?"

Darren nodded. "I'll meet with the judge tomorrow, after I've spoken with the aunt and her attorney. My argument will focus on how disrupting Storm's routine now would be detrimental—especially considering the bond she's already formed with you both."

Etta straightened, determination blazing through her.

"Let's do that. Let's do whatever it takes."

Darren met their eyes, tension easing slightly from his shoulders.

"All right," he said. "I'll make sure the judge hears our case."

Chapter Twenty-Nine

ETTA LOOKED UP AT the night sky as James pulled the car out of the parking spot.

The stars seemed unusually bright, scattered across the dark canvas like tiny promises.

But her mind refused to settle. The weight of their meeting with Darren clung to her, filling the silence in the car with unspoken fears.

She glanced at James.

His eyes were fixed on the road, but the crease in his brow betrayed his silent worry. Without a word, she reached over and took his hand, lacing her fingers with his.

He gave her hand a gentle squeeze, his lips twitching into a faint, weary smile.

"We're going to be okay," he said, though the tremor in his voice hinted that he was trying to convince himself as much as her.

"I know," she whispered, leaning her head back against the seat. "We just have to believe."

The hum of the tires on the asphalt filled the space between them, a rhythmic reminder of the path they were on—not just the road home, but the fight they were determined to win for Storm.

The light ahead turned red, and James eased the car to a stop. The low, amber glow from the dashboard accentuated the worry lines etched into his brow.

Etta looked up at the sky, her voice barely above a whisper.

"I just hope she knows how much we fought for her."

James glanced at her. "We haven't stopped fighting, Etta. Not for a second."

Etta turned to him, tears filling her eyes.

"But this woman—her aunt. How can we compete with that? She's family, James. What if the court sees that as enough?"

"We're family too. Maybe not by blood, but by choice. And sometimes, that's stronger."

The light turned green, and James pressed gently on the accelerator. The soft hum of the engine offered a momentary balm for their frayed nerves.

Neither of them noticed the speeding car barreling toward them from the side until the headlights flooded their vision.

The impact came hard—a violent eruption that tore through the stillness. Glass exploded into tiny shards, scattering like falling stars.

Metal groaned and twisted, the force flipping their world into a dizzying spiral of chaos.

The car spun out of control, the screech of tires and the roar of colliding steel echoing into the night. It finally slammed into a streetlight, the frame crumpling under the force.

And then—silence.

A suffocating, deafening quiet, broken only by the faint sound of sirens growing louder in the distance.

Inside the wreckage, Etta's head rested against the seat, her eyes half-open as though still searching the stars. James' hand remained in hers, their fingers intertwined—unbroken even in the stillness of their final moment.

The sirens drew nearer, but the stars above shone on, unchanging, as if bearing witness to the love they both would leave behind.

Chapter Thirty

MAY SAT ON THE edge of her bed, the funeral program for Etta and James trembling in her hands.

Tears traced silent paths down her cheeks as her eyes locked onto their photo, frozen smiles staring back at her from a moment untouched by the grief now suffocating her.

She ran her fingertips over the glossy paper as if the gesture could somehow bring them closer and let out a shuddering sigh.

No words came to her—not from her mother, whose wisdom had always been her anchor, nor from her own heart, which felt hollowed out and raw.

There was nothing that could quiet the relentless ache deep within her chest.

In an hour's time, she would say goodbye to her best friend. The thought was unbearable. She couldn't even bring herself to say Etta's name aloud; it caught in her throat every time she tried. The silence that followed each failed attempt was louder than any words could have been.

Her eyes drifted to the closet door, where her black dress hung limply on its hanger.

It seemed out of place there, a shadow against the soft earth tones of the room.

The sight of it made her chest tighten further. The dress looked as forlorn as she felt, its presence a grim reminder of the finality of the day ahead.

The phone rang, cutting through the oppressive quiet.

She wiped her eyes quickly and answered, "Hello."

"I'm on the way," Darren said, his voice heavy with sadness. "I should be there in about ten minutes."

"Did you speak to her?" May asked, hesitant.

"Yeah," Darren replied after a brief pause. "She's coming, and she's bringing Storm. Are you sure having the aunt there is a good idea?"

May closed her eyes, releasing a sigh that felt as though it had been held in for days.

"They would have wanted Storm there," she said quietly. "She belonged to them. I don't care what any judge or aunt might say otherwise."

"I understand. I'll see you soon."

May nodded even though he couldn't see her, then slowly returned the phone to the receiver. Her attention drifted back to the black dress hanging on the door, its presence a burden she still wasn't ready to carry. But she had to.

Rising from the bed, she walked over to the dress, her fingers brushing against the linen fabric. The day ahead would be one of the hardest of her life.

But for Etta, for James, and for Storm, she would face it head-on.

Taking a deep breath, she whispered, "A storm may test your strength, but it will never break your spirit if you stand tall and face it with courage."

Etta's voice echoed in her mind, the memory of her first day on the job sharp and vivid.

Those words had anchored her then, and now they acted as a lifeline, pulling her through the unbearable grief threatening to consume her.

May reached for the dress, her fingers trembling as she carefully slipped it off the hanger. With tears brimming, she began to prepare for the awful goodbye that would forever leave an imprint on her soul.

Sarah Michaels entered Oak & Haven Funeral Home, her presence drawing brief glances despite her attempt to slip in unnoticed. The room was illuminated by delicate pendant lights hanging from the high ceilings, their warm glow reflecting off the polished mahogany pews.

The walls, painted in muted taupe, were adorned with tasteful floral arrangements and framed landscapes evoking a sense of quiet peace. A faint scent of lilies and cedar hung in the air, mingling with the soft hum of whispered condolences.

She carried a baby in one arm and a car seat in the other, moving with the quiet grace of someone accustomed to managing both elegance and responsibility.

She was thirty minutes late, so she settled into a seat in the back row. With careful movements, she placed Storm's car seat down and gently eased the baby inside.

Her cream silk dress shimmered softly under the diffused lights, the fabric clinging delicately to her poised frame. She had paired the dress with solid gold earrings that framed her face, enhancing her rich mahogany complexion. A black hat, trimmed with fine cream stitching, added a touch of sophistication, while freshwater pearls at her neck swayed slightly as she adjusted Storm's blanket.

Sarah's eyes swept the room, searching for the man who had called her and urged—no, demanded—that she be here today. Darren Johnson. He sat near the front.

Frustration swirled within her as she looked at him, seated with quiet resolve. She still wasn't entirely sure why she'd come, but here she was anyway, watching him as he focused intently on the woman in the sheath-style black linen dress approaching the podium.

The striking contrast of the woman's bright red lipstick against her somber attire seemed to speak of inner strength—a boldness against the heaviness of grief.

Around the room, the audience opened their programs to the obituary. Sarah followed suit, her eyes darting between the printed words and the woman's trembling yet determined voice as she began to read.

When the woman finished, she remained at the podium, her hands gripping its edges. Silence filled the room as she wiped away the tears streaming down her face, her breaths coming in uneven bursts. Finally, she raised her head, clearing her throat.

"If you don't mind," she began, "I'd like to say a few words."

The audience nodded quietly.

"I met Etta ten years ago when we started working together. I'll never forget my first day on the job. It came at one of the darkest times in my life. I had just experienced a tragedy, and in a desperate attempt to find some semblance of normalcy, I walked into that hospital determined to throw myself into my work. But as I stood in the locker room later that day, the weight of losing my husband and daughter overwhelmed me. I broke down, unable to stop the tears that soaked through my nurse's uniform. Etta came over. She didn't hesitate.

"She put her hand gently on my shoulder and said, 'A storm may test your strength, but it will never break your spirit if you stand tall and face it with courage.'"

"Those words—those words got me through my shift. They got me through life. They are getting me through today as I stand here remembering Etta and James. My friends. My family."

When the woman at the podium said Etta and James' names, Sarah's heart tightened. She glanced back at Storm just as the baby's small hand lifted, her fingers splaying in a gesture that seemed almost intentional.

A sharp breath escaped as she leaned closer, gently smoothing Storm's blanket.

"You understand what's going on, don't you?" Sarah whispered.

Storm let out a faint coo.

Chapter Thirty-One

THE LINE OF PEOPLE waiting to offer their condolences was long, so Sarah lingered at the back of the room, watching silently until the line dwindled down to just a few. She glanced down at Storm, thankful the baby had drifted off to sleep. Carefully, Sarah picked up the car seat, cradling it with an awkward gentleness as she made her way toward the front row.

How women happily lug these things around is beyond me, she thought, adjusting her grip as she set the car seat down gently in an empty seat near the front.

From a few feet away, May leaned slightly toward Darren and murmured under her breath, "Here comes the long-lost aunt."

Sarah paused mid-step, catching the words but choosing not to react. Instead, she straightened her posture, smoothed the fabric of her dress, and closed the remaining distance between them, her expression calm but unreadable.

Sarah extended her hand toward May. "Hi, I'm Sarah Michaels."

May shook Sarah's hand, her grip firm, but her focus shifted almost immediately to Storm, nestled in the car seat. "She's asleep,"

Sarah said quickly, her tone softening as if to explain herself. "Poor thing sleeps most of the day, but the second her eyes open, the crying starts."

May raised an eyebrow, her lips curving into a faint, knowing smile. "That's what babies do. I take it you haven't been around many."

Sarah nodded, feeling the weight of May's words settle heavily in her mind. "I'll admit, this is all new to me," she said, her tone betraying a hint of defensiveness. "But I'm a quick learner."

She hesitated briefly, then added, "My condolences on the loss of your friends."

"They weren't just my friends," May said, her voice edged with quiet defiance. "They were my family. Just like that little girl is."

Sarah hesitated before speaking again.

"If you're ever in Atlanta, you're welcome to come and see Storm whenever you like." As soon as the words left her mouth, regret washed over her. This wasn't the time to bring up her plans to take Storm to Atlanta once legal guardianship was secured.

"Nothing has been settled yet," Darren interjected, cutting through the tension.

Sarah blinked, her brows furrowing slightly. "What is there to settle? Storm is my sister's child. I'm her biological aunt. The foster parents aren't fighting for her anymore, and—"

"Thank you for coming," May interrupted, her tone polite but carrying an unmistakable finality. "And thank you for bringing Storm. I know you didn't have to, but I also know they would have wanted her here."

Sarah met May's eyes, her shoulders square and her voice even. "I came out of respect. I know they loved her. That's why they fought so hard to adopt her. But the truth is, I'm her family."

May's lips pressed into a thin line.

"Respect? You didn't come here out of respect. You came to measure them up. To see if a nurse and a baker could ever compare to what someone like you—with your designer cream dress and pearls—could offer. But, like I said, thank you for coming."

Sarah nodded curtly. Without another word, she lifted the car seat, Storm still peacefully sleeping inside, and made her way to the door.

As she stepped into the bright Saturday afternoon sunshine, she paused and turned back.

Her eyes locked on May, a silent challenge in the air.

May exhaled, her shoulders falling as the tension of the moment lingered. Darren stepped closer once Sarah was no longer in view. "You handled that better than I expected."

May smirked faintly, though her eyes stayed fixed on the door through which Sarah had just exited. "I don't think I've handled anything yet. But I will."

Chapter Thirty-Two

THE COFFEE SHOP WAS a cozy spot tucked into a quiet corner of May's neighborhood. The scent of freshly brewed coffee mingled with the faint sweetness of baked goods, creating a warm, inviting atmosphere. Soft jazz music played in the background, its soothing melody blending with the occasional hiss of the espresso machine.

May was seated at a small table near the window, her caramel-colored trench coat draped neatly over the back of her chair. She wore a long-sleeved burgundy sweater tucked into a plaid wool skirt, the rich tones complementing the vibrant leaves visible through the glass.

She absently traced the rim of her water glass with her finger, her mind restless despite the comforting aroma of the shop.

When the door opened, the bell above it jingled, instantly pulling May's attention. Darren stepped inside, the crisp October air clinging to him as he unwound a dark gray scarf from around his neck. He wore dark jeans and a white polo shirt under a navy sweater—a stark contrast to the suits she was so used to seeing him in. The casual look suited him, though, and May found herself thinking that he seemed far more relaxed.

She offered a small wave as Darren's eyes found her, and he made his way over, his warm smile cutting through the chill of her thoughts.

His eyes lingered for a second longer than usual.

"You look lovely," he said as he pulled out the chair across from her.

May smiled, a touch of color rising to her cheeks. "Thank you. You do too! It's the first time I've seen you in something other than a suit."

Darren let out a quiet laugh as he sat down. "It's the first time I've seen you in something other than scrubs—or that black dress from yesterday. It was a nice dress, by the way."

"Thank you." Her smile faded slightly, but she recovered quickly, gesturing toward the menu. "What'll it be?"

"Black coffee," Darren said, his tone light. "You?"

"Same," May replied, waving to the barista.

As they placed their orders, Darren leaned back slightly, his eyes scanning the room before resting on May again. "I wasn't sure if you'd want to meet today. Yesterday was… a lot."

"It was," May admitted, smoothing the fabric of her skirt. "But moments like this help you keep moving forward. Etta would've said the same."

Darren nodded, his expression thoughtful. "You're right. It's why I threw myself into work after Michelle passed away. Staying busy—it felt like the only way to keep from falling apart."

May held his eyes, the shared understanding between them filling the space. "Sometimes, busy is the only thing that keeps us sane."

Their coffees arrived, and for a moment, they sat in silence. The hum of the shop, punctuated by soft conversations and the whiff of coffee beans, created a comforting backdrop.

Darren finally broke the quiet. "May, as your friend, I need to be honest with you. This is going to be a heck of a fight. Not impossible, but it could get ugly."

May nodded, her fingers curling around her mug. "I appreciate the warning, but I've thought about it, Darren. I thought about it all night. And I'm doing this—for Etta, for James, and for Storm. That woman doesn't know the first thing about raising a child. Did you see her with the car seat? She was fumbling like it was a jigsaw puzzle."

Darren gave a low, light laugh—his first genuine smile of the morning. "I noticed. But don't underestimate her attorney. He's good. Real good."

"He might be," May said, her tone level. "But I have you, right?"

Darren reached across the table, placing his hand on hers. "Of course."

May glanced down at his hand.

Let's keep things in the friend zone, girl. He isn't ready—but are you?

The barista called their names. Darren stood, gesturing for May to follow him. As they walked to retrieve their drinks, May said casually, "You know, we both look different today."

Darren raised an eyebrow, handing her the coffee with a small smile. "Different can be good."

May nodded, cradling the warm cup in her hands before taking a sip. "My mama used to say that different is what changes the world."

Darren let out a low laugh as they made their way back to the table. "You and your mother, May," he said with a fond shake of his head. "She must have been something else."

"Well, the apple doesn't fall far from the tree," May said, her lips forming a playful smile.

"I'm sure it doesn't," Darren said, shaking his head again before taking a sip of his coffee.

"There's a park nearby," May said, setting her empty cup gently on the table. "How about a walk? We could talk strategy and enjoy that crisp wind hovering out there."

Darren smiled, a hint of laughter escaping him, but he shook his head. "I'd love to, but I need to get back. My mother has a date."

May's eyebrows shot up. "Your mother? A date?"

He nodded, clearly amused by her surprise. "Yeah, she met him while taking Isaiah for a stroll. They got to talking, and before the conversation ended, he was asking her to dinner. Now, she swears tonight isn't a date, but I know better."

May placed her hand on her heart, her smile warm. "Isaiah. I haven't seen him since he was just a couple of days old, and that was six months ago. He's probably grown so much since."

"He has," Darren said, standing as he pulled his car keys from his pocket. "You know, I don't live far from here. Fifteen minutes, tops. Why don't I pick up Isaiah and meet you at the park?"

May hesitated. "I don't want to put you through all that."

Darren shook his head, his smile unwavering. "You're not putting me through anything. He needs to see his Aunt May."

May's lips curved into a soft smile, the warmth of the nickname settling over her. "All right," she said finally. "Then Aunt May would love to see him too."

Chapter Thirty-Three

MAY SAT ON A wooden bench beneath an old oak tree, its branches nearly bare, with only a few golden leaves clinging to the ends. The crisp air carried the faint scent of damp earth and the distant smokiness of burning leaves. Around her, the park was quiet except for the rustling of fallen leaves and the occasional laughter of children playing in the distance.

In front of her, a small pond reflected muted sunlight, its surface rippling gently as a mother duck glided gracefully across the water, her ducklings trailing behind in a wobbly, endearing line. The scene held a serene beauty, but the chill in the air mirrored the ache in May's chest, making the moment feel bittersweet.

She watched the little family, her vision blurring as tears spilled over.

The mother duck gently nudged her ducklings forward, their tiny, hesitant movements a bittersweet reminder of life's delicate and uncertain journey.

May reached into her pocket, pulling out a tissue to dab at her cheeks.

Her thoughts drifted to Etta, and a sharp pang of grief claimed her chest.

Work had been a fog this past week without her. Each shift had felt hollow, and every quiet moment an echo of Etta's absence. The hospital halls, once bustling with shared purpose, now felt strangely empty, as if the world had shifted just enough to feel off balance.

Now that the funeral was behind her, the weight of the void left by Etta settled heavily on her shoulders. It was as though the finality of saying goodbye had left her standing alone at the edge of a vast emptiness. But as the ducklings paddled clumsily behind their mother, May thought of the words she had so often shared with others.

One step at a time. Keep moving forward.

Now, it was her turn to live by them. She straightened her posture, inhaling deeply, as if to breathe in a renewed sense of purpose.

Storm needs you.

A soft crunch of gravel broke through her thoughts, and May turned to see Darren approaching, pushing a sleek black stroller along the park's winding path. Isaiah sat snugly inside, bundled in a navy coat, his wide eyes taking in everything around him, while his feet kicked with boundless energy. Darren navigated toward her with an easy, warm smile.

"Hey," he greeted, stopping the stroller in front of the bench. "Sorry to keep you waiting. It took me forever to find Isaiah's coat. Definitely a humbling moment. Makes me even more grateful my mother's decided to move in."

May laughed, her eyes falling to Isaiah, who clutched a familiar stuffed bear tightly in his tiny hands. "I remember that bear," she said, reaching out to gently brush her fingers over Isaiah's hand. The little boy looked up at her curiously, his grip on the bear unrelenting.

"Yeah," Darren said with a smile. "He doesn't go anywhere without it. It's his favorite thing in the world right now."

"So, all that digging through the lost and found," May said, giving the bear's head a tender rub, "was worth every second."

"I'm sure Isaiah would say so," Darren replied, taking a seat, "and for what it's worth, I'm still grateful too." His eyes lingered on her face, softening as he noticed the faint trace of tears she was trying hard to hide. "You okay?" he asked gently.

May turned her attention to the stroller as Isaiah babbled softly to himself. "Yeah," she said, her voice a little too quick, a little too curt. "It's just been… a lot, you know?"

Darren nodded, leaning forward slightly, his elbows resting on his knees.

"I do know," he said quietly. "And you don't have to pretend with me, May. I'm your friend. You know I understand the pain of loss."

May's eyes followed the mother duck gliding across the pond, her ducklings paddling behind her in close formation. "It's a lot of responsibility to raise a child on your own," she said. "I want you to know that I understand that. I'm not going into this blindly or with my emotions on my sleeve. I'm doing this because I want to give that little girl everything Etta wanted for her."

She turned to Darren, her eyes focused despite the tears threatening to surface.

"I will love her as if she were my own. And I'll make sure she knows who her parents could have been. She'll know them through my eyes, Darren."

He offered a weary smile. "Sounds like you're taking your own advice for once."

May let out a small laugh, but it was filled with sorrow. "I have to. I've been telling myself that every day since the accident."

She took a deep breath, her hands folding tightly in her lap.

"I know it's a long shot—getting guardianship of Storm—but I have to try. I have to..." Her voice trailed off, thick with hesitation.

Darren's brows creased. "What is it, May?"

A quiet tremor ran through her as the words pressed at the edge of her lips. "I need to tell you something."

"Okay."

"I was married before."

Darren's expression didn't shift. "I know."

"No," she said, shaking her head. "You don't. The husband you know about—that was my second husband. What I'm telling you now isn't something I share often. But I know you have to do your due diligence, so you need the full story. I don't want there to be any surprises."

He sat up straighter, a gentle expression on his face urging her to go on.

"I was eighteen when I met my first husband. I thought I was in love, Darren. My mama told me I wasn't. She told me a hundred times, but I didn't listen, thinking I knew better."

Her voice wavered slightly, the memories pulling at her.

"We got married at the courthouse, and for two years, life felt perfect. He was five years older, had his own place, and I thought I'd made it—thought I'd found my forever."

She paused, looking back at the pond as though searching for something in the ripples.

"Then one day, there was a knock at the door. I answered it, and standing there was a girl about my age. She was holding a baby and asking for her husband."

Darren frowned slightly, sensing where the story was heading.

But he let her speak at her own pace, letting her tell this in her own words.

"I told her she had the wrong apartment, but then she started describing him—my husband, Bryon. Turns out, she wasn't wrong. They'd gotten married a few months before Bryon and I did. Her marriage was legal. Mine wasn't."

May let out a bitter laugh, her hands unclenching as she wiped at the corner of her eye.

"I dragged my sorry self back to Mama's house, only to find out she'd been battling cancer the whole time I'd been gone. She didn't tell me, didn't want to pull me from my 'perfect' life."

Her voice broke slightly. "She'd passed before I got there, so I never got to say goodbye. Just like Etta. Both of them—gone, just like that."

Darren reached out, his hand resting gently over hers.

"I'm so sorry, May. That's… a lot for anyone to carry."

May nodded, her voice quivering. "It is," she admitted, swallowing hard. "My mother was a nurse. She inspired me to follow the same path. Losing her felt like losing a piece of myself. And now, losing Etta… it feels like reliving that pain all over again." Her eyes glistened as she paused, her words catching in her throat. "That little girl, Storm, she's my way of honoring Etta. Of making sure her love, her kindness, and everything she stood for doesn't disappear."

A fire lit in May's eyes. "You know Sarah will never tell Storm about Etta and James. She'll erase them from her life like they never existed. I can't let that happen, Darren. I just can't."

Darren shifted closer. "And you won't. We'll make sure Storm knows who they were. We'll make sure she knows the love they had for her, May. I promise you that."

His words carried conviction, but it was the way Darren looked at her—with quiet understanding and unwavering support—that unraveled her resolve.

His lips were close enough for her to catch the faint aroma of coffee, mingling with the warmth of his breath. The activity around them seemed to fade, the gentle rustle of leaves and distant laughter replaced by the rapid rhythm of her heartbeat.

Don't go there, May. Pull back.

But before she could retreat, Darren leaned in slightly, his eyes locked on hers, as though searching for permission. May's heart answered before her mind could intervene.

Their lips met softly, the touch tentative at first, as if testing the waters of a connection neither had fully acknowledged until now. It wasn't hurried or forceful, but sweet—an exchange of unspoken pain and hope. Darren's hand rested lightly on the back of her neck, pulling her closer.

May closed her eyes, releasing the burdens she had held so tightly.

Every ounce of pain. Every drop of grief.

In that moment, nothing else existed but the quiet comfort they found in each other.

When Darren's lips finally left hers, his eyes searched May's as if silently asking a question he wasn't ready to voice. May felt a rush of emotions rise to the surface, emotions she wasn't ready to name, let alone confront.

"I—" Darren started, but May raised a hand.

"Don't," she whispered. "Let's just… Well, let's just let it be for now."

Chapter Thirty-Four

DARREN SAT IN HIS office chair, staring out of the large window overlooking the bustling Chicago streets below. The world outside moved in its predictable rhythm—cars honking, people rushing, a city alive with purpose. Yet inside his office, Darren felt unmoored. His work had always been his anchor, the one place where logic and preparation outweighed emotion.

But now, his thoughts were consumed by the park, by May, by the kiss.

It hadn't been planned, not in the slightest. They were both grieving, carrying the weight of Etta and James's absence in ways neither of them fully understood yet. The kiss was spontaneous, born of shared pain and an unspoken connection. But it lingered with him—not just because it had happened, but because of what it might mean.

Darren ran a hand over his head, his fingers pausing as he replayed the moment in his mind. May's expression afterward—part surprise, part hesitation—mirrored his own internal conflict.

They had been leaning on each other so heavily these past months, bound by a shared commitment to Storm and to Etta and James.

Was this something more? Or was it just the product of raw emotions and vulnerability?

He exhaled deeply, rubbing his temples. May had always been a guiding force, a source of warmth and strength in the chaos of their shared mission.

He admired her resilience, the way she fought tirelessly for Storm, her ability to find purpose even in the face of profound loss. But this? This added layer between them felt like stepping onto uncharted ground, and Darren wasn't sure if he was ready—or even capable—of navigating it.

Then there was Isaiah to think about, the child who needed to be at the center of everything, no matter what. His son had been his world since Michelle's passing, a constant reminder of both his greatest joy and deepest pain. Darren had spent every day since her death focusing on being the best father he could, pouring everything he had into making sure Isaiah felt loved, protected, whole. Bringing someone else into that carefully constructed world was not something he had considered—not yet. No, it was way too premature to be jumping into something new.

This could potentially turn little Isaiah's world upside down.

Darren's eyes shifted to a photo on his desk, one of him and Michelle on their wedding day. Her laughter had been captured mid-motion, a light that seemed to leap out of the frame.

He couldn't accept that she was gone—gone forever. He had loved her deeply, and though time had dulled the sharp edges of grief, the scars of losing her still remained.

Could he really open himself up to something new? Could he even consider what it might mean to care for May in a way that went beyond friendship, knowing how much he still carried?

And what about May herself?

A crease formed between his brows as he thought of her, sitting on that bench, her pain and determination etched into her every word. She deserved clarity, not hesitation.

She deserved someone who could match her resolve, her heart.

Was he that person? Could he possibly hope to become that person?

Or would letting her in only complicate an already fragile situation? Perhaps it would be kinder to let her go before they became too enmeshed in one another's tangled lives... She could find someone else, someone who could give her one hundred percent, not mere fragments.

The sound of his office door opening startled him out of his thoughts. His assistant poked her head in, a stack of papers in her hand as usual. "Mr. Johnson, the background checks for Ms. Michaels and Ms. Jones are ready. Should I leave them here for you?"

Darren nodded absently, gesturing to his desk. "Yes, thank you."

As the door clicked shut, Darren leaned closer, his elbows resting on the wood surface.

Now he was already back inside his mind, entrenched in his thoughts. Sweet thoughts, yet painful too. His thoughts had wandered right back to the kiss.

The kiss had opened a door he hadn't even realized was there. Now, he had to decide whether to step through it or close it gently before it could change everything.

One thing was clear: whatever happened next, it couldn't distract them from Storm.

She was the thread tying them together, the reason for their fight, the heart of their shared purpose. But as Darren sat there, lost in thought, he couldn't help but wonder if that kiss was also the beginning of something neither of them had expected.

May stood at the nurse's station, her hands gripping the edge of the counter as she tried to ground herself in the rhythm of the hospital around her. The usual chaos—doctors rushing to pagers, the murmur of patient monitors, the shuffle of nurses exchanging updates—should have been enough to pull her back into her routine.

But her thoughts were elsewhere, stuck on the park, on Darren, on the kiss.

She let out a slow breath, willing her heart to ease. What had she been thinking?

The answer came swiftly: she hadn't been thinking at all. It wasn't a moment of reason or logic. It had been a raw, unfiltered reaction to everything they'd been through together. The shared grief, the long conversations, the way Darren had been her anchor since Etta and James' accident—it had all culminated in that fleeting, unexpected moment of intimacy.

But was it that unexpected?

May leaned back against the counter, her eyes unfocused as the memory played on a loop in her mind. She could still feel the warmth of his hand on hers, the way his voice had softened when he spoke to her, the faint aroma of coffee lingering on his breath.

It wasn't just the kiss itself that unsettled her; it was what it revealed.

Somewhere along the way, her feelings for Darren had shifted, evolving into something she hadn't anticipated and wasn't sure she was ready to face.

She shook her head slightly, trying to dispel the thought. Darren wasn't just anyone.

He was a widower, a father, someone who carried his own share of loss. And she? She was a woman still picking up the pieces of her life after losing her best friend.

Her attention fell to the gold pin on her uniform, the light catching on its polished surface as she traced the delicate design with her thumb. Etta's parents had given it to her at the funeral, their quiet way of passing on a piece of their daughter.

Etta had worn the pin often at the hospital, a small but constant reminder of her unwavering dedication and care. May could almost hear Etta's voice in her mind, calm and controlled as ever: *"You've been through storms before. You'll make it through this one too."*

They were such distant words, and she could barely remember sweet Etta's voice now, but she'd never forget her words of light and encouragement for as long as she lived.

May ran her thumb over the cool metal, her chest tightening.

Back to the kiss.

The kiss had felt… good. But she knew she couldn't afford to fall for someone like Darren. Not now. Not when everything was so fragile, when Storm's future hung in the balance.

And yet, she couldn't deny the comfort he brought her.

Darren understood her pain in a way few others could. He didn't try to fix it or offer empty platitudes; he just was. His reliable presence had become a balm for her grief, a reminder that she wasn't alone in the harshness of this world. But was it fair to lean on him like that?

To blur the lines of their friendship when both of them were still carrying so much?

The sound of a baby's cry echoing from the nursery pulled May from her spiraling thoughts.

She straightened, drawing in a slow breath as she moved with practiced efficiency toward the source. The familiar rhythm of her work offered a momentary reprieve, her hands soothing the infant as she hummed a gentle tune.

But as the baby's cries softened and the room grew quiet again, the weight of her emotions returned, settling over her as she made her way back to the station.

She thought about going to see Darren later.

They needed to talk, to figure out what that kiss had meant—not just to her, but to him. But the idea of seeing him, of risking the awkwardness that might follow, made her hesitate.

What could she even say? *Sorry about kissing you? Let's just pretend it didn't happen?*

Let's both forget the sparks and the tenderness of your warm lips on mine.

May sighed, pulling a notepad from her pocket and jotting down a reminder to call Darren's office tomorrow. She didn't want to leave things unresolved, but she also didn't trust herself to handle the conversation face-to-face. Storm's future was the priority, and whatever her feelings for Darren were, they couldn't distract her from the fight ahead.

But even as she busied herself with her work, the thought of Darren lingered in the back of her mind, resembling a song she couldn't quite shake.

And for a fleeting moment, she allowed herself to wonder:

What if?

Chapter Thirty-Five

MAY WALKED INTO DARREN'S office building just after six, the day's exhaustion clinging to her like the faint antiseptic scent from her shift at the hospital. Her scrubs were wrinkled from hours of work, and her practical black flats scuffed softly against the polished floors with each step.

She had rehearsed what she wanted to say to Darren a hundred times on the drive over: *Let's stay friends. Keep the focus on Storm.*

But the words felt tangled now, caught in a web of emotions she couldn't quite shake.

Just as she reached the elevator, a familiar voice stopped her.

"Well, if it isn't Auntie May," Sarah Michaels said, her tone sharp, layered with mock politeness.

May froze, her hand hovering near the button. Slowly, she turned to face Sarah, who stood a few feet away, her perfectly tailored navy pantsuit and black Prada purse radiating the kind of effortless elegance May could recognize but had never admired.

To her, this show of affluence was pretentious and grandiose—and pointless.

"Sarah," May greeted, her voice cool and even. "What brings you here?"

Sarah smirked, taking a step closer. "I could ask you the same thing. But I'm guessing you're here to strategize with Darren about how to undermine me."

Her eyes narrowed, the tension between them palpable.

May squared her shoulders, refusing to be rattled. "I'm here to talk to Darren about Storm. About what's best for her."

Sarah's expression shifted, a subtle hint of raw emotion breaking through her composed facade. "You think you know what's best for her? Her family. Real family. That's what's best for her."

May lifted her chin, her voice calm but unshakable.

"Family isn't just blood, Sarah. It's love. It's stability. And if you cared so much about your sister, where were you when she needed you most? Where were you when Storm needed you?"

Sarah's lips thinned, her polished demeanor cracking just enough to reveal the pain beneath.

"You don't know anything about what I did or didn't do," she snapped, but her words lacked their earlier sharpness.

"Then tell me," May pressed. "Because from where I'm standing, this feels like guilt, not love. And Storm needs love. Every baby needs love, stability, security. Nothing less."

Sarah's shoulders sagged, her breath hitching as she glanced at the floor.

"I knew Allie's husband was controlling," she admitted. "He had this… presence, you know? But I didn't know he was hurting her. Not until it was too late."

May frowned, her arms crossing as she listened.

"She called me one day," Sarah continued, her voice wavering. "She asked if she could stay with me for a while. I said yes, but she never showed up. The next time I saw Allie, she was pregnant… and wearing sunglasses inside." Sarah's breath hitched again. "I knew then. I should have done more. I should've fought for her. But I didn't."

The vulnerability in Sarah's voice surprised May, her arms loosening slightly. "Sarah—"

"When she passed away," Sarah interrupted, her tone bitter with regret, "I was devastated. But I didn't even know Storm had survived until recently. That's why I'm here now, you see? I can't change what happened to my sister—and I would do anything to turn back the clock and save her—but I can make sure her daughter knows her—knows who her mother was."

A dull ache settled in May's chest as she took in Sarah's words, the raw pain in them undeniable. But so was her own determination.

"Then honor your sister," May said, her voice resolute despite the turmoil inside her. "Honor what she wanted for her child. Because Etta and James loved that little girl like their own. And I will fight to make sure that love doesn't get erased."

Sarah looked at May, her expression unreadable for a fleeting moment before her lips pressed into a thin line. "You won't win this, May," she said, her tone suddenly sharp again. "I promise you, the judge will rule in my favor, and Storm will be coming back to Atlanta with me."

With those words, Sarah turned on her heel, the leather soles of her polished shoes clicking against the tiled floor with an air of finality. Her head held high, she strode toward the exit, her silhouette framed briefly by the glass doors before they slid closed behind her.

Chapter Thirty-Six

JUST AS MAY REACHED out to press the button on the elevator panel, the doors slid open with a soft chime. Her pulse stumbled as Darren stepped out, his expression warm but touched with surprise. He held a file in one hand and clutched a cup of coffee in the other.

"May," he said, "I wasn't expecting to see you here."

"And I wasn't expecting to catch you coming down," she replied, forcing a small smile. "I thought I'd meet you upstairs."

Darren gestured toward the waiting area nearby. "You've caught me just in time. Why don't we talk in the conference room? It's just over here."

May nodded, following his lead, her mind racing as she prepared for the conversation she had been rehearsing all day.

"Darren," May said the moment he stepped into the conference room, closing the door behind him. "I..." Her voice faltered when their eyes met. "I just ran into Sarah Michaels," she finally said, glad to have something else relevant to talk about when her courage failed.

Darren's brows lifted slightly, but his calm demeanor remained.

"Sarah was here with her attorney," he said, nodding.

May placed her bag on the edge of the conference table. "Well, we had… words."

She folded her arms across her chest, her emotions still simmering from the confrontation. "She's convinced she's already won."

Darren hesitated, his lips pressing into a thin line as he chose his words carefully. "Her attorney presented me with proof that the hospital didn't inform her that baby Storm had survived the delivery. Apparently, the paperwork was never filed correctly, and she only found out about Storm recently. So in that regard, she will certainly win empathy from the judge."

May's stomach tightened, and her voice grew more anxious. She felt quite sick.

"Really? Is that going to help her case?"

There was unspoken worry in her tone, and without thinking, he reached over and placed his hand on top of hers. The warmth of the gesture caught her off guard, but she didn't pull away.

"It complicates things," Darren admitted gently. "The judge will certainly see it as mitigating circumstances. It supports her argument that she didn't abandon Storm intentionally. But it's not the only thing the judge will consider."

May's brows furrowed, her free hand gripping the edge of the table.

"Then what else will they consider? Because I'm ready to fight, Darren. I just can't let that little girl be uprooted from everything Etta and James built for her."

Darren looked at her, full of reassurance. "The judge only wants what's in the best interest of Storm. That's where we'll focus. We'll prove that you're the one who can give her the most love, the most certain stability, and the sense of family and constancy she needs."

Tears began to form in May's eyes. "But if I lose, Darren... If I lose, it'll feel like I've failed them, and like I've failed Storm."

"You won't fail," Darren said firmly. "Even if the court rules in Sarah's favor, you'll have shown Storm what it means to fight for someone with your whole heart. And that will matter, May—more than you know. These attempts will always be part of her records, for the rest of her life. Adopted children almost always seek out their records when they turn eighteen. If she doesn't know it much sooner, she'll certainly read about it then."

"If that's supposed to make me feel better, it's not."

"It's the truth, May."

Her voice was unsteady, weighted with doubt. "Truth. It's not always easy to hear, is it?"

Darren shook his head slowly. "It isn't—and sometimes, it's even harder to say."

"I... I believe Sarah loves her. I could hear it in her voice, Darren. The regret, the guilt, the determination. And the judge will hear that too."

Darren leaned back slightly, giving her space but keeping his focus locked on her. "Sarah might love her, May, but love isn't the only thing that makes a family. Stability, understanding, a cohesive framework in which to care for her, as well as demonstrating a sound comprehension of what Storm needs—that's what matters. That's what the judge will look at."

May wiped at her cheeks, her fingers trembling. "But what if I'm wrong? What if this fight does more harm than good? Am I doing the right thing? Am I doing it for selfish reasons?"

"You're doing what you believe is right, and that's all anyone can do," Darren said, reaching out to wipe away her tears. "You're fighting for Storm's future, May. That's not wrong—it's extremely brave. The fact that you are not related to this baby only makes it braver."

May let out a shaky breath. "Thank you, Darren. I needed to hear that."

"You don't have to thank me, May. I'm here for you, no matter what happens."

Her eyes lingered on his, drawn to the calm strength she hadn't realized she'd been searching for. Darren—always composed, always stabilizing—was suddenly so much more than just an ally in her fight for Storm. He was a refuge, a quiet reassurance she hadn't dared to expect.

Before her mind could catch up with her heart, May shifted closer, her pulse quickening.

"Darren…"

His name was barely a whisper, her voice tinged with hesitation.

His hand shifted, cupping hers fully, his fingers brushing lightly over her knuckles in a touch that was both grounding and electrifying.

"May," he said softly, his voice a low murmur hanging in the air between them.

The space separating them dissolved, and their lips met in a kiss that didn't demand explanation, a connection that didn't require words. It wasn't about the battles they were fighting or the weight they were carrying; it was simply about them, in this fleeting, unguarded instant.

Chapter Thirty-Seven

MAY SAT OUTSIDE WHAT had once been Etta and James' home, her car idling quietly at the curb.

The headlights illuminated the *For Sale* sign staked firmly into the ground.

Its bold red letters seemed to glare at her, an undeniable declaration of change, a severing of ties that she wasn't yet ready or willing to accept.

The house itself sat in stillness, its once warm and lively presence now feeling hollow.

The porch light flickered softly, casting a dim light over the front steps as May closed her eyes and allowed the memories to flow.

She'd walked up those steps hundreds of times.

The garden that Etta had tended so lovingly was now slightly overgrown, the bright bursts of flowers replaced by blades of brown grass.

May could almost hear Etta's laughter as she knelt in the soil, her hands dirty, her face glowing with pride as she talked about planting tulips for next spring.

The mailbox still bore their last name in black letters: *Harris.*

Seeing it made May's chest tighten.

She hadn't let herself come here until now. It had felt far too raw, too final. But tonight, she needed to see it, to feel close to them again, if only for a moment.

She shut off the engine and stepped out of the car, the cool evening air brushing against her skin. The familiar creak of the gate made her stomach flip as she pushed it open and stepped onto the walkway.

The front door was adorned with a wreath, one Etta had made herself. It was slightly askew now, the bow grown faded from the sun. May imagined she could hear her friend's voice teasing James for not hanging it straight, and James laughing, insisting it gave the house character.

She looked toward the window beside the door, where the curtains Etta had picked out years ago still hung neatly in place. Behind that window was the living room, the heart of the home.

May could almost see Storm's toys scattered on the floor, Etta perched on the couch with a glass of wine, and James in his chair, flipping through the TV channels.

That's how it was supposed to be for them.

She blinked back tears, the ache in her chest almost too much to bear.

She stepped closer to the porch, her flats brushing the wood, creaking softly under her weight. She sat down on the steps, her hands resting on her knees as she stared out at the yard. The neighborhood was quiet, save for the faint chirp of crickets and the occasional bark of a distant dog.

"This was their dream," she whispered to herself, barely audible. "This house. This life."

May's fingers traced the edge of the step, her mind replaying memories she hadn't dared to let herself revisit. The laughter, the warmth, the sense of belonging that had radiated from this place—it all felt so close, yet so impossibly far away.

A single tear slid down her cheek, and she let it fall, unashamed.

The weight of the day, the funeral, the kiss—both pressed heavily on her chest. Her mind replayed Darren's words from earlier: *"Even if the court rules in Sarah's favor, you'll have shown Storm what it means to fight for someone with your whole heart."*

If I lose, though, how will she know? The thought gnawed at her, a cruel echo of self-doubt that she couldn't silence. Sure, Darren had given her the speech about how, when Storm was eighteen, she could request her adoption records. It was too far away, and Storm would have had eighteen years of not even knowing about Etta and James by then.

They would count for nothing at all in Storm's world.

May took a shaky breath, the quiet of the night stirring a strange kind of memory. Her thoughts drifted back to when she was eight years old, standing in the corner of the school auditorium, tears stinging her eyes after losing the spelling bee. She had refused to go and congratulate the winner, her pride and disappointment too heavy to overcome.

She had always been stubborn, and it wasn't about to change.

Her mother had knelt down beside her, her warm hands settling on May's trembling shoulders. "May, waving that white flag doesn't mean defeat," she'd said, her voice carrying both firmness and love. "That white flag is a sign of strength. It takes courage to understand you can't win every single battle. If you did, the effort would be pointless."

Reluctantly, May had listened, her small legs feeling like lead as she walked over to the spelling bee winner.

With a shaky voice, she had muttered quiet congratulations, her mother standing close, her unwavering presence a reminder that even in moments of loss, there was room for grace.

Now, as May sat outside Etta and James' home, the memory felt as vivid as if it had just occurred. Her mother's words echoed in her mind, wrapping around her heart like a balm.

It takes courage to understand that you can't win every single battle.

She rose slowly from the step, her scrubs creased from the long period of sitting. She inhaled deeply. As she walked back to her car, she stopped and looked back at the house.

For a fleeting moment, she could almost see Etta waving from the porch, her laughter ringing in the air. But reality pulled her back. The *For Sale* sign was an unyielding truth.

She had never wanted to raise her white flag—but knew she might have to.

Chapter Thirty-Eight

THE CONFERENCE ROOM WAS bathed in the late afternoon sunlight streaming through the floor-to-ceiling windows. The air was thick with tension, the kind that made every creak of a chair or shuffle of papers seem amplified. The polished wood of the long table reflected the solemn faces of those gathered around it.

Darren sat at one end, his expression calm but watchful. To his right, May sat upright, her fingers clasped tightly in her lap, a visible effort to calm the trembling that betrayed her nerves. Across from her, Sarah's face exuded defiance and uncertainty. Beside her sat her attorney, a man in his early fifties with a composed demeanor and a rich mahogany leather briefcase resting by his side. He observed silently, occasionally adjusting his glasses or making brief notes.

Darren cleared his throat, his voice breaking the silence. "Thank you all for coming. May has asked me to arrange this meeting because she has something important to say."

May inhaled deeply, her eyes darting toward Darren before settling on Sarah.

"I asked for this because I think we've all been so focused on the fight, on the legalities, that we've forgotten who this is really about—Storm."

Sarah straightened, a wary look in her eyes. "I haven't forgotten. That's why I'm here, May."

"I know," May said, her tone gentle but controlled. "And that's why I'm ready to step back."

The room seemed to hold its breath.

Even Sarah's attorney paused mid-note, his pen hovering over his notepad. His brows lifted, and there was a fleeting look of empathy on his face, as if seeing that the opposition was human after all.

"What are you saying?" Sarah asked, her voice cautious.

May looked at her, eyes shimmering with unshed tears. "I'm saying that I believe you love Storm. I believe you want what's best for her, and I don't want to put her through a drawn-out court battle just to prove who loves her more. Etta and James wouldn't want that. And it's definitely not what's in Storm's best interests."

Sarah's lips parted, her composed exterior faltering for a moment. She glanced at her attorney, who gave a small nod as if to say, *Listen.*

"But," May continued, "if I step back, I need your word. I need your promise that you'll let me be a part of her life. That you'll make sure she knows who Etta and James were, how much they loved her, and how hard they fought for her."

Sarah's fingers loosened. "I never intended to erase them from her life," she said. "I just… I've been so focused on making up for what I couldn't do for my sister. Maybe I didn't see how it looked to you."

May nodded slowly. "I'm sorry for assuming the worst. I was scared. Scared of losing her, of losing another piece of Etta and James. But I really do believe you love her, Sarah. I can see it."

"I do love her very much," Sarah said, her tone almost breaking under the weight of her emotions. She looked directly at May. "And I promise, she'll know who they were. And she'll know them through you. You'll always be Auntie May to her."

May blinked rapidly, trying to keep her tears in check, but the relief in Sarah's words broke through her defenses. "Thank you," she whispered. "That means absolutely everything to me."

Darren leaned back in his chair, the tension in his posture easing as a small, approving smile crossed his face. "It sounds like we're finally finding common ground."

Sarah's attorney cleared his throat, breaking the emotional moment with practicality. "I'll draft an agreement outlining visitation rights for May—spring, summer, and some of the winter break, if you like, May. We can present it to the judge as part of our guardianship proposal."

"Good," Darren said, glancing at May with quiet pride. "That's a step in the right direction."

The room settled into a contemplative silence as May and Sarah exchanged a look. It wasn't trust—not yet—but it was understanding, a shared determination to do what was best for Storm.

As the meeting drew to a close, May stood, smoothing the front of her Kelly green dress. "Thank you, again," she said, her words directed at Sarah but carrying across the room.

Sarah extended her hand. "For Storm," she echoed.

May clasped Sarah's hand, her grip firm yet warm. "For Storm, Etta, and James."

Sarah nodded in agreement.

Darren watched the exchange, a sense of pride settling over him. He gathered his papers with deliberate care, his smile understated but genuine.

The road ahead was still uncertain, but in this moment, they had all taken an important step toward building a future rooted in love, understanding, and the memory of those they had lost.

Chapter Thirty-Nine

MAY SLID INTO THE seat across from Darren, her soft gray dress brushing lightly against her knees as she settled into place. Her hair was neatly tucked behind one ear, with a few loose strands softly framing her face. Silver earrings swayed gently, catching the warm glow of the restaurant's pendant lights.

Her usual bold red lipstick had been swapped for a more understated shade, complementing her natural warmth.

"I feel like we haven't spoken in weeks," Darren said, his eyes resting on her, taking her in.

"It does feel like that, doesn't it?" May said, her voice carrying a hint of something she dared not say out loud. She'd missed him.

Her eyes briefly swept across the bustling restaurant, but the way Darren was looking at her was impossible to ignore.

There's something different about him.

She pulled her attention back to the room, taking in the clinking of chopsticks and the murmur of conversations mingled with the mouthwatering aroma of fried rice and stir-fried dishes wafting through the air. For a moment, the atmosphere felt surreal, as though the rest of the world had hit pause on its problems, creating a fleeting illusion of perfection and kindness.

Darren shifted slightly, leaning in just enough for his focus to linger. "You look… amazing."

"Thank you." May smiled, a faint blush warming her cheeks. "It feels good to finally get a day off and come here not wearing my scrubs."

"Work keeping you busy?" he asked, his tone filled with genuine concern.

May let out a soft sigh, tucking a stray strand of hair behind her ear. "Busy doesn't even begin to cover it. The hospital's been nonstop, and without Etta, it's been…" She hesitated, searching for the right words. "Without Etta, it's been rough. Every day feels like I'm just trying to keep my head above water, you know? I'm just going through the motions."

"I do know what you mean," Darren said. "I meant to call, but every time I picked up the phone, it felt like there was something I couldn't quite put into words."

May looked up, meeting his eyes. "Maybe we're both guilty of that."

A brief silence settled between them, the kind that wasn't uncomfortable but one that acknowledged everything left unsaid. Around them, life carried on. Servers darted between tables to the soft scraping of plates and the ebb and flow of laughter.

But just here, in their small corner of the restaurant, the world seemed to pause.

"I've missed this," May finally said. "Just… talking to you. Being here."

"Me too," Darren admitted, meeting her eyes with a quiet intensity. "I've…"

Before he could finish, the waitress arrived at their table, her cheerful demeanor breaking the moment. "Are you ready to order?" she asked, pen poised over her notepad.

Was he about to say that he missed me?

May exchanged a quick glance with Darren. "You go first," she said, gesturing for him to start.

Darren laughed lightly, glancing at the menu as if he hadn't already decided.

"I'll take the spicy fried rice, and a side of steamed vegetables," he said, handing the menu back to the waitress.

"And for you?" the waitress asked, turning to May.

May closed her menu. "The pepper steak, please. And a hot green tea."

"Great choices," the waitress said, collecting the menus with ease. "Your food will be out shortly."

As the waitress walked away, May leaned back slightly in her chair, letting the moment settle. Darren's unfinished words lingered in the air between them, but neither seemed in a rush to fill the space. Sometimes, silence carried its own kind of understanding.

"How did the date with your mother go?" May asked, her eyes sparkling with curiosity.

"It's turned into four more, actually."

May's laughter bubbled up, warm and genuine. "Good for her. Sounds like she's got herself a little romance going."

"She does," Darren said, shaking his head with an affectionate smile. "I don't know who's more surprised—her or me."

"Well," May said, pausing to give Darren a sly smirk, "every woman—and man—deserves all the happiness they can get from this crazy thing we call life."

Darren matched her smirk with one of his own. A familiar warmth passed between them as the waitress approached the table with their food.

"When's your first visit with Storm?" Darren asked, picking up his fork and taking a small bite.

"Funny you should ask," May said, swirling her straw in her glass. "Sarah called me yesterday. She's going to some ski resort during the Thanksgiving holiday and asked if I could take care of Storm that week."

Darren raised an eyebrow, impressed. "Wow. That's a big step. How do you feel?"

May nodded. "It is a big step, and I think she's finally starting to trust me."

"Nice." Darren set his fork down, leaning in slightly. "It's a wonderful outcome. Listen, why don't you bring Storm to my house that Saturday? She and Isaiah can have a play date."

May's lips curled into a teasing smile. "You sure Isaiah is ready for a date?"

Darren laughed softly. "I think he can handle it." His eyes met May's as she took a sip of her hot tea. "I think we both can."

Chapter Forty

AS THEIR MEAL CAME to a close, Darren leaned back in his chair, savoring the last bite of his fried rice. He set his fork down and looked across the table at May, who was finishing the last bite of her pepper steak.

"Don't tell me the night ends here," he said, his tone light but hopeful.

May glanced up, her brow arched in curiosity. "What do you mean?"

"Well," Darren said, leaning forward slightly, his signature playful smirk tugging at the corners of his mouth, "since it's Friday night, how about we go salsa dancing?"

May froze mid-sip of her tea, lowering her cup slowly. "Salsa dancing?" Her voice carried equal parts surprise and disbelief. "You? Salsa?"

"Why does that sound so impossible to you?" Darren asked, feigning mock offense.

May laughed, shaking her head. "Because you're Darren Johnson. Suits, ties, spreadsheets, and courtrooms. You're telling me you salsa dance?"

Darren leaned back with a confident grin. "There's a lot you don't know about me, May. And trust me, I've got moves."

"Moves?" May repeated, trying to suppress her laughter. "I'll believe it when I see it."

"Well, then," Darren said, standing and offering her his hand, "you'll just have to see it."

May stared at his outstretched hand, her mind racing. "Darren, I don't even have the right shoes for dancing," she said, motioning to her modest heels.

"Excuses," Darren teased. "The May I know never backs down from a challenge."

May rolled her eyes but couldn't stop the smile creeping onto her face. "All right, Mr. Johnson. Let's see these so-called moves of yours."

Darren's grin widened as he left cash on the table for their meal. "You won't regret it."

As they walked out of the restaurant and into the cool November evening, May pulled her jacket tighter around herself. "I can't believe I'm letting you talk me into this," she muttered.

"You're going to thank me," Darren said confidently, his stride full of purpose as they walked down the street. "There's this little place just a few blocks from here. One of the attorneys from the office told me about it. Great music, great energy—it'll be perfect."

May gave him a skeptical side-eye, slowing her pace slightly. "Perfect, huh?"

"Trust me," Darren said, a playful grin on his face.

"Of course I trust you," May replied, narrowing her eyes at him. "But just so we're clear—if I twist my ankle trying to keep up with you, you're carrying me back to my car."

"You know I'd carry you in a heartbeat," Darren said without hesitation.

May's heart skipped a beat. She forced a laugh, pushing the fluttering feeling aside. "You better be as good as you claim," she teased, trying to keep the moment light.

Darren's smirk deepened as he glanced over at her. "Like I say, you'll see."

May shook her head, a smile forming despite herself. "Don't make promises you can't keep."

"You'll be impressed."

"With this place or you?"

"Why can't it be both?"

As the rhythmic beats of salsa music began to drift down the street toward them, May couldn't help but feel a sense of anticipation.

As they walked past a few of the shops along the way, most closed for the evening, May stole a glance at Darren walking confidently beside her. His excitement seemed at odds with the composed professional she was so used to seeing, but it suited him—perhaps too well.

Her thoughts wandered back to the restaurant, to his words, *"I think we both can."*

She hadn't dared to ask what he truly meant. Was it just about the playdate for Storm and Isaiah? Or had there been more behind those words?

"Something on your mind?" Darren's voice broke through her thoughts, drawing her back to the present.

May blinked, caught off guard. "What? No. Just… taking in the moment," she said, her voice a little too quick, betraying her internal conflict.

Darren's lips curled into a knowing smirk. "Uh-huh. Sure you are."

She narrowed her eyes at him, half tempted to brush it off, but something pushed her forward. If he could be confident, why couldn't she? "Fine, then. Since we're asking questions, what did you mean earlier when you said, 'I think we both can?'"

Darren slowed his pace slightly, the music growing louder as they neared their destination. His teasing smirk shifted into something more sincere. "I meant exactly what I said."

May's pulse quickened at his directness.

Darren stopped walking, turning to face her fully, the glow from a nearby streetlamp illuminating his expression. She searched his face, looking for the catch, the teasing remark that would undercut the weight of his words. But it wasn't there.

"Darren," she began, unsure of what she wanted to say next, when the sound of a vibrant Latin beat jolted them both back into the moment. Darren gestured toward the glowing sign of the salsa club, his expression lightening as he offered her his hand.

"Come on," he said with a grin.

May hesitated for a split second before slipping her hand into his, letting his warmth and confidence guide her forward. If tonight was about taking chances, maybe it was time to let the music lead the way.

Chapter Forty-One

THE AIR INSIDE THE salsa club was electric. Raw, untamed energy seeped into every corner of the room. A web of string lights stretched above, illuminating the crowd with soft hues of amber and gold. The rhythmic beat of the music pulsed through the floorboards, vibrating up through May's heels as Darren led her to the edge of the dance floor.

"Ready?" Darren asked. His hand hovered just above hers.

May glanced up at him. "I guess we'll find out."

With that, Darren slipped his hand into hers, his fingers warm against her palm. His other hand came to rest lightly at the curve of her waist, drawing her just close enough for their movements to synchronize without crowding her space. For a man who spent most of his days in suits and courtrooms, he moved with surprising ease, his steps confident and fluid.

"Don't overthink it," he said, his voice a teasing whisper near her ear as she stumbled slightly. "Feel the music."

May laughed softly, nervousness and delight blending together. "Easier said than done when I'm trying not to step on your toes."

"If you do, I can handle it." His hand at her waist tightened just enough to ground her. "Just follow me."

May could feel the music wrapping itself around them as she mirrored his lead.

The crowd around them blurred, their laughter and cheers fading into the background. All she could focus on was the way Darren's hand guided her, the gentle pressure of his palm against hers, and the confident rhythm of his body leading hers.

She hadn't felt the presence of a man like this in years.

Darren, for his part, was captivated. There was something about the way May's lips curved when she let out a quiet laugh, the way her shoulders relaxed as she surrendered to the music, the way her trust in him felt like the greatest victory he'd ever earned.

Holding her this close felt intimate in a way that words couldn't touch, and for the first time in a long time, he let himself lean into that feeling.

As the tempo of the music shifted to something slower, May paused, her eyes dropping to her feet. "I need a second," she said, slipping out of her shoes. She held them in one hand as she turned back to Darren, the gentleness of the lights catching the sheen of sweat on her brow and the flush of her cheeks.

"You're going barefoot now?" he teased. "How brazen!" His grin was cheeky.

"Don't judge me." She stepped closer to him, her bare toes curling slightly against the smooth wooden floor. "You ready? Now I'll show you my moves."

Darren let out a quiet laugh, taking her hand once more and pulling her in.

This time, the space between them evaporated. His arm wrapped firmly around her back, holding her steady as their bodies moved in unison. The slower pace of the song pulled them into a movement that was both deliberate and welcome.

May felt her breath catch as Darren's hand slid from her back to the small of her waist, his fingers splaying gently against the fabric of her dress. She rested her free hand on his shoulder, feeling the tension beneath his shirt easing as they swayed. Her heart raced—not from nerves, but from the way every step seemed to close the distance between them emotionally.

"You're amazing at this," May said softly, her voice barely audible over the music.

"So are you," Darren replied, his tone equally hushed but full of sincerity.

She looked up at him, their eyes locking.

Darren's hand brushed lightly along her waist as they turned, the gesture more instinctual than intentional, yet it sent a spark through her. She felt vulnerable and safe all at once, as though the walls she kept carefully constructed were finally allowed to come down.

The music began to fade, replaced by the sound of applause as the song ended. Darren's hand remained at her waist, fingers brushing gently against her side. May felt a blush rise to her cheeks as she stepped back slightly, but the way he looked at her held her in place.

"I really missed you, May."

She opened her mouth to respond, but the depth in his eyes and the sincerity in his tone spoke the words she hadn't been able to say until now.

"I missed you too," she finally whispered.

Her voice trembled slightly, but there was no hiding what she felt.

Darren's lips curved into a faint smile, one that seemed to hold both relief and something deeper. His hand, still resting gently at her waist, gave the faintest squeeze before he let it fall.

The crowd began to shuffle, couples moving toward the bar or back to their seats, but May and Darren remained in place.

"You want to get some air?" Darren asked, tilting his head toward the door.

May nodded, her heart racing. "Yeah. That sounds good."

As they walked side by side toward the exit, May knew something between them had shifted. Something neither of them could ignore.

Chapter Forty-Two

THE AIR NIPPED AT them as they stepped outside, a welcome contrast to the warmth of the club. The streets were quieter now, with only the occasional sound of a car passing by or the distant chatter of late-night strollers. They walked side by side in silence, their steps falling into a rhythm that gave them time to gather their thoughts.

May glanced at Darren from the corner of her eye, taking in the sharp line of his jaw and the thoughtful expression that rested on his face.

"Did you always know how to dance like that?" she asked, breaking the silence.

Darren gave a low laugh.

"Well, not from birth!" he quipped, and they chuckled. "It's not something I get to practice much these days, but yeah, I've always loved it. My mom used to say it was the only time I looked completely at ease."

May smiled. "It suits you."

He stopped walking, turning to face her. "You suit me, May."

May froze, her breath catching in her throat at Darren's words.

"You suit me," he repeated, his voice laced with purpose. "And that terrifies me."

May's heart raced as she took a step closer, her voice barely above a whisper. "Why?"

Darren exhaled deeply, his hands brushing hers, hesitant yet deliberate.

"Because I didn't think I'd ever feel this again. After Michelle..." He trailed off, glancing up at the sky as though searching for the right words.

May swallowed. "Darren, I—"

"No, let me finish," he interrupted gently, his eyes meeting hers, laying bare all his fears. "I feel like I'm betraying her, May. As if loving you means letting go of her, and I know that it's too soon. But at the same time..." He paused, his voice breaking slightly. "At the same time, I'm just as afraid of walking away from this—whatever this is—without seeing it for all the possibilities it could offer. For the love it could be... or is."

A wave of emotion swelled in May as she reached out, her fingers lightly brushing his. "Darren, I don't want to replace her. I couldn't, even if I tried. And I know what it's like to carry that kind of guilt." She looked down, her voice trembling. "I thought I'd never feel this way about anyone again. But then you came into my life, and it's like..."

She trailed off, her words hanging in the air.

"Like what?" Darren asked, leaning in closer.

"Like I've been given a second chance," May admitted, her eyes brimming with tears she feared to shed. "And it scares me too. Because what if I'm wrong? What if I let myself feel this, and it all falls apart?"

Darren took her hands into his. "Like I mentioned earlier, the May I know doesn't back down from a challenge. Love has no promises, no guarantees. But the way I see it, we're just two people trying to find our way forward—together."

May's tears spilled over.

Darren lifted one hand, his finger brushing gently across her cheek, wiping away the last trace of doubt that lingered there. "We deserve love, May," he said softly. "Fully, completely, without fear or guilt. I know Michelle would have wanted me to be happy. And you—May, you make me happy. Do I make you happy, May? Do you love me?"

Her fingers tightened slightly around his. "Yes," she whispered, the word trembling on her lips. As it left her, she felt something shift deep inside her, a release of the grief and doubt that had been weighing her down for so long. Her voice grew stronger as she continued, "You make me happy, Darren. Happier than I ever thought I could feel again. And yes, I love you."

Darren let out a breath, his smile deepening as his hands gently cradled hers.

"You have no idea how much I needed to hear that."

May closed the small space between them, their hands still entwined. The night air wrapped around them both, cool but comforting, as if it too acknowledged the quiet promise they had just made to each other—the promise to move forward.

Darren leaned in, his breath warm against her cheek as he whispered, "I've been waiting four long weeks to finally kiss you again."

"What took you so long?"

Darren let out a soft laugh, his forehead gently brushing against hers as his hands tightened slightly around her fingers. "I wanted to make sure it was right. That I wasn't rushing something that deserves to be everything."

"And now?"

His lips quirked into a small, teasing smile. "Now, I'm done waiting."

Chapter Forty-Three

MAY PULLED HER CAR into Darren's driveway, her eyes scanning the quiet, tree-lined street. His neighborhood, just a few minutes inside the River Forest city limits, was charming, with wide sidewalks, neatly trimmed lawns, and the kind of homes that looked as though they had been plucked from the pages of a lifestyle magazine. Darren's five-bedroom home stood near the end of the cul-de-sac, a classic red-brick house with large windows and a black mahogany front door. Flowerbeds flanked the walkway, bursting with marigolds and asters, their warm colors a cheerful contrast to the crisp fall air.

As May stepped out of her car, the sound of leaves crunching under her flats accompanied her approach to the front door. She paused for a moment, adjusting the strap of Storm's diaper bag on her shoulder. Storm, nestled in her car seat, gurgled softly, her tiny hands gripping the edge of a blanket.

"You ready for some fun, little one?"

May offered Storm a big smile before ringing the doorbell.

The door opened almost immediately, revealing Darren with Isaiah perched on his hip. His smile was warm, the kind that made her stomach flip.

"Hey," he greeted, stepping aside to let her in. "Come on in. It's warmer inside."

May stepped into the foyer, the scent of something baking in the oven welcoming her. Darren's house was inviting, a perfect blend of contemporary and cozy. Hardwood floors gleamed beneath their feet, and the walls were painted in soft, neutral tones, accented with family photos and tasteful artwork. A large sectional sofa anchored the living room, scattered with throw pillows in varying shades of blue and gray.

"Something smells good," May said as she set Storm's car seat down near the sofa.

"My mom's doing," Darren said with a slight laugh, nodding toward the kitchen. "She insisted on baking cookies before heading out for the afternoon. She's been eager to meet you."

As if on cue, Darren's mother appeared from the kitchen, wiping her hands on a towel.

She was petite, with a neatly styled bob that framed her face, the silver streaks in her hair adding a touch of mature elegance. Her warm, hazel-brown eyes mirrored Darren's, carrying the same spark of kindness that May had grown to admire so much.

"You must be May." Her eyes shifted to the baby nestled in the car seat. "And this, of course, must be baby Storm," she added with a smile, reaching in to gently rub the baby's cheek with the back of her fingers. Storm responded with a happy gurgle, her dimples deepening as if she already knew she was in the presence of someone profoundly kind.

"I'm Helen," Darren's mother continued, standing upright. "I'd hug you, but I see your hands are quite full."

May returned the smile, a sense of ease settling over her. "It's so nice to meet you, Helen. Darren's been raving about your cooking, by the way, so I'm glad I finally get to meet the chef behind those meals."

They both glanced at Darren, who suddenly seemed very interested in adjusting Isaiah's shirt.

"I love to cook," Helen said with a wink. "Now, let me get out of your way. Enjoy the cookies—they're on the counter."

With that, Helen grabbed her coat and purse, offering a wave before disappearing out the door.

May settled into the plush sectional sofa as she set Storm down on the play mat. Darren moved to a corner of the mat, but his attention drifted to the baby with the biggest smile May had ever seen. Storm, dressed in a soft mint onesie dotted with tiny white triangles, wore a pink headwrap tied in a perfect bow, framing her round, cherubic face.

Her deep, expressive eyes seemed to sparkle against her light-tinted skin. Long lashes fluttered every time she blinked, and her dimples deepened with every giggle she let out.

"She's so beautiful," Darren said softly, watching as Isaiah, sitting nearby, tilted his head and observed Storm too. His curiosity quickly turned into excitement as he babbled something unintelligible and reached toward her.

"Tell me something I don't know," May replied with a grin, her heart swelling with pride. She adjusted the bow on Storm's head. "And that smile… it's dangerous, isn't it?"

"Absolutely. You're in for some trouble when she gets older," Darren joked, settling onto the floor beside the babies.

The playful melody of cartoons floated through the living room as Isaiah sat with a collection of colorful blocks scattered in front of him. His tiny fingers grasped one block, bringing it to his mouth before banging it against another with curious delight.

"You've got quite the setup here," May remarked, watching as Darren picked up one of the blocks, giving it a playful toss before setting it down.

"Well, Isaiah keeps me on my toes," he said, flashing her a grin. "Gotta make sure he's entertained."

Storm let out a happy squeal, and May laughed softly, leaning forward to move her beside Isaiah. "All right, Storm," she said playfully, arranging a few soft blocks in front of her. "Show him how it's done."

The two babies turned their attention to each other, their expressions curious and intent.

Isaiah reached out with one chubby hand, brushing against Storm's arm.

She responded with a delighted giggle, her tiny hands flailing with excitement, as though inviting him to join in the fun.

"They're naturals," Darren remarked, adjusting himself to sit cross-legged on the floor beside them. He picked up another brightly colored block and handed it to Isaiah.

Isaiah inspected the block for a moment before letting it tumble to the mat.

Again, Storm squealed with excitement, her arms waving.

Darren laughed, grabbing another block and holding it out to Isaiah. "Here you go, buddy. Let's try this again."

Isaiah's small fingers wrapped around the block, and he stared at it briefly before letting the block drop again. When Storm squealed anew, he joined in.

May grinned, shaking her head. "They're adorable together," she said, her tone gentle as she watched the interaction. "I think Storm likes him."

Darren smiled, amusement in his eyes. "Who wouldn't? The kid's got charm."

His smile deepened as he glanced at May, who was watching the two with a soft smile, her eyes lit with an expression he hadn't seen in a while—joy.

The afternoon unfolded in an easy rhythm, filled with baby giggles, soft coos, and the occasional rustle of toys being dropped and picked back up. The living room felt alive, blending warmth with the simple comfort of watching two babies explore together.

May glanced down at her watch just as Storm's whimper turned into a low cry. "She's tired," May said, her voice filled with the knowing tone of a seasoned caretaker.

Darren got to his feet. "I think I've got just the thing."

He quickly grabbed Isaiah's well-loved teddy bear from the pile of toys, its fur slightly worn but still as comforting as ever. He held it out to Storm with a small smile.

Storm's cries quieted almost immediately as she clutched the bear to her chest, her tiny fingers curling around its soft, plump paw.

Darren returned to his spot on the floor, watching her with quiet satisfaction.

"You sure that's okay?" May asked.

Darren gave her a reassuring smile. "Of course. I think he can manage to share it for a bit."

May nodded.

Isaiah, noticing Storm with the teddy bear, paused for a moment. His curious eyes darted between her and the toy, as if weighing his options. To May's relief, he extended a hand toward a nearby block instead, giving it a satisfying shake before bringing it to his mouth.

"Looks like Isaiah is okay with it too," May said with a smile, her tone gentle as she watched the babies interact.

Darren leaned back, his arms crossed comfortably as he observed the scene. "I have a feeling he'll always be okay sharing anything with Storm."

Storm let out a small yawn, her tiny fingers loosening their grip on the teddy bear as her eyelids grew heavier. "I think it's time to put them down for a nap," May said.

Darren stood and stretched.

"I'll grab Isaiah. We can lay them both down in his crib. His room's just down the hall, first door on the right. The baby monitors are always on, so we'll hear them even from here."

"I can get both of them. You just lead the way."

"You sure?"

May rose to her feet, lifting both Storm and Isaiah with ease.

Darren led May down the softly lit hallway, glancing back occasionally to check on her. She cradled both babies with a tenderness that made something in his chest tighten.

"They're not heavy," May said quietly, noticing his concern. "Believe me, I've done this more times than I can count."

Darren stopped at the doorway to Isaiah's room, pushing the door open gently.

"Here we are."

May stepped inside and paused, her eyes sweeping over the cozy nursery.

The walls were painted a calming yellow, dotted with tiny white stars that glowed faintly in the soft light of the nightlight. A navy-blue recliner sat in one corner, and shelves filled with books and stuffed animals lined the opposite wall. Above the crib hung a mobile of clouds and stars, turning lazily as it caught the faint current of air.

"This is beautiful, Darren," May said, her voice filled with quiet admiration. "It's perfect for him."

"Thanks," Darren replied, his tone gentle. He watched as she crossed the room to the crib, her movements careful and deliberate. She placed Isaiah down first, adjusting the blanket around him before gently settling Storm beside him. Storm stirred briefly, her hand brushing against Isaiah's.

His little fist opened and closed once before he settled back into the rhythm of sleep.

May stood over the crib, a smile of happiness touching her lips as she watched them. Darren leaned against the doorframe, his gaze fixed on her. There was something about the way she looked at the babies—her expression showing love, awe, and quiet resolve—that left him momentarily speechless.

"They're peaceful," May said, not looking up. "As if nothing in the world could touch them."

Darren nodded, stepping into the room. "Because they're safe. You have a gift, May. You make people feel that way."

She turned to him, her smile deepening before she stepped back. "No, I think it's because they have each other," she whispered, moving toward the door.

Darren smiled, closing the door halfway behind them.

Back in the living room, May sank into the couch with a soft sigh, the day's events settling over her, comforting and full. Darren joined her with a mug in each hand.

"Here you go," he said, handing her a mug. "Peppermint tea."

"Thank you," May said, wrapping her hands around the drink.

They sat in companionable silence for a moment, the soft hum of the baby monitor filling the space between them. Darren rested his elbows on his knees as he spoke.

"May, can I ask you something?"

"Of course," she said, her brow lifting slightly.

"Would you ever consider having another child?"

The question caught her off guard.

May hesitated, her fingers tightening slightly around the mug as she searched Darren's face for the meaning behind his words. There was no pressure in his eyes, only a quiet curiosity.

"Honestly?" she began, setting the mug down carefully on the coffee table. She took a breath. "I've thought about it. After losing my daughter, I didn't think I could open myself up to taking that chance again. The pain was… unbearable. But Storm… she's shown me that loss doesn't mean the end of love. It just means love must grow differently, in ways you didn't expect." Her lips curved into a faint smile. "So while I don't think I could risk giving birth to a child of my own again, I've come to understand that there are a lot of ways to become a mother."

Darren nodded slowly. "Seeing you today with Isaiah, with Storm… it's hard not to wonder about what's possible."

May tilted her head slightly. "What about marriage? Would you ever consider remarrying?"

Darren hesitated, not because he didn't know the answer, but because of the weight of the admission. "Yes," he said. "I would marry again, if it felt right. Marriage is a wonderful gift."

Their eyes met. May's voice was soft when she spoke. "I think I would want it too."

For a moment, neither of them said anything. Darren reached over, covering her hand with his. "It's nice to know we're on the same page."

May's fingers curled around his, her smile growing.

"It is," she whispered, as the sound of the babies' soft breaths came through the monitor, a reminder of the life and love that had already begun to blossom between them.

Chapter Forty-Four

THE NEON SIGN OF their favorite Chinese restaurant bathed May's windshield in a muted red-orange glow. She sat in the parking lot for a moment, fingers drumming lightly on the steering wheel as a familiar wave of nostalgia washed over her. It had been over a year and a half since she'd first walked into this place with Darren, unsure of so many things—her future, her feelings, her ability to love again. Now, everything felt… different. Fuller. Happier. Like she was exactly where she was meant to be.

She smiled, thinking about Isaiah and Storm, who would turn eighteen months old in a week. Both were walking—or, in Storm's case, running everywhere—and keeping her and Darren constantly on their toes. Storm's fearless streak never failed to make May laugh and worry at the same time, while Isaiah's quieter, more observant nature was equally endearing. Watching the two of them grow and bond had been like watching the start of something extraordinary.

Her cell phone rang, pulling her from her thoughts. May grabbed it, flipping it up.

"Are you coming in, or should I bring the food out to you?"

May couldn't help but laugh. "On my way in."

She stepped out of the car, a brisk gust of wind trailing behind her as she walked toward the restaurant. She paused briefly at the door, smoothing her shoulder-length hair before stepping inside. The warmth of the restaurant greeted her instantly, along with the familiar scent of sesame oil and soy sauce. Darren was already at their usual table by the window, and when his eyes met hers, his face broke into a grin that made her stomach flip.

"Hey," he said, standing to pull out her chair. "Right on time."

May returned his smile as she slid into her seat. "Hey. You know me—always punctual."

Darren gave a short laugh as he sat down. "One of the many things I love about you."

May tilted her head, teasing. "Only one? Should I be worried?"

He smirked, tilting his head with a playful glint in his eye. "There are too many to count, but punctuality definitely makes the list."

Their laughter blended with the restaurant's lively energy. The waitress approached to take their drink orders, and once she left, Darren turned his full attention back to May.

"How was your day?" he asked, his voice warm with interest.

May sighed, resting her chin in her hand. "Busy. Storm decided this morning that she didn't like the socks I picked out, so we had a ten-minute standoff before I gave in and let her wear her favorite pair of gym shoes with no socks. Little Ms. Fashion still had no socks on when I dropped her off at your mother's place."

Darren laughed, his eyes crinkling.

"Sounds about right for Storm. Isaiah's latest thing is he won't eat unless I sing the ABCs first. And I mean every single time." He shook his head, chuckling. "Kid loves music—got it naturally. Michelle had a voice, and she played the guitar."

"I've always wanted to learn an instrument, but I never got around to it. What about you?"

Darren smirked. "Oh, I got nothing. My mom plays the piano, but I never had the patience for it. Isaiah, though—he might be the musician in the family."

"Oh?"

Darren laughed, shaking his head at the memory. "I came home one day and found him banging away on the toy piano my mother got him. Completely off-key, making all kinds of noise, but in his little mind, I'm sure he was jamming."

May grinned. "These kids are going to run our lives, aren't they?"

"They already do," Darren said, his smile softening. "But honestly, I wouldn't have it any other way."

"Same," May said as she settled into her chair. But she noticed a trace of distraction in Darren's expression. His fingers were tapping lightly against the edge of the table—a rhythm she recognized as nervous energy.

She narrowed her eyes slightly but didn't comment. Instead, she said, "Your mother's place is really coming along. I saw that they've already finished the kitchen."

"Good thing her new boyfriend owns his own home remodeling company."

May raised an eyebrow, smirking. "You think this one will stick?"

Darren let out a light, quiet laugh, shaking his head. "With my mother's track record, who knows? But hey, at least she's happy. That's all I can ask for."

The waitress approached, interrupting their conversation as she set down their drinks. "Are you two ordering your usual?" she asked with a grin.

Darren and May exchanged a glance before bursting into laughter.

As the waitress walked away, May shifted closer, resting her elbows on the table. "All right, what's going on? You've been fidgeting since I got here."

Darren blinked, then let out a sheepish laugh. "Am I that obvious?"

"Oh, only a little. Like that neon sign outside!" May teased. "Come on—out with it."

Darren rubbed the back of his neck, his eyes lowering for a moment.

"I've just been thinking about how far we've come, you know? How much has changed since the first time we were here."

May tilted her head, her playful demeanor softening into something more thoughtful. "It really has been a lot, hasn't it? But this past year, it's been all good things."

"More than good," Darren said, his voice quiet but deliberate. He paused. "Do you remember that day at Isaiah and Storm's first playdate, when I told you I'd remarry if it felt right?"

He reached into his pocket, pulling out a small velvet box and placing it gently on the table between them.

May's heart skipped a beat as her eyes darted to the box, a short breath catching in her throat.

"May," Darren began, his eyes locking onto hers, "this feels right. You've shown me what it means to love again, to believe in second chances, and to build something beautiful out of life's broken pieces. You've been my partner, my confidante, my best friend—and I can't imagine my life, or Isaiah's, without you."

Tears welled in May's eyes as Darren opened the box, revealing a simple yet elegant diamond ring that caught the light perfectly.

"I want to spend the rest of my life with you," he said. "Will you marry me?"

For a moment, May couldn't speak. Her heart overflowed with emotions she could barely name—joy, gratitude, love. She reached out, covering Darren's hand with hers as a tear slipped down her cheek.

"Yes," she whispered. "Yes, Darren. I'll marry you."

Darren's face broke into a grin as he slid the ring onto her finger. "I love you, May."

"I love you too," she said, her voice carrying the weight of everything her heart felt.

Just then, the waitress returned with their plates and paused when she saw the scene.

"Oh, congratulations!" she exclaimed, beaming. "Finally!"

May laughed, wiping her eyes. "Thank you."

As they dug into their meals, the moment settled into a comforting warmth between them. They talked about the kids, about their hopes for the future, and the life they wanted to build together. It was easy, natural, as if all the pieces of their journey had finally slotted into place.

When they left the restaurant, hand in hand, the brisk night air greeted them. Darren glanced at May, his smile as wide as when she'd said yes.

"You know you've made me the happiest man tonight," he said, squeezing her hand.

May looked up at him, her heart full. "And you've made me believe in love again."

Chapter Forty-Five

THE SPRING MORNING WAS painted in soft hues, the sky a pale blue dotted with wisps of white clouds drifting lazily by. A gentle breeze carried the scent of blooming flowers through the rows of chairs arranged in the park where May and Darren had first glimpsed the mother duck and her ducklings.

It was the perfect day for a wedding—serene, bright, and full of promise.

At the center of the scene stood the gazebo, transformed for the occasion. Champagne and peach-colored flowers cascaded from its beams, their delicate petals catching the sunlight. Draped fabrics framed the structure, creating a romantic backdrop against the lush greenery.

May stood just out of sight, the soft cream fabric of her dress shimmering in the sunlight. The fitted silhouette hugged her frame gracefully, and Etta's gold pin caught the light with each step. Her hair was swept into a loose chignon, a few curls framing her glowing face, and a simple veil cascaded softly down her back.

"You look breathtaking," Sarah said, her voice sincere as she adjusted May's train.

Sarah's champagne dress complemented the palette, but more than that, her smile held none of the tension it once had. The two women were genuinely happy to be standing side by side.

"Thank you," May said, her voice calm despite the butterflies in her stomach. "I'm so glad you're here."

"I wouldn't miss this for the world," Sarah said, placing a hand briefly on May's arm before stepping back to take her seat.

The sound of Ming's voice floated through the air as Darren took his place under the gazebo, holding Isaiah's tiny hand. Darren looked handsome in his navy suit, the crisp lines softened by a champagne bow tie.

Little Isaiah, dressed to match, clutched a small satin pillow that held the rings. His wide eyes scanned the crowd, occasionally darting to Storm, who stood nearby in her champagne-colored gown, clutching a basket of peach rose petals.

When the music shifted to a lilting melody, all eyes turned to May.

She stepped onto the grass aisle, her heart racing as she took in the sight of Darren waiting for her. Etta's parents sat in the front row, watching with teary eyes. Helen sat beside them, her boyfriend offering a quiet squeeze of her hand as she dabbed at her eyes.

May looked up, catching Darren's loving gaze. The sunlight glinted off his smile, and for a moment, the park held just the two of them.

When she reached him, Darren extended his hand. "You're stunning," he whispered as she took her place beside him.

"Ming's voice is amazing," May said, barely audible, enough to make him give a low laugh.

"You'll never doubt me again."

"Not about Ming," she said with a smirk.

The officiant began, his voice blending with the gentle rustle of leaves and the distant calls of ducks from the pond. As Darren and May exchanged vows, their words carried the weight of their journey—doubt, joy, and the deep love that had brought them here.

Darren's voice shook with emotion as he promised to love and cherish her, his eyes never leaving hers. When May vowed to stand by Darren and Isaiah, to build a life filled with love, laughter, and hope, a tear slipped down Darren's cheek.

The ring exchange brought a tender moment. Darren knelt to Isaiah's level, whispering something that made the boy nod solemnly before handing him the rings.

Isaiah's small, careful gesture drew a collective sigh from the guests.

"You may kiss the bride," the officiant declared.

Darren cupped May's face, his hands gentle, his eyes searching hers as he leaned in. The kiss was soft, filled with all the unspoken promises they had made long before this day.

The crowd erupted into cheers and applause, and when they pulled apart, May's radiant smile mirrored Darren's.

As they turned to face their guests, Storm and Isaiah took the lead. Storm swung her now-empty basket proudly as Isaiah toddled beside her, his tiny suit slightly rumpled. Their small hands suddenly clasped together.

"Here's to beginnings," Darren whispered.

"Here's to love."

Chapter Forty-Six

THE SUN RESTED LOW in the sky as rows of neatly arranged chairs lined the freshly cut grass. At the center of the high school football field, a stage adorned with blue and gold banners stood proudly, its backdrop framed by the school's emblem. A gentle spring breeze carried the mingled scent of blooming flowers through the gathering crowd.

The weather was glorious—balmy and serene, not too hot or cool. The rustle of swaying trees added to the soft, celebratory atmosphere.

May sat beside Darren, her fingers interlaced with his as they watched the sea of caps and gowns shuffle into place. She still couldn't believe how fast the years had passed. It felt like only yesterday that she had stepped into Darren's life, Isaiah just a newborn then. Now, here they were, watching that tiny baby walk across a stage into adulthood.

Her eyes scanned the students, easily finding Isaiah among them.

Darren's boy stood taller than most, his broad shoulders filling out his navy-blue graduation robe. His cap was tilted slightly, as if he had put it on in a rush, and even from a distance, May could see the tension in his posture.

She knew why.

Because Storm wasn't here.

Isaiah had been looking forward to this day for months—not just because it marked the end of high school, but because he had wanted to share the moment with the one person who had been by his side through it all. Storm.

Their graduations had fallen on the same day, nearly seven hundred miles apart. Storm was in Atlanta, walking across a different stage in a different cap and gown, surrounded by her own friends. The reality of it stung, and May had seen it in Isaiah's eyes the moment they'd arrived.

Darren leaned in closer, his voice low enough that only May could hear.

"He hasn't smiled once since we got here. You know, my heart breaks for him. It's supposed to be his special day, but just look at his face."

May sighed, watching Isaiah too. "I know," she murmured. "He barely spoke this morning. I think he kept hoping she'd find a way to make it, but there was no way around it."

Darren exhaled through his nose, his expression filled with the kind of understanding only a father could have. "It's hard. She's been part of his life forever. This is the first big moment they've had to do separately. Let's hope it's the only one, but knowing how life plays out, I know it won't be."

His words fleetingly made May wonder if he ever thought about Michelle. Years ago, she might have felt sensitive at what he'd just said. But now, she knew his life revolved around their world—the one he, May, Isaiah, and Storm had built together.

May nodded, her heart aching for Isaiah too.

She knew what Storm meant to him. The two had been inseparable since the moment they'd met. They had learned to crawl side by side, taken their first steps together, spent summers tangled in adventures only the two of them understood.

To anyone else, they were childhood best friends.

To those who truly knew them, they were so much more.

The crowd erupted into cheers as the principal stepped up to the microphone. "Welcome, families, friends, and most importantly, the graduating class of 2012!"

The ceremony carried on in a blur of speeches, laughter, and applause, but Isaiah barely reacted. Even when his name was finally called and he made his way up to the stage, there was only the faintest hint of pleasure as he shook hands with the principal and took his diploma.

May and Darren stood, cheering for him as loudly as they could, but May noticed the way his eyes skimmed the crowd, searching for someone who just wasn't there.

Later, as the evening breeze cooled the warm air, they stood outside by the car, Isaiah's cap in his hands. He hadn't spoken much since the ceremony ended.

May let him have his silence, knowing he'd speak when he was ready.

Finally, Isaiah let out a slow breath. "It doesn't feel right," he admitted, his voice quiet but firm. "She should've been here."

May exchanged a glance with Darren before stepping closer. "I know," she said gently. "She really wanted to be. You do know it wasn't Storm's choice, Isaiah."

Isaiah shook his head. "Well, it's not the same." His lips pressed together, frustration creeping into his features. "We were supposed to do this together."

Darren clapped a firm hand on his son's shoulder. "You and Storm have shared a lot of things in life," he said. "This might not have been one of them, but that doesn't change what you mean to each other. Sometimes, when you have someone special, you can be far apart geographically, but your hearts are still united. You know that."

Isaiah nodded, his jaw tight, but his expression barely shifted. "Guess so."

It seemed difficult for him to even force out the few words.

May reached into her purse, pulling out a small envelope. "She left this for you."

Isaiah's expression tightened as he took the envelope, hesitating before carefully tearing it open. A simple card slipped into his hands, Storm's familiar handwriting filling the inside.

> *Isaiah,*
>
> *Since we were kids, we've done everything together. And while I hate that we're not in the same place this Thursday evening, nothing—no distance, no separate stages—can change the fact that we got here together. I am so proud of you, and I know that wherever life takes us next, we'll always have each other's back.*
>
> *P.S. You better save me a dance at your graduation party because I have been waiting for an excuse to outshine you.*

Isaiah let out a breathy laugh, shaking his head as he reread the words. May and Darren watched as some of the weight on his shoulders seemed to lift.

"She's impossible," Isaiah muttered, but the corners of his mouth twitched into a real grin.

Darren squeezed his shoulder. "That's better."

May's expression lifted, relief washing over her as well. "Is she coming to your party on Saturday?"

"Sounds like it." He slipped the letter into his pocket, patting it lightly. "Thanks… for giving me this."

May nodded. "Anytime. And I don't even need to tell you that while you're thinking of Storm, she's thinking of you too, right?"

As he climbed into the car, Isaiah paused for a moment, glancing over at his father and May, both still beaming with pride.

I'll tell them tomorrow.

As his high school drifted out of view, he wasn't sure why he was hesitating. Maybe because once he said it out loud, everything would feel real. The decision he'd made. The next step he was about to take.

With Storm.

Chapter Forty-Seven

LAUGHTER AND MUSIC INTERTWINED with the rhythmic hum of cicadas, filling the summer evening with a vibrancy that seemed to echo the promise of new beginnings. Friends and family gathered around tables in Darren and May's backyard, wildflower arrangements dotting each surface as conversation and the faint aroma of grilled food lingered in the air.

Storm stood near the edge of the makeshift dance floor, her pink silk blouse catching the soft light. At eighteen, she radiated a natural confidence and warmth that seemed to brighten any space she entered. Her curls framed her face, and her dark eyes held that familiar spark of curiosity and determination.

Isaiah watched her from across the yard, his gaze lingering on her smile. To him, it had always been her most captivating feature—broad, genuine, and touched with a playfulness that hinted at her spirited heart. The kind of smile that had always made him feel at ease.

Storm's style was simple and effortless—a white tee she'd designed herself and light-wash jeans—but to Isaiah, it was her grace that defined her most.

She looked calm on the outside. Inside, she was anything but.

Storm watched guests sway to a slow melody, her thoughts tangled in the conversation she hadn't yet had.

"Hey."

The familiar voice grounded her instantly. She turned to see Isaiah standing beside her, his hands tucked casually into his pockets. The boy she'd grown up with was now a man, and for a moment, she couldn't quite find her words.

"You okay?" he asked.

Storm lifted a small smile. "Yeah. Just taking it all in. It's a great party."

Isaiah studied her, his warm brown eyes searching hers. Then, without warning, he held out his hand. "Dance with me."

Caught off guard, Storm hesitated. "I don't know, Isaiah—"

"Come on," he said with a teasing grin. "One dance won't kill you. Besides, you were the one who said you were going to outshine me."

Reluctantly, she placed her hand in his.

The moment their fingers touched, a spark shot up her arm. Isaiah led her onto the dance floor, his hand resting lightly at her waist.

The DJ shifted to *It Will Rain* by Bruno Mars.

"You know," Isaiah murmured, "this is the first time we've ever slow-danced together."

Storm let out a soft laugh. "I guess it is."

"I don't hate it," he admitted.

The way he looked at her—soft, focused, as if she were the only person in the yard—made her chest tighten.

"You're acting weird tonight," she teased, though her voice came out softer than she intended.

Isaiah smirked. "Maybe I am."

The closeness, the familiarity, the years of shared history—all of it pressed in on her at once. And with it came the weight of what she had to say.

"I need to tell you something."

Isaiah's hand tensed slightly. "Okay."

She hesitated, then forced the words out. "I got into Marist. And… I've decided to go."

Isaiah's steps faltered. His expression shifted—surprise, disbelief, something deeper.

"That's in New York," he said quietly.

Storm nodded. "I know."

A crease formed between his brows. His hand loosened at her waist. "How long have you known?"

"Long enough that I should have said something sooner."

"Why didn't you?"

"Because I didn't know how to tell you without—"

"Without what?"

"Without it sounding like we're breaking up or something."

"We'd have to be dating for that," he said, his voice calm, though his eyes held hurt. "Are we dating?"

Storm's fingers curled into his shirt as she tried to steady herself. "Isaiah…"

Before she could finish, the music cut off as Darren stepped up to the microphone.

Isaiah stepped back, his eyes still locked on Storm's. "We're not done talking about this."

Storm could only nod.

Darren's voice echoed across the yard. "Come on up here, son. Say a few words."

Isaiah exhaled and forced himself to look away. His hand lingered on Storm's arm for a second before he let go.

As Isaiah climbed onto the stage, the crowd quieted.

"This wasn't what I planned to do tonight," Isaiah began, gripping the microphone stand. "But I was reminded recently that sometimes plans change."

He reached for the guitar.

A murmur rippled through the crowd.

"I wrote this song about chasing dreams," he continued. "About love. And about what you sometimes have to leave behind to move forward."

The first chord silenced everything.

His voice carried across the yard—raw, honest, full of everything he hadn't said out loud. Storm stood frozen, every lyric landing like a confession meant just for her.

By the final chord, the backyard erupted in applause.

But Isaiah never took his eyes off Storm.

He stepped down from the stage, moving toward her—until Sarah tapped Storm on the shoulder.

Storm's eyes told him they were leaving.

Before he could reach her, Darren and May approached.

"You were incredible," Darren said, clapping Isaiah's shoulder. "I had no idea you could do that."

"Thanks, Dad."

May followed Isaiah's gaze. "Sarah's not feeling well. Storm's driving her back to the hotel."

Isaiah nodded, his chest heavy. "She's going to New York. You knew that already, didn't you?"

May nodded. "Yes."

Darren's concern sharpened. "What's going on?"

"She's going to Marist," Isaiah said flatly.

May touched his arm. "She didn't want to hurt you."

Isaiah let out a bitter laugh. "So why am I hurting?"

Darren stepped closer. "Son, if Storm's going to Marist, it doesn't mean you lose her. It just means it'll take more effort."

"That's just it," Isaiah said quietly.

"I'm not trying to stay best friends."

Chapter Forty-Eight

STORM PERCHED ON THE edge of her hotel bed, her fingers tracing the edges of a small photo of her and Isaiah. It was from four years ago, taken during spring break in Destin. They stood side by side on the beach, their grins wide enough to rival the waves behind them.

She closed her eyes, holding onto the memory—the crash of the ocean, their laughter tangled with the salty breeze, the warmth of the sun on her skin.

For a fleeting moment, it felt as if nothing had changed.

But everything had.

She tucked the photo back into her wallet and pulled out another—an old, worn image of her mother, Allie Olivia Jamerson. The corners were soft and crumpled, the color slightly faded, but the woman in the picture was still striking.

You look just like her, Sarah had always said.

Storm stared at the face of the woman she had never met, a shadow of her own reflection. She had spent her life piecing her mother together through stories, secondhand memories, and photographs like this one.

Her father, though, was a void. A name never spoken. A past her aunt refused to touch.

Storm had stopped asking when she was younger, sensing how the air grew heavy whenever she did. But now, at eighteen, the silence felt unbearable.

How could she know so little about the two people who had given her life?

It was time to ask. Time to demand the truth.

A voice broke through her thoughts.

"Storm?"

She looked up to see Sarah standing in the doorway, hesitation written across her face.

"You told him, didn't you?"

Storm slipped the photo back into her wallet. "Yeah. I told Isaiah I'm going to Marist."

Sarah stepped inside. "How did he take it?"

Storm let out a slow breath. "He was upset. Just like I thought he'd be."

Sarah sighed and sat beside her, patting Storm's hand. Silence stretched between them, heavy and awkward.

"I know you'll miss him," Sarah said quietly. "But you're too young to be thinking about relationships and marriage. You just graduated."

Storm frowned. "Who said anything about marriage?"

Sarah hesitated.

"All I'm saying is that Isaiah is following his dreams, and you should do the same."

Storm studied her aunt's face. "What aren't you telling me?"

Sarah barely hesitated. "Isaiah is moving to California."

Storm's heart stopped. "What?"

"Darren and May don't know yet. He's going to pursue his music career. He's signed with a record label."

Storm's stomach twisted. "How do you know this?"

Sarah inhaled. "Because he called me."

Storm's brows drew together. "Why would he tell you before telling me?"

Sarah hesitated again. "He told me because he wanted you to go with him. And he wanted my blessing to ask you."

Storm's breath stalled. "Ask me what?"

Sarah met her eyes. "To marry you."

Storm stared at her. "What?"

"He said he couldn't imagine his future without you. That he loved you. That the thought of you going away—and possibly meeting someone else—broke his heart."

Storm shook her head. "And what did you say?"

"I told him no."

The words cut clean.

"You told him what?" Storm whispered.

"I told him no because you're eighteen. Marriage would change everything—your plans, your future. You've already chosen Marist. Being engaged would pull you in an entirely different direction."

"That wasn't your choice to make."

Sarah reached for her hand. Storm pulled away.

"Sweetheart, I was protecting you."

"You decided for me."

"Yes," Sarah said firmly. "Because it's my job."

Storm's voice shook. "From what?"

"I won't let you make the same mistakes your mother did."

Storm froze. "What mistakes? Having me?"

"No, you know that's not what I meant."

"Then what?" Storm demanded. "What mistakes did my dead mother make that give you the right to control my life?"

"Eighteen is not grown," Sarah snapped.

"You had no right."

"I had every right. As your guardian."

Storm's fists clenched. "So what mistakes did my mother make that you're making me pay for?"

Sarah stiffened. "If you're going to be like this, then forget I said anything."

"No. You are going to tell me."

"Storm—"

"Tell me!"

Sarah finally shouted, "She married that horrible man! That's what she did!"

Storm went still.

"He took her away from me," Sarah continued, her voice shaking. "From her family. And then he—"

"He what?" Storm whispered.

Sarah squeezed her eyes shut. "He tried to kill her."

The room seemed to tilt.

"No," Storm whispered. "That's not true."

"Yes, it is," Sarah said. "On the night you were born, your father was beating her. She thought she was going to lose you."

"She what?" Storm demanded.

"She stopped him."

Storm collapsed onto the bed, her body trembling.

"You're saying my mother… killed my father?"

"I'm saying your mother loved you more than anything. That she protected you. That she saved you."

Storm sobbed. "I don't believe you."

Sarah stood slowly.

"Where are you going?"

Sarah paused at the door. "To get you proof."

Chapter Forty-Nine

STORM COULD HEAR HER heartbeat pounding in her ears as Sarah stepped back into the room, her expression unreadable.

A lump rose in Storm's throat. "What's that?" she asked hesitantly.

Sarah didn't answer right away. Instead, she walked over to the bed, lowering herself onto the edge with a quiet sigh. Between them, she placed a small white box, its edges slightly worn, as if it had been held onto for years.

Storm hesitated, her fingers hovering over the lid before she slowly lifted it.

Inside, nestled carefully, was a clear plastic bag containing a collection of small, timeworn mementos. A delicate silver bracelet, its charm glinting under the dim hotel light. A folded piece of paper, creased from being read and reread. A tiny hospital band, yellowed with age, with the words *Jamerson, Baby Girl* printed in faded ink.

Storm's breath hitched.

Her hands trembled as she reached for the paper, carefully unfolding it. The handwriting was delicate, slanted slightly to the right, and though the ink had softened over time, the weight of the words crashed over her.

To my daughter,

I wanted so much to be there for you, to watch you grow. I can only imagine how beautiful you are.

Eyes like mine, I'm sure.

I want you to know that I did everything I could to make sure you had a life filled with love, even if I couldn't be there to give it to you myself.

There are things I wish I could shield you from. Things I never wanted you to know.

But if there comes a day when you begin to question, when you start searching for answers, I want you to have access to the truth.

Your father was not a good man. He hurt me in ways I can't explain, and when I found out I was pregnant with you, I knew I had to leave. But he wouldn't let me go.

The night you were born, I was so afraid. Not of the pain, not of what was happening to me—but of what would happen to you if I didn't stop him.

So, I did.

I fought for you.

His blows landed harder than ever before. He was trying to take you away from me, but I stopped him this time. He can't hurt either of us anymore.

He can't hurt anyone anymore.

I don't regret what I did, not for one moment.

And if there is only one thing you ever know about me, let it be this—that I loved you with a strength greater than fear, greater than pain, greater than life itself.

You were my reason.

The only thing I got right.

And even though I am not with you, I need you to live, Storm.

Live bravely.

Live fully.

And never let anyone tell you that you are anything less than extraordinary.

With all the love in my heart,

Your mother,

Allie

Storm's hands trembled as she reached the end of the letter.

The tears came fast—hot and unstoppable—dripping from her nose, sliding down her jaw, cascading over her cheeks. She pressed the letter to her chest, her breaths coming in short, broken gasps. The walls of the hotel room seemed to close in, the air thick and suffocating.

Sarah reached out again, but Storm stood abruptly, the letter still clutched in her grasp.

"You knew," she whispered, her voice trembling. "You knew about my father all this time, and you never told me?"

Sarah's face was lined with pain. "I wanted to protect you."

Storm let out a sharp, bitter laugh.

"Protect me? You kept the truth from me." Her voice wavered between anger and disbelief.

Sarah's eyes filled with tears.

"I did, Storm. Yes. Because I was afraid that knowing about him would break you."

Storm shook her head, stepping back as if distance could make sense of everything unraveling inside her.

"I spent my whole life hating her—" Her voice cracked.

"Storm—"

"It's true." Storm's fingers tightened around the letter. "I hated her because she left me. I hated her because my father never came for me. And now I find out that he's dead. That my mother died after trying to protect me from him."

A weighted hush settled between them.

Storm inhaled sharply, trying to steady the storm inside her. It didn't work. She folded the letter carefully and placed it back inside the box.

"Were you ever going to tell me the truth?" she asked quietly. "Or was keeping it from me just another decision you thought you had the right to make for me?"

Sarah blinked, searching for the right words. "Yes … I was going to tell you. When, I don't know."

Storm scoffed, shaking her head. "Unbelievable."

She turned abruptly, grabbing her jacket from the chair.

"Storm, please." Sarah's voice cracked with desperation. "It's late. Isaiah's probably out with his friends or already asleep."

Storm heard her, but she didn't stop.

She yanked open the hotel door, stepping into the dimly lit hallway.

She had to see him.

And if he asked her the question she knew was coming …

She already knew her answer.

Chapter Fifty

THE PARK LAY STILL, the evening breeze whispering through the trees in a way that should have brought comfort. But for Storm, peace was an illusion. Her mother's words clung to her, a weight settling deep in her stomach, while the pressure tightening around her chest came from something far heavier. The truth. The kind that didn't just unsettle her—it splintered her.

She spotted Isaiah sitting on a bench, his elbows resting on his knees, his head tilted slightly, as if he already sensed she was carrying something too heavy to bear alone.

"Thanks for coming," she murmured, lowering herself onto the bench beside him.

Isaiah glanced at her, his dark eyes scanning her face. He didn't need to ask if she had been crying. The redness, the slight puffiness around her eyes—it was all there. But what really worried him was the look behind them. Something was different.

"What's going on?" he asked.

Storm leaned her head on his shoulder. "I never noticed how empty this park is," she said absently. "There aren't any swings.

We've been coming here since we were kids, and I never noticed it until now. I look around and all I see is emptiness. It's sad, isn't it?"

Isaiah frowned, turning his head slightly toward her. "Storm …"

She sat up, wiping at her face as fresh tears fell. "For eighteen years, I hated my mother."

Isaiah stiffened. "Why?"

"It's hard to explain. But I guess I'd see you with Darren and May, and resent that I didn't have that. That I didn't have a father or a mother. Just my aunt."

"You forget that I lost my mother as well."

"But you never went without one, Isaiah. I love my aunt, don't get me wrong. But I wanted my mother. I wanted to have the same home life that other kids had." Her voice shook, and she took a deep breath, trying to compose herself. "So, I hated Mom for not being here. And I hated that my father never came for me, that I never knew anything about him. He was just this … this hole in my life, filled with questions I could never get answers to."

Isaiah sat quietly. He had known, on some level, that she struggled with her past. But he hadn't realized how deep it ran.

"I didn't even know what he looked like," Storm continued, her voice growing harsher. "And now? Now, I don't care if I never see his face."

Isaiah's stomach tightened. "What changed?"

Storm let out a hollow laugh. "You ever hear that saying? The truth shall set you free?"

Isaiah nodded. "Yeah."

"Well, tonight, I found out the truth." She turned to him, her dark eyes flashing with something raw and painful. "But I don't feel free."

Isaiah's chest ached at the way she looked at him, as if she were standing at the edge of something she couldn't step away from.

"What do you feel then?" he asked softly.

Her hands curled into fists in her lap. "Anger," she whispered. "I'm angry that I wasted eighteen years hating a woman who died trying to save me from a monster."

Isaiah's whole body went still.

Storm let out a ragged breath. "That's what my father was, Isaiah. A monster." She forced herself to say the words out loud. "A monster who nearly killed my mother and me the night I was born."

Isaiah closed his eyes for a second before turning fully toward her.

"Storm ..." His voice was careful, measured. But she caught the flicker of something else in his eyes.

"You knew," she whispered. The realization hit her all at once.

Isaiah didn't answer right away, his hands gripping his knees as if bracing for impact.

Storm's heart slammed against her ribs. "You knew. And you never said anything to me!"

Isaiah exhaled sharply. "Storm, it's not—"

"How long, Isaiah?" she demanded, her voice rising. "How long have you known that my entire life had been built on a lie? Right now, I feel you're as bad as my aunt. So, how long?"

Isaiah's jaw tightened. "Since I was ten."

"What?" Her whole body went stiff, as if she recoiled into herself. "That long?"

Her words nearly drifted into nothingness, so weak he could barely make them out. It felt as if the idea of him knowing sucked all the breath out of her.

Isaiah let out a heavy breath. "Please don't be angry ... I heard May and Sarah on the phone one day. They were talking about a letter Etta had found—a letter your mother had written."

Storm leaned back, as though his words had physically struck her.

"Eight whole years?" Her voice was barely a whisper, laced with disbelief and devastation. "We've been so close, and you never thought to say a word to me. Unbelievable."

Isaiah stood abruptly, his frustration bubbling to the surface. "Look, it wasn't my truth to tell, Storm. And I didn't want you to be hurt."

Storm let out a sharp, bitter laugh. "That's funny, because I feel pretty darn hurt right now. I feel about as hurt as it's possible to be. Thanks a lot."

Isaiah's lips thinned as he stepped closer, his eyes locking with hers. "Kinda like I felt tonight."

"Excuse me?"

"You knew you were leaving for Marist. You knew for weeks, Storm. But you waited until tonight—at my graduation party—to tell me."

Storm's chest tightened. "Are you kidding me right now?"

"No, I'm not kidding," Isaiah shot back. "Today was supposed to be about us. May knew. Sarah knew. But me? I had to find out while we were dancing?"

Storm let out a humorless laugh. "Unbelievable. You've known my entire life was a lie, but I'm the one in the wrong for not telling you about college soon enough? So now you turn it around on me because you're not man enough to accept responsibility."

Isaiah shook his head. "You're not listening. That's not what I'm saying."

"Then what are you saying?" she snapped.

He opened his mouth, then closed it, his expression torn.

"That's exactly what I thought." Storm folded her arms tightly across her chest, trying to keep herself from unraveling. "You don't get to act like this—like you're the one who got blindsided."

For a moment, neither of them spoke. The weight of everything—truths kept hidden—settled between them.

Storm sat back down on the bench, her fingers gripping the wooden edge as if it were the only thing holding her together.

Isaiah sat beside her, his face a mask of emotions—hurt, frustration, love.

"You know, don't you?" His voice was quiet, but something raw lived underneath it. "You know I was going to ask you to come with me to California. That I was going to ask you to marry me."

Storm looked at him, but the intensity in his eyes was too much to bear.

"Yes, I know."

This should have been a tender moment between them, but instead, Storm felt as though she might explode with anger and bitterness.

Isaiah let out a slow breath, his hands twitching as if he wanted to reach for her but didn't know if he still had the right to. "Would you have come with me?" The vulnerability in his voice sliced straight through her. "Would you have married me?" A beat. "Would you?"

Storm placed her hands in her lap, forcing herself to stay together when all she wanted to do was break down. "I've loved you since I first started to really understand what love was," she admitted. "All the way here, I thought about that, convinced that saying yes—if you asked me—would be the right answer. But now ..." She exhaled, feeling the crack in her heart. "Now, I see that saying yes wouldn't have been right after all. Not when you can let me down like this."

Isaiah's fingers curled against his knees. He was in pieces.

Storm's voice was quiet, but it didn't waver. "It just shows that my aunt was right about something she said to me ... that love isn't enough. You need love and trust. And I'm not sure we have that anymore." She turned to face him, her eyes searching his. "Are you?"

Isaiah's lips parted as if he wanted to argue, to fight for them—but then nothing. His shoulders sagged, and his face twisted with something Storm couldn't bear to see: acceptance.

"I love you, though, Storm," he whispered.

She swallowed the lump in her throat. "I know. And I love you too."

The words felt heavy. Final.

A breeze moved between them. The kind of breeze that carried finality.

"I don't know how we fix something that has a crack so deep," she admitted. "Maybe … maybe we were only ever meant to be best friends."

Isaiah rose slowly, reluctantly, the pain in his eyes unmistakable.

Storm felt it too.

As he began walking away, she hated how much the sight of it hurt. Deep down, she wanted him to stop and turn back, to run toward her and beg her to give him another chance.

But he didn't.

As his presence disappeared, it was the first time in her life she wasn't sure she would ever see him again.

Chapter Fifty-One

STORM WAS ALREADY RUNNING late.

Two gallons of soft cream paint balanced awkwardly in her arms, the plastic handles biting into her fingers as she hurried down a busy Brooklyn sidewalk. The late afternoon sun beat down, heat radiating off the concrete, the city alive with horns, footsteps, and shouted conversations.

She was halfway past a sleek, black-awninged restaurant when her phone buzzed in her pocket.

Dasha — her best friend from Marist — was calling again.

Storm shifted her grip to check it — and that was all it took.

One of the paint cans slipped.

"Dang it—"

The lid popped loose as it hit the pavement, a splash of pale cream arcing dangerously close to a pair of polished Italian shoes.

Storm froze.

"Oh my goodness, I am so—"

A hand shot out, steady and quick, catching the can before it tipped completely.

"I've got it," a man said calmly.

Storm looked up.

He was tall. Broad-shouldered. Dressed in a tailored navy suit that probably cost more than her first semester of tuition. His dark hair was perfectly styled, his expression composed — but his eyes held something warmer. Curious. Appreciative.

He set the can upright, checking the lid before handing it back to her.

"Crisis avoided," he said smoothly.

Storm let out a breath she hadn't realized she was holding. "You just saved me from a very public paint disaster. Thank you."

"Happy to help," he said. "Though I have to admit — carrying paint down the sidewalk suggests you're in the middle of something important."

Storm adjusted her grip. "Opening a boutique. Doing some last-minute touch-ups myself."

His gaze swept her — not in a way that felt invasive, but observant. Intentional.

She was wearing a tailored linen jumpsuit in a rich terracotta shade, cinched at the waist with a wide fabric belt. Clean lines. Effortless. Elevated — but practical enough for a long day on her feet.

"You designed that," he said.

It wasn't a question.

Storm blinked, surprised. "I did."

His mouth curved slightly. "It shows. The cut is impeccable. Confident. Functional. Most designers forget that real women move."

Something warm sparked in her chest.

"I design for women who live in their clothes," she said. "Not just pose in them."

"I can tell," he said. "You look like someone who builds things — not just dreams about them."

Storm held his gaze.

Not just another pretty man in an expensive suit.

"You sound like someone who understands that," she said.

"I do," Roman said easily. No hesitation. No qualifiers. Just certainty.

The restaurant door opened behind him, and a hostess glanced his way.

"We're ready for you, Mr. Carter."

He gave a small nod but didn't take his eyes off Storm.

"One moment."

The hostess stepped back inside.

Storm arched a brow. "Looks like I interrupted something important."

"Nothing more important than meeting a woman who designs her own clothes and carries her own paint," he said. "That combination alone tells me plenty."

She laughed softly. "I'll take that as a compliment."

"You should." He extended his hand. "I'm Roman."

"Storm."

They shook hands.

His grip was warm.

Confident — in a way that felt grounding, not overpowering.

"Much success with your boutique, Storm," Roman said. "Something tells me it's going to be worth seeing."

She smiled. "Maybe you'll see for yourself."

"Count on it."

They held each other's gaze for a beat — just long enough for something unspoken to pass between them.

Storm shifted the paint cans in her arms.

"I should go before gravity tries to embarrass me again."

"Probably wise," he said with a faint smile.

She took a few steps, then glanced back.

"Roman?"

"Yes?"

"If you get a grand opening invite with my name on it… now you'll know why."

His smile deepened. "I'll be watching for it."

Storm walked away, her pulse a little quicker than before.

Behind her, Roman watched her go — not with curiosity alone, but with intention.

She didn't know his story yet.

But she felt the shift.

Chapter Fifty-Two

STORM STOOD IN FRONT of the gleaming glass door, where **S. Jamerson Studio** was elegantly etched in gold. A smile tugged at her lips.

It was finally real.

This place was hers.

It had taken three years longer than she'd planned — delayed dreams tangled in the uncertainty of a world turned upside down by the pandemic — but standing outside her soon-to-open boutique in SoHo, Storm felt nothing but pride.

Built from the ground up.

Financed with nearly every dollar of her inheritance.

And still, despite the overwhelming joy, a quiet ache lingered.

Her aunt wasn't here to see it.

Sarah had passed away a year ago, and Storm still reached for her phone sometimes, forgetting for just a second that she couldn't call to share moments like this.

The thought tightened her chest, but she didn't let the sadness take over.

Sarah would have been so proud.

"Dang, girl."

A familiar voice pulled her back.

"Three years late, but here we are."

Storm turned to Dasha, who stood beside her with a grin that matched the excitement bubbling in her own chest.

Storm let out a grateful breath. "Yeah. Here we are."

"And this is just the beginning," Dasha said, nudging her. "I can already see store number two in the works."

Storm laughed softly. "Let's get customers for this one first."

Dasha scoffed, flipping her braids over her shoulder. "Please. With the marketing I've done, the line's gonna wrap around the block. Our grand opening is about to be a whole event."

"I hope so."

"I know so." Dasha gave her a pointed look. "It's what I do."

Storm smiled. Humility had never been Dasha's strong suit — but when it came to marketing, she was unmatched.

Dasha waved a hand dramatically. "Let's get inside. I do not play well in this May sun."

Storm shook her head, smiling as she pulled open the door.

Inside, warm lighting bathed the boutique in an inviting glow. Soft neutrals and earthy tones filled the space. A sleek white marble checkout counter gleamed at the back, trimmed with delicate gold accents. Floor-to-ceiling open shelving displayed hand-sewn garments luxurious silk blouses, structured blazers, flowing midi dresses — each piece reflecting the effortless sophistication of Storm's brand.

Mannequins stood near the oversized windows, dressed in the boutique's signature looks. Timeless, yet modern. Classic femininity with a contemporary edge.

A plush seating area anchored the center of the shop — a cream velvet couch, a glass coffee table stacked with high-end fashion magazines, and a single vase of fresh white peonies. The air carried a faint scent of sandalwood and vanilla, warm and inviting.

Dasha let out a low whistle. "You really did this."

Storm scanned the space.

Every detail.

Every fabric.

Every choice.

Hers.

"Yeah," she murmured. "I did."

The door chimed.

Storm turned, expecting to see a delivery man.

Instead, her breath caught.

Roman.

He stepped inside like he belonged there — tall, composed, impeccably dressed in a tailored cream suit. The same confidence. The same detailed presence.

But this time, when his dark eyes met hers, recognition sparked instantly.

A slow smile curved his mouth.

"Well," he said. "I was hoping that paint incident would lead me somewhere interesting."

Storm blinked — then laughed softly. "You followed up."

"I told you I would," Roman said easily. "Storm Jamerson, right?"

She lifted a brow. "You remembered."

"I don't forget women who design their own clothes and carry their own paint," he said. "Especially when they invite me to a grand opening."

Dasha's eyes darted between them. "You two know each other?"

Storm glanced at Roman. "We met briefly — over paint — in Brooklyn."

"Brief, but memorable," Roman added with a sly smile.

His gaze swept the boutique — slower this time. More deliberate.

"Beautiful space," he said. "Even better than I imagined."

When he looked back at Storm, it felt personal.

Her pulse quickened. There was something familiar that lingered around the corners of his eyes.

For a fleeting second, he reminded her of someone — Isaiah.

She immediately pushed the thought away.

"Thank you," she said casually. "We're opening tomorrow."

"I know," Roman said. "Your brand's been making waves. I keep an eye on up-and-coming designers. You're one of the most interesting I've seen in a long time."

Storm tilted her head.

"Wait," she said with a sly smile. "You're Roman Carter. *NY Fashion Magazine.*"

A corner of his mouth lifted. "I hope that impresses you."

"It surprised me when we first met," she said honestly.

"You mean when you almost spilled paint on my thousand-dollar shoes?"

"Let's not forget the almost part."

"I never will."

Dasha's hand flew to her mouth. "I knew you looked familiar."

Roman's gaze settled on Storm again.

"So," Dasha said, finding her voice, "what do you think about the place?"

His eyes swept the boutique once more. "Impressive. Bold without being overdone. Classy, but wearable."

"All of that in one take?" Storm said, meeting his gaze.

"I'm happy to look deeper," he said smoothly, "if you want."

Before Storm could respond, he glanced at his watch. "I won't keep you. You have a big day tomorrow."

"We do."

He pulled out a sleek black card and handed it to her. "After the opening, someone will be in touch to arrange a formal interview."

Storm glanced down.

Roman Carter

NY Fashion Magazine

Owner

She looked back up. "Thank you."

A smile etched across his face. "Your work deserves to be seen."

Then, just like that, he turned and walked out.

The bell chimed softly.

Silence.

Then Dasha squealed, grabbing Storm's shoulders. "Are you kidding me? Roman Carter was just here. In this store!"

Storm stared at the black card in her hand.

"Girl, why didn't you tell me you met him?"

"There wasn't anything to tell."

Dasha smirked. "Right. The way the two of you were staring into each other's eyes tells a very different story."

"We were not staring into each other's eyes."

"Please. There was enough chemistry between the two of you to light up this place if the lights went off."

Storm blurted out a laugh.

"Girl, you are a hot mess," she said as she walked over to the counter and placed Roman's card on top of it.

Storm's eyes drifted toward it.

She told herself it was professional. Her pulse disagreed.

Chapter Fifty-Three

"IT'S BUSY IN HERE," Storm said as she stepped into the shop, her arms weighed down with a bag of fabric.

Dasha barely looked up from the register, sliding a credit card through the reader. "Same as yesterday. And last week. And for the last two months, for that matter. I'm exhausted — like, I've never worked so hard in my life."

Storm smirked, setting her bag on the counter. "Must be the marketing."

"Absolutely. The stunning clothes you design help too," Dasha quipped, handing the customer a receipt. "Just a little."

Storm leaned against the counter, feigning humility. "Just trying to do my part."

Dasha rolled her eyes, though the grin on her face gave her away. They shared a quiet laugh before Storm swept a hand over the back of her neck.

"I cannot believe how hot it is," Storm said, fanning herself dramatically.

"You sound like me," Dasha shot back. "It's July, so it's supposed to be hot, remember?"

"No, it's supposed to be warm. Not skin-melting hot. I hate feeling sweaty."

"Well, brace yourself," Dasha said, amusement dripping from her voice. "It's about to get even hotter. Your boyfriend is about to walk in."

Storm straightened. "He's not my boyfriend."

Dasha snorted. "Oh, really? Let's see — you've gone out with Roman Carter at least ten times. In my book, that's called dating."

Storm grabbed a bottle of water, twisting off the cap. "And I call that a friend."

If Storm was being honest, it still surprised her how quickly Roman had become a regular presence — lunches, gallery openings, late dinners squeezed between deadlines.

It was a feeling she recognized.

With Isaiah.

Dasha didn't wait two seconds. "Whatever helps you sleep at night."

"It's the truth."

"Mmm-hmm," Dasha mimicked, eyeing her. "Then why are you blushing?"

"I'm not blushing."

"Sure. And I'm not the best marketing strategist in New York."

Storm sighed just as the shop bell chimed.

Dasha's grin turned smug. "Well, would you look at that. Your close friend is here — probably angling for his eleventh non-date."

Storm shot her a glare and turned.

Roman strolled in.

"Ladies," he greeted, his eyes lingering on Storm.

Dasha leaned close. "You're telling me that man is just a friend? Girl, please."

Storm ignored her.

Roman leaned casually against the counter, polished as ever in a charcoal suit, his top button undone just enough to be distracting. His ease made Storm wary.

It was a feeling she recognized.

With Isaiah.

"Busy day?" Roman asked, glancing at the fabric bag.

"Always," Storm said.

"She's been running all day," Dasha chimed in. "Barely takes a break. Someone should fix that."

Roman smiled. "Sounds serious."

Storm shot Dasha a look.

"All work, no play?" Roman asked lightly.

"I take breaks," Storm muttered.

Dasha scoffed. "You drank water ten minutes ago. That doesn't count."

Roman tilted his head. "Then I have a solution."

Storm arched a brow. "Do you?"

"Dinner," he said. "At my place. Tonight."

Storm's stomach flipped.

Dasha inhaled dramatically. "That sounds intimate."

Storm swatted at her. "Go organize the scarves."

Dasha winked and disappeared.

Storm crossed her arms. "Roman, I—"

"You're about to say we're not at that stage," he said.

She stopped. That was exactly what she'd been about to say.

He stepped a little closer. Not crowding her. Just enough to make her aware of him.

"We've had dinner plenty of times," he said. "Only difference is the location."

"That's exactly the point. Your place is… different."

His teasing faded. "It's just dinner. No pressure. No expectations."

She studied him. No smirk. No game.

He stepped back. "You pick the wine."

Storm laughed. "Oh, how generous."

She hesitated — then sighed. "Fine. But if your cooking is terrible, we're ordering takeout. You're paying."

Roman grinned. "Deal."

Dasha popped out. "I cannot wait to hear about this."

Storm groaned. Roman laughed.

It was the kind of laugh that settled into your chest and stayed.

Chapter Fifty-Four

STORM STOOD OUTSIDE ROMAN'S brownstone, breathing in the thick Brooklyn summer air before knocking.

The door opened almost instantly.

Roman stood there in a dark gray dress shirt, the top three buttons undone, sleeves neatly rolled up, a glass of red wine in hand. The look was effortless — the kind of casual that was clearly intentional. Relaxed. Confident. A man comfortable in his own space and skin.

For just a second, Storm forgot to speak.

"Hi," she finally said.

"Right on time," he said. "I like that."

She stepped inside, aware of how his eyes followed her.

She'd chosen her outfit carefully.

A fiery red dress, fitted through the waist with a soft side slit that revealed just enough movement when she walked. Her hair was brushed loosely to one side, soft waves framing her face. Gold earrings brushed her neck when she shifted, catching the light.

Roman's gaze flicked over her — not rushed, not careless.

Appreciative.

"One of your designs, I assume?" he said.

"It is."

Something like approval crossed his face.

His home was modern and warm — dark wood floors, shelves of books and vinyl, a white leather sectional, soft lighting. The kitchen gleamed with black marble and gold accents.

"You definitely hired a designer," she teased, needing something light to anchor herself.

"Guilty," he said. "But I picked the art."

She smiled. "Points for taste."

He gestured toward the kitchen. "Wine first?"

"Yes, please."

He poured two glasses, the soft sound of liquid against crystal filling the space. Storm leaned against the counter, watching him move — comfortable here, unhurried, like this space truly belonged to him.

He handed her a glass. Their fingers brushed.

"Red?" she asked.

"Red. Always. It forces you to slow down," he said. "You can't rush a good glass of red."

She took a sip. "I like that philosophy."

"Most people don't slow down enough to taste anything," he said. "Life included."

Storm studied him over the rim of her glass. "That sounds like experience talking."

He shrugged. "Trial and error."

They moved to the living room, settling into opposite ends of the couch at first. The city hummed faintly through the windows.

"So," she said. "How does a man like you end up cooking dinner instead of hosting at some impossible-to-get-into restaurant?"

A corner of his mouth lifted. "Because I spend most of my life in rooms where people want something from me. It's nice to be in a place where I don't have to perform."

Storm nodded.

"That, and the fact that I love to cook. My mother did as well," he added.

"Are you and your mother close?" Storm asked lightly.

His expression shifted — not sad, but thoughtful. More open.

"She was a seamstress," he said. "Worked out of our apartment when I was a kid. Clients everywhere. Fabric draped over chairs. Pins in places they absolutely shouldn't have been."

Storm smiled. "Sounds familiar."

"She worked nonstop," he continued. "People thought because she worked from home, it wasn't real work. Like she was playing dress-up instead of building a business."

Storm's chest tightened slightly. "That still happens."

"All the time," Roman said. "She'd take on impossible deadlines. Alterations overnight. Wedding gowns for women who barely said thank you."

"Why?" Storm asked quietly.

"Because she believed if she worked hard enough, people would finally take her seriously." He paused. "They didn't. Not really. But she never stopped trying."

Storm felt something shift. Not just respect — recognition.

"She taught me to see talent," he said. "Real talent. Not just the kind with fancy degrees and big names attached. She taught me that brilliance often looks like exhaustion to people who don't bother to look closely."

Storm swallowed. "That sounds like her legacy talking."

He met her eyes. "It is."

A beat passed between them.

"That's why your work stood out to me," he added. "It's not trying to impress. It's trying to build. I recognize that kind of ambition."

Storm looked down at her glass, then back up. "Most people just see clothes."

"I see intention," Roman said.

The air between them shifted — warmer now. Heavier.

"Come," he said gently. "Dinner's ready."

They stepped out onto the balcony.

Candles flickered. Fairy lights glowed softly. Salmon, roasted vegetables, rosemary, and garlic filled the air.

Storm took it in. "Okay. Now I'm officially impressed."

"That was the goal."

They ate slowly. Talked. Laughed. Shared stories.

Storm told him about Marist. About Dasha. About starting with nothing but sketches and stubborn hope.

Roman told her about New York in his twenties. About taking risks that almost broke him. About learning when to fight and when to walk away.

By the time they finished, something unspoken had settled between them.

After dinner, they moved back to the couch.

This time, they sat closer.

The space between them pulsed with possibility.

Roman leaned in.

Their first kiss was slow. Curious.

Then deeper.

Storm melted into it — just for a moment — before placing a hand on his chest and pulling back.

"Not that kind of girl," she said softly.

His smirk returned — different now. More intrigued. "Noted."

"You're not used to being told no," she added.

He laughed. "Fair."

"I don't think you've ever really been with someone," she said evenly. "Not the way it actually matters."

He studied her. "I want to date you, Storm. Properly."

She exhaled. "So, you're asking for something real?"

"That's exactly what I'm asking for."

He leaned in again — slow this time. A question, not a demand.

This time, she didn't pull away.

The kiss was softer. Deeper. Different.

Then Roman pulled back.

She blinked.

"Impressed?"

She smirked. "Maybe."

"I want this," he said quietly. "I want you."

She met his gaze. "Why me?"

He didn't joke this time. "I've never been in love. But you make me want to know what it feels like."

Storm held his eyes for a long moment.

"All right," she said finally. "Let's see if you're as serious as you think you are."

"For you?" Roman said, his voice low. "I'll be better than serious."

Chapter Fifty-Five

THE WARM AUGUST EVENING buzzed with energy as Roman and Storm strolled down the bustling streets of Manhattan. The air was thick with summer heat, but a faint breeze stirred, rustling the edges of Storm's dress. She adjusted the strap on her shoulder, glancing up at Roman as he walked beside her, exuding his usual quiet confidence.

"This show better be good," she teased, side-eyeing him. "Because the last time you picked, we ended up watching a play about two people staring at a fish tank for an hour."

Roman murmured a laugh. "It was art, Storm. You have to let yourself be moved by the experience."

"I was moved, all right. Moved to fall asleep."

He shook his head, grinning as he reached for her hand, intertwining their fingers. "Trust me. This one will actually have a plot."

"I'll believe it when I see it."

They reached the entrance of the theater, where a small but eager crowd gathered outside. Roman placed a light hand at her back as they moved inside.

As they found their seats, Storm glanced around, admiring the grand chandeliers and rich velvet curtains framing the stage.

"Okay," she admitted, leaning toward him. "This looks promising."

Roman smirked. "Told you."

She rolled her eyes. "Don't get ahead of yourself."

The lights dimmed. As the performance began, Storm found herself drawn into the story—but she was also aware of Roman beside her. The quiet intensity of him. The way he occasionally glanced at her, as if her reactions mattered just as much as the show itself.

Halfway through, he leaned in. "Enjoying it so far?"

She tilted her head. "I have to admit—you redeemed yourself with this one."

Roman laughed softly. "I always redeem myself."

She smiled, turning back to the stage, but the way he looked at her made her pulse quicken.

When the final act ended and applause filled the theater, Roman reached for her hand again. "Come on. I made late dinner reservations."

They stepped into the night, the warm air wrapping around them as they walked a few blocks to an intimate rooftop restaurant. String lights glowed overhead, the city stretching out below in a glittering sprawl of movement and light.

Storm exhaled softly. "You do have a way of making things… romantic."

Roman grinned. "I told you I'd be better than good at this."

As they settled in, a waiter poured their wine. Conversation flowed easily, the night stretching between them like something lifted from a perfect movie scene.

After a moment, Roman spoke. "We've spent the last few weeks having fun—but tell me something real. Something I don't know about you."

Storm hesitated, swirling her wine. "What do you want to know?"

He studied her. "Tell me about your last relationship."

She exhaled, setting her glass down. "You don't hold back, do you?"

"I don't see the point in games," Roman said simply.

She gathered her thoughts. "His name was Isaiah. We grew up together. He was my best friend before anything else."

Roman nodded. "And?"

"And..." Storm's lips curved into a faint, bittersweet smile. "We thought we'd always be in each other's lives. But sometimes, life has other plans."

"You still talk?"

"No." The word came out softer than she expected. "He left. I left. Our dreams didn't fit in the same place."

Roman leaned back slightly. "Do you still love him?"

She blinked, caught off guard.

"I told you," he said calmly. "I don't hold back."

Storm sighed. "I'll always care about him. He mattered. But our chapter closed a long time ago."

Roman nodded. "I get that."

She tilted her head. "What about you? Any long-lost loves?"

He gave a measured laugh. "No long-lost loves. Just short-lived ones."

Storm smirked. "Why doesn't that surprise me?"

Roman's voice lowered, playfulness edged with sincerity. "Maybe I just hadn't met anyone like you."

She held his gaze. "I bet you say that to all the women you take to Broadway shows."

He shook his head. "No, Storm. I don't."

She looked out over the city for a moment.

After a quiet beat, Roman spoke again. "You lost your mom, right?"

Storm turned back. "She died when I was born."

"I lost mine a few years ago. Cancer."

"I'm sorry."

He exhaled. "Losing her was a kind of loneliness I wasn't prepared for." His eyes lifted to hers. "That's part of why I don't take this lightly."

"Take what lightly?"

"You," he said. "Us."

Her breath stalled.

"I know it's early," Roman continued. "Maybe reckless. But I'm all in, Storm."

Her heart pounded. "Roman…"

"I know," he said gently. "But I won't pretend I don't feel it. Even if it's a first for me."

Storm stared at him, thoughts colliding in her mind. No one had ever spoken to her like that—so certain, so unapologetic, so present.

His certainty pressed gently against the walls she'd built.

Not breaking them.

But making her wonder how long she could keep them standing.

Chapter Fifty-Six

SNOW DUSTED THE SIDEWALK outside as Dasha locked up the shop for the night. She turned, shivering slightly, and called toward the back.

"Storm! Put that fabric down and come look at the snow. It's beautiful!"

Storm appeared in the doorway wearing a stark white evening gown that flowed delicately around her. The soft fabric hugged her curves, the silken hem trailing just enough that she lifted it lightly as she walked.

"What do you think?"

Dasha raised a brow, crossing her arms with a grin. "What, you were back there designing your wedding dress?"

Storm laughed. "Stop it. You know this is for my new spring collection. I'm already behind."

"Looks like a wedding gown to me."

"No one is getting married."

Dasha leaned against the counter, studying her. "But if he asked, would you say yes?"

The question wasn't new. Dasha had been teasing her about Roman since they'd made things official in July. But this time, it landed differently.

Six months.

Long enough to know she had real feelings for him. He was smart, charming, devastatingly handsome—fine, as Dasha would say.

He loved her openly. Without hesitation.

And she trusted him.

Completely.

"He does like things a certain way," Storm said lightly. "But I understand him."

Dasha tilted her head. "That's not what I asked."

Storm rolled her eyes. "Six months is not forever."

"My mother would disagree. She was ready to marry that last guy after three months."

"Your mother is… an exception."

Dasha snorted. "Which is why I avoid all that relationship mess."

"You say that, but one day you're going to meet some super-fine man and two months later, I'll be designing you a gown just like this."

Dasha gasped. "Two months? Have some faith in me!"

They both laughed, the warmth of years of friendship filling the shop.

"So," Dasha said, "where's Roman taking you tonight? You two have been inseparable since you officially started dating."

Storm groaned. "Stop with the air quotes."

"Seriously though. You've done everything in New York. What's left?"

"Who said we're staying in New York?" Storm teased.

Dasha's eyes widened. "Don't tell me he's pulling out that private jet again."

"I think we're flying to California for a fashion show. Just the weekend. I'll be back Sunday night."

Dasha whistled. "Must be nice. You sure you trust me to run things without you?"

"Of course. But have Mrs. Dungan's daughter come in again. Saturdays get crazy."

Dasha nodded. "California, huh?" A pause. "Isn't that where he is?"

Storm stiffened—just slightly.

"Isaiah," she said evenly. "Last I heard, he was touring in Europe."

"I can't believe you grew up with him. Every record he's put out has been fire."

Storm nodded.

"So... you still keep up with him?"

"No," Storm said quickly. "I just saw a post."

Dasha smirked. "Right."

"Stop giving me that look."

"What look?"

"That look."

Dasha grinned but let it go.

Storm checked her watch. Almost six. Roman's car would be at her place at seven.

"Come help me get out of this dress so I can get out of here," Storm said.

Dasha stepped forward, reaching for the zipper—then paused.

"Hey. What's that bruise on your back?"

Storm flinched, turning slightly. "Nothing. I was moving boxes the other day. One slipped."

Dasha frowned. "That looks like it hurt."

"It did."

For a second, Dasha looked like she wanted to say more.

But she didn't.

"All right," she said lightly. "Let's get you out of this dress before your crazy-rich boyfriend whisks you away to the West Coast—where your ex may or may not be."

Storm laughed. "Girl, stop."

"If this were a movie," Dasha said, "this would be the part where your past shows up right when your present gets serious."

Storm stepped out of the gown and reached for a red dress draped over a chair. "Good thing this isn't a movie."

Dasha shrugged. "Could've fooled me. Billionaire boyfriend. High-end fashion designer. Famous musician ex. Sounds cinematic."

Storm smirked. "You forgot the part where I work too much for unnecessary drama."

"Uh-huh. Just make sure your little weekend trip doesn't turn into one."

Storm slipped on her boots. "I promise it won't."

Dasha raised a brow. "Girl, your man looks at you like you're a limited-edition Birkin."

Storm laughed and tossed a pillow at her. "Get out."

Dasha dodged it easily. "Fine. But you better call me the second something interesting happens."

"Nothing interesting will happen. But if it does, you'll be the first to know."

"Here's a thought," Dasha added. "Instead of going home to pack, why don't you shop in your own boutique. Market that label."

Storm smiled. "Now that is excellent advice."

Chapter Fifty-Seven

THE CALIFORNIA NIGHT AIR was warm and inviting as Storm and Roman stepped onto the red carpet leading into the exclusive West Coast Elite Fashion Show. The sprawling glass-walled venue perched on the cliffs of Malibu offered an unparalleled view of the Pacific, its waves shimmering under the moonlight.

Photographers lined the entrance, flashes popping in rapid succession.

A stream of A-list celebrities, designers, and investors arrived one after another, each new face adding to the electric energy of the night.

Roman placed a guiding hand at the small of Storm's back as they moved inside.

The venue was breathtaking. Chandeliers hung from vaulted ceilings, casting golden light across sleek marble floors. Floor-to-ceiling windows framed the dark, endless ocean. The air carried the scent of expensive perfume and chilled Champagne. In one corner, a live jazz ensemble played a sultry melody that blended into the hum of conversation.

Storm wore one of her own designs—a midnight-blue gown that clung to her like liquid silk. The structured bodice cinched her waist before falling into a flowing train, the off-the-shoulder sleeves framing her collarbones. Her diamond earrings caught the light with every movement.

Roman, immaculate in a tailored black tuxedo, exuded effortless power. Though Storm had risen quickly, Roman was already a legend—his name opened doors before he even spoke.

As they moved through the room, Storm recognized faces she had admired for years. Julien Moreau. Elena Reyes. Miranda LaVelle. People who once felt untouchable.

Now, they were only a few steps away.

"I see someone I need to speak with," Roman said, releasing her hand. "I'll meet you at our seats."

"Wait here. I won't be long." His gaze softened. "You look beautiful. I should've said that earlier."

Storm smiled. "It's okay. I could tell your mind was elsewhere."

"I want this weekend to be special for you."

Before she could ask what he meant, he disappeared into the crowd.

Special?

"You're the woman everyone's talking about."

Storm turned to see Liam Sinclair—young, powerful, and unmistakably confident.

"I do my best," she said coolly.

Liam smiled. "Your best is redefining the game. I've seen your pieces everywhere. And I'm guessing the dress you're wearing is yours."

"It is."

"Stunning. Your work feels fresh in an industry that's gotten lazy." His gaze lingered. "You should be showing here."

"I design and sew every piece myself."

"That's rare. And impressive." He extended a hand. "I'd love to talk more. Maybe over dinner."

Before Storm could respond, Roman's arm slid firmly around her waist, pulling her in.

"She's spoken for," Roman said.

Not loud.

But unmistakably firm.

Liam's smirk deepened. "Of course. Strictly business."

Storm forced a polite smile. "Another time, Liam."

He lifted his glass in mock salute and moved on.

Roman's hand remained at her waist long after Liam disappeared.

The drive back to their hotel was silent.

Tight.

"You were enjoying it," Roman finally said.

Storm turned to him. "Enjoying what?"

"Him. Flirting with you."

Storm scoffed. "Roman, that's what happens at these events. Networking. Conversation."

"He wasn't interested in your designs," Roman said flatly. "He was interested in you."

"And even if he was?" Storm challenged. "That doesn't mean I was."

Roman exhaled sharply, dragging a hand through his hair. "I don't like men looking at you like that."

"You don't get to control how men look at me," Storm said, her voice measured. "This is my industry. Flirting happens. That doesn't mean I invite it."

Roman's hands clenched on his knee. "I expect you to shut it down. It's embarrassing."

Storm stared at him. "Embarrassing for who?"

She reached for the door handle.

Before she could open it, Roman's hand shot out and wrapped around her wrist.

Not crushing.

But firm.

Firm enough.

Storm froze.

The limo went still.

Roman's gaze dropped to her hand. To the skin paling beneath his grip. To the red mark already blooming.

He released her immediately.

"Storm..." His voice shifted. Quieter. "I didn't mean—"

Storm pulled her hand back, holding it protectively. "That hurt."

Roman ran a hand down his face. "I'm sorry. I shouldn't have done that."

She said nothing.

"I swear it won't happen again."

Storm studied him. Then looked down at her wrist.

Another bruise.

"Let's just go inside," she said quietly. "I need to put ice on this."

"I'm so sorry," Roman said again.

He leaned in and kissed her—intense, urgent. A silent plea for forgiveness.

She kissed him back.

But when his hand slid to the back of her neck, pulling her closer, Storm gently stopped him.

Roman searched her face.

After a moment, he nodded.

He understood.

Chapter Fifty-Eight

MORNING LIGHT SPILLED THROUGH the hotel suite's floor-to-ceiling windows as Storm stirred beneath the sheets. Warm sunlight brushed her skin—but it was the quiet presence near the window that pulled her fully awake.

Roman stood with his back to her, gazing out at the city below.

The crisp lines of his tuxedo were gone, replaced by gray pants and a white dress shirt. He looked composed, but the way his hands rested in his pockets, his shoulders held just a little too tight, told her his thoughts were far from settled.

"You're beautiful even when you sleep," he murmured.

Storm blinked against the light. "How long have you been standing there?"

"Not long." He turned to face her. His gaze softened—then stopped.

At her wrist.

The bruise stood out against her skin, deepening in color. A dull ache pulsed beneath it.

"It's just a bruise," Storm said quietly. "You scared me, but it will heal."

Roman crossed the room and sat at the edge of the bed, his hands braced on his knees. "It shouldn't have happened," he said. "I promise you, I'm not that kind of man."

"What kind of man?" Storm asked gently.

He exhaled, eyes dropping before lifting again. "My father… he put his hands on my mother. He was a drunk. A coward." His jaw tightened. "I almost killed him once."

Storm's breath caught. "Roman… I'm so sorry."

"One night he broke her arm," Roman said. "She tried to hide it. Said it was an accident. I knew better. The next night, I was waiting for him. I hit him so hard he dropped in the doorway. He left after that. Packed and disappeared."

Storm reached for his hand, threading her fingers through his. "You protected her."

Roman gave a hollow laugh. "She was angry with me. Said we'd starve without him. I got two jobs. I made sure she never had to depend on a man like that again." His voice dropped. "I swore I'd never be him."

"I know you're not," Storm said softly.

But his eyes drifted back to her wrist.

"I hate that I did that to you," he said. "I hate myself for it."

She lifted her hand and brushed his jaw, guiding his gaze back to hers. "I know you're sorry. I know you didn't mean it. And I believe you won't do it again."

He searched her face for a long moment. Then nodded.

Still, something lingered in his expression.

"Roman?" she asked quietly.

"I'm in love with you," he said. "That's why I lost control. I want everything between us to be perfect. I want to give you the life you deserve."

Storm felt the weight of his words settle in her chest.

She wrapped her arms around his neck. "I'm in love with you too."

He held her tightly, as if grounding himself in her.

Then, softly, almost casually, he asked, "Do you love me more than you loved him?"

Storm stiffened slightly. "Who?"

His eyes didn't waver.

"Isaiah?" she whispered.

"I didn't even have to say his name," Roman said quietly. "You were in love with him. I could tell."

Storm swallowed. "That was a long time ago. I've moved on."

He traced her jaw gently. "Then it should be easy. Tell me. Do you love me more than you loved him?"

There was something desperate in his eyes.

Needing.

Storm held his gaze. Then leaned in, pressing a soft kiss to his neck.

"Yes," she whispered. "I love you more. More than Isaiah."

Roman closed his eyes briefly.

When he opened them, something had settled into place.

Without a word, he stood and reached into his pocket.

Storm's breath caught as he dropped to one knee.

He placed a small velvet box on the bed between them.

For a moment, the room seemed to go quiet—as if the world itself had leaned in to listen.

"Then marry me."

Tears filled Storm's eyes.

"Yes," she whispered. "Yes, I'll marry you."

The words felt right.

Certain.

Final.

And still, Storm couldn't explain it—but the moment they left her mouth, another name surfaced in her mind.

Uninvited.

Unwelcome.

Isaiah.

"I knew it!" Dasha practically shouted through the phone. "What does the ring look like? Is it huge? I know it's huge."

Storm laughed, glancing at her hand. "It's a good size."

"That's not enough detail. How many carats are we talking?"

"Probably three. Maybe four."

Dasha gasped. "Four carats? Girl, can your hand even support that?"

"I'm managing."

"I'm officially calling you Mrs. Storm Carter."

"We're not married yet."

"Yet." Dasha laughed. "So where is Mr. Billionaire right now?"

"In his room. Business calls."

"Of course. Proposes, then goes right back to billionaire mode."

"You are ridiculous."

"Wait—his room? Separate?"

"Obviously."

Dasha sighed dramatically. "Can I be you when I grow up?"

Storm laughed. "I cannot with you."

"How was the shop?"

"Insane," Dasha said. "We need help."

"Then let's hire."

Dasha squealed. "Store Manager promotion? Raise?"

"We'll talk raises when I get back."

Dasha laughed. "Look at you—making billionaire moves."

Storm smiled.

But as she ended the call, her gaze drifted back to her wrist.

The bruise was darker now. Nothing she couldn't cover up.

Chapter Fifty-Nine

MORNING LIGHT SPILLED THROUGH the hotel suite's floor-to-ceiling windows as Storm stood by the glass, staring out over Los Angeles. She sipped her coffee, still reeling from everything that had happened.

The proposal.

The ring.

The dinner.

The way Roman had looked at her—as if she were his entire world.

It was overwhelming in a way she hadn't expected.

Behind her, Roman emerged from his connecting bedroom, already dressed in a crisp white button-up and dark slacks. He slipped an arm around her waist and kissed her temple.

"Happy Monday to my fiancée."

Storm turned with a small smile. "Morning."

"Are you ready?" he asked softly. "To start our life together?"

Her fingers traced his shirt absently. "Of course. It's just… a lot to take in."

"That's why I've been thinking," Roman said. "Why wait?"

"Wait for what?"

"To get married." He brushed his thumb over her ring. "We're already here. I have a friend with an estate in Beverly Hills. Private. Beautiful. We could have an intimate ceremony tonight."

Storm's breath caught. "Today?"

"Yes." His tone was calm. Certain. "We love each other. We're doing this anyway. Why not now?"

Her mind spun.

Roman watched her hesitation closely. "I know you'd want Dasha here. I'll fly her in. Whatever you need."

It was fast. Too fast.

He lifted her chin gently. "You love me, right?"

"Yes."

"Then be all in with me."

"I am all in."

"Then prove it," he said softly, his lips brushing hers. "Say you'll marry me today."

Storm swallowed. With Roman, everything always felt inevitable—like saying no wasn't really an option.

"Let me call Dasha," she said quietly.

Chapter Sixty

DASHA BURST INTO HER hotel room with a suitcase and a grin. “Girl, a private jet? I could marry a man like Roman if it came with perks like this.”

Storm laughed weakly.

“But honestly,” Dasha added, softening as she set the suitcase down, “I’m here for you. That’s what matters.”

They shared a brief, fragile laugh—the kind that barely covered what neither of them wanted to say out loud.

Then Dasha’s expression shifted.

“Storm… I love you. So I need to ask—are you sure this isn’t happening too fast?”

Storm forced a small smile. “I’ve thought about it. I love him. He loves me.”

Dasha studied her face. Not just her words.

“Okay,” Dasha said slowly. “If you’re sure.”

“I am.”

“All right,” Dasha said, trying to lighten the moment. “Now show me those carats.”

Storm held out her hand.

Dasha's smile vanished.

"Storm… what happened to your wrist?"

Storm's body went still.

Dasha gently reached for her arm, carefully pulling back her sleeve.

The dark, fingerprint-shaped bruise was unmistakable.

"And don't you dare tell me you ran into a door."

"It was an accident," Storm said too quickly. "Roman would never—"

"You know what every woman in an abusive relationship says?" Dasha cut in, her voice sharp with fear more than anger.

"Don't," Storm whispered.

"I will," Dasha said, softer now. "Because I love you. No man who truly loves you puts his hands on you like this."

Storm looked down, her shoulders curling inward.

"Tell me the truth," Dasha said gently. "That bruise on your back… that was him too, wasn't it?"

Storm swallowed hard.

"He pushed me into a wall," she whispered. "But he apologized. He cried. He said he lost control."

Dasha closed her eyes for a moment, steadying herself.

"And the next time?" she asked quietly.

"There won't be a next time."

"You don't know that," Dasha said. "There have already been two."

Storm pressed her fingers to her temples. "He grew up watching his mother get abused. He swears he'll never be that man."

"And yet," Dasha said softly, "here you are. With bruises."

Storm's voice broke. "I love him."

"I know," Dasha said. "But love doesn't leave marks."

The room felt heavy. Airless. Like the walls were pressing in.

"I won't watch you do this," Dasha said. "If you marry him, I'm done. I won't stand by and watch you disappear into excuses."

Storm looked up, her eyes shining. "You're giving me an ultimatum?"

"I'm giving you the truth," Dasha said. "Because I'd rather lose you angry than lose you broken."

Storm's throat tightened. After a long moment, she whispered, "Okay."

"Okay?" Dasha asked carefully.

"I'll talk to him."

"No," Dasha said firmly. "You leave him. Now."

Before Storm could respond, her phone rang.

She froze.

The name on the screen made her chest tighten.

May.

Storm's pulse spiked as she answered. "Hey—"

"Storm…" May's voice broke. "It's Darren."

Storm sat straighter. "What about him?"

"He passed away."

The world tilted.

"What?" Storm whispered.

"He had a heart attack."

The words didn't make sense. Not at first. Darren was solid. Constant. The one who always had a plan.

"I—I'm so sorry, May," Storm said, her voice shaking. "I didn't even know he was sick."

"It happened a week ago," May said softly. "I should have called sooner. It's just been… hard, Storm. Everything feels unreal."

Storm swallowed. Her throat felt tight. "I understand."

There was a pause on the line.

"The funeral is tomorrow," May said. "Will you come?"

Storm didn't hesitate.

"Yes," Storm said quietly. "Of course. I'll be there."

She ended the call, but the phone stayed pressed to her ear for a second longer, as if letting go might make it real.

The room felt too still.

Too quiet.

Dasha was the first to move.

Storm barely registered it at first—the sound of drawers opening, the soft zip of a suitcase. It wasn't until Dasha crossed the room with purpose that Storm looked up.

"I'll book flights," Dasha said. "You go to Chicago. I've got the store."

Storm nodded, but it felt like someone else was moving her head for her.

"I should've stayed in touch," Storm said. "Twelve years, Dasha. I let twelve years go by."

Her voice cracked on the number.

"That's not fair," Dasha said gently. "Life happened. You were a kid when everything blew up."

Storm shook her head. "I still should've called. Written. Something. Darren was always there for me when it mattered. Always."

Her throat tightened. "And I just… kept moving forward like he was frozen in time."

Dasha crossed the room and sat beside her on the edge of the bed.

"Grief doesn't run on logic," she said softly. "It runs on regret."

Storm pressed her lips together, nodding once.

After a moment, Dasha asked, "What about Roman?"

Storm stared at the wall. "I'll handle it."

Dasha studied her. "I don't trust that."

Storm turned. "What's that supposed to mean?"

"It means you avoid hard conversations until they become harder," Dasha said gently. "You always have."

"Please," Storm said, her voice thinning. "Just… drop it."

Dasha hesitated. "If you don't walk away now, you never will."

Storm's jaw tightened. "I said I'll handle it."

Dasha went quiet. When she spoke again, her voice was steadier—but heavier.

"If you marry him, I won't be there."

That landed harder than Storm expected.

She looked at Dasha, searching her face. "You don't mean that."

Dasha held her gaze. "I do. Because I won't stand by and watch you disappear into someone else's life while you're still running from your own."

Storm didn't answer.

She picked up her phone instead.

She needed to hear Roman's voice.

"Hey, baby," Roman said smoothly. "Everything's set for tonight."

The word *baby* felt wrong in her ear.

"Roman," Storm said. "I'm going to Chicago."

"For what?"

"Darren died. The funeral is tomorrow."

There was a pause.

"I'm sorry," he said. "But we have plans."

Storm closed her eyes. "I have to go."

"You have to?" His tone sharpened, just slightly.

"Yes."

Silence stretched.

"I'll come with you," he said.

"No." Storm glanced at Dasha. "I need to go alone."

A low laugh. Not amused. Not warm.

"Alone," he repeated.

"Yes."

"So the moment we decide to start our life, you run off?" he said.

"Darren was family," Storm said. "He helped raise me."

"Family," Roman said quietly. "Or him?"

Her chest tightened. "Not now."

Another pause.

"Fine," he said. "The jet will take you."

Storm stiffened. "Roman—"

"But when you come back," he continued, "we're getting married."

It wasn't a question.

Storm closed her eyes.

The words felt heavy in her mouth. Permanent.

"Okay," she said.

She ended the call before he could say anything else.

Dasha was watching her.

"We'll do it your way," Dasha said. "For now."

Storm forced a smile that didn't reach her eyes.

As she walked out of the room, suitcase in hand, the truth settled quietly in her chest.

Two storms were coming.

One waited in Chicago.

The other was waiting for her when she returned.

Chapter Sixty-One

THE CHICAGO SKYLINE CUT a dark silhouette against the pale winter morning as Storm stood by the hotel window, arms wrapped around herself, staring out at the city below. Snow clung to the streets, softening the harsh edges of sidewalks and buildings—yet everything still felt cold.

Empty.

She had stayed in this very hotel countless times with her aunt Sarah, back when she was a child. Back when the world had still made sense.

Storm sat on the edge of the bed, rubbing her hands together to chase the chill from her fingers. Her suitcase rested in the corner. The black dress she'd bought the night before lay folded neatly on the bed.

Her hands trembled as she reached for it.

She was going to a funeral.

Darren's funeral.

She hadn't seen him much since leaving Chicago all those years ago, yet his death pressed heavily on her chest, growing heavier with every passing second.

A tear slipped free.

Her mind drifted—to another room, another bed, another truth held in her hands.

The letter.

The letter that had changed everything.

She could still feel the paper beneath her fingertips. Delicate. Weighted. Her mother's final words pressing into her heart.

Love protects. Love sacrifices.

That was what her mother had shown her.

But now, looking down at the faint bruise circling her wrist like a tarnished bracelet, she heard Dasha's voice in her mind.

Love doesn't hurt. Love doesn't leave marks.

Storm blinked back tears and slipped off her engagement ring, setting it on the nightstand as if it weighed more than it should have.

She had thought she understood love—what it meant, what it required.

Now, she wasn't so sure.

The funeral had already begun when she arrived.

Storm paused just inside the doors of the funeral home, scanning the crowded pews. Most faces were unfamiliar. But at the front sat May, her posture straight, hands clasped, grief etched into every line of her face.

Storm's hands curled into fists.

She should have been here sooner.

She slipped quietly into a seat in the back row, letting the eulogy wash over her. The words blurred, her mind drifting between past and present, regret and grief.

Then—something pulled her gaze forward again.

Isaiah.

The breath left her lungs, sharp and sudden, like she'd been struck.

He sat in the second row, head bowed, hands folded tightly in his lap.

Even after all these years, she would have known him anywhere.

He was different now. Older. Broader. The boy she'd known had become a man whose presence filled space without effort. His hair was still cropped short, styled with the kind of ease that suggested he barely thought about it and yet somehow always looked perfect. His shoulders were wider, his posture marked by the quiet confidence of someone who had spent years on stages across the world.

But it was his face that undid her.

The same strong jawline.

The same unmistakable kindness in his eyes.

Fame hadn't hardened him. Success hadn't taken that away.

Then, as if he could feel her watching, he turned.

Their eyes met.

A moment passed between them—heavy with sorrow, regret, and a thousand things left unsaid.

Storm's fingers tightened in her lap.

She had spent years convincing herself that what they'd been was only a memory. That she had moved past it.

But in this moment, she knew that wasn't true.

Isaiah held her gaze just long enough to make her chest ache—then turned back toward the front.

After the service, Storm stepped outside.

The winter air cut into her skin, sharp and biting. She welcomed the sting.

Snowflakes drifted down, melting the moment they touched the pavement. She exhaled, watching her breath cloud and disappear.

"Storm."

She turned to see May standing beside her, wrapped in a thick wool coat, her expression tired—but warm.

"May..."

May squeezed her hands gently. "Thank you for coming."

"I wouldn't have missed it," Storm whispered. "I wish I had been here sooner. I should have stayed in touch. I'm so sorry."

May sighed softly. "Life pulls us in different directions. Darren would have been happy to see you here today."

The lump in Storm's throat dropped heavy into her chest.

"Come to the house," May said gently. "For the repast."

Storm hesitated.

The house. The memories.

Then Isaiah stepped past them, his coat draped over his arm.

His eyes met hers again.

Another silent moment.

Another weight pressing against her ribs.

"You should be with family right now," May urged.

Storm's hands trembled, but she nodded. "Okay."

May gave her a small smile and walked ahead.

Storm remained where she was.

Isaiah lingered.

For just a moment, his eyes searched hers.

Then, with a small nod, he turned and followed the others.

Storm released a shaky breath as she watched him disappear.

This was going to hurt.

More than she had expected.

Chapter Sixty-Two

THE HOUSE LOOMED BEFORE her, both familiar and distant—a memory frozen in time. The porch light flickered softly, illuminating the same welcome mat that had been there since she was a child. Inside, she could hear muffled voices and laughter—sounds of warmth, of family.

But tonight, they felt like they belonged to someone else's life.

Not hers. Not anymore.

Storm hesitated, fingers hovering over the doorbell. She had been here a hundred times before—but never like this.

The air felt thick with regret before she even stepped inside.

Before she could knock, the door swung open.

"Storm," May whispered, pulling her into a hug.

Storm exhaled into the warmth of her embrace, but the tightness in her chest didn't ease. Guilt wrapped around her ribs.

How had she let so much time pass? How had she let everything slip away so easily?

"I'm so glad you came," May murmured.

"Of course I came," Storm said softly. "What else would I have done?"

May pulled back, studying her face—searching for something Storm couldn't name.

"Come inside," May said gently. "You're always home here."

The words landed softly—and still managed to hurt.

Was she?

Storm crossed the threshold, her heels clicking softly on the wooden floor. The scent of vanilla and freshly baked bread filled the house. Laughter drifted from the living room, where friends and family swapped stories about Darren.

She took a breath. It didn't steady her.

And then she saw him again.

Isaiah.

Isaiah felt her before he saw her.

A shift in the air. A pause in the conversation. A pull in his chest.

Then he turned.

Storm.

She stood near the doorway, hesitation in her posture—but she was stunning.

Thirty looked good on her.

Her face had sharpened, her confidence woven into the way she held herself. But her eyes—those eyes—were the same. Always saying more than she let on.

She wasn't the girl he used to know.

She was more.

And yet… still Storm.

He had followed her success from afar. The boutique. The fashion world. The headlines. The interviews.

He had watched without ever stepping closer.

But seeing her now, it felt as though the years collapsed in on themselves. Like they were kids again, standing across a room, waiting for the other to speak first.

Neither of them moved.

Neither of them spoke.

And then May stepped in.

"You two, come with me," May said, looping an arm through each of theirs. "There's something in here for both of you."

Storm's pulse spiked as she was guided down the hallway, Isaiah's presence solid beside her.

Too close.

Too far.

Not close enough.

Not far enough.

"May—" Isaiah started.

"Enough," she said gently but firmly.

She pushed open the door.

Darren's office.

Dark mahogany shelves. The scent of old books and leather.

But it was the small, familiar shape on the desk that stole Storm's breath.

The teddy bear.

Her chest tightened painfully.

Isaiah stilled beside her, his brow furrowing.

Their childhood sat there.

Frozen in time.

"Darren kept this all these years," May said softly. "He wanted you both to have it."

Isaiah exhaled slowly. "He kept everything, didn't he?"

May nodded, pulling a worn scrapbook from the shelf and placing it on the desk.

Storm's hand flew to her heart.

Newspaper clippings. Magazine spreads. Photos.

Isaiah's sold-out tours.

Storm's fashion launches at Marist.

Side by side.

As if they had never stopped being connected.

Storm traced the pages with trembling fingers.

"I had no idea he kept all of this," Isaiah said, voice rough.

"He was proud of you both," May said, emotion thick. "Even when you thought he wasn't."

Isaiah looked down. "We fought before I left for California. He wanted me to go to college. To follow him."

His voice cracked.

"We barely spoke after that."

May sighed. "He was hurt. But he never stopped loving you. Never stopped being proud."

Isaiah swallowed hard.

"I'll give you two some time," May said quietly.

And just like that, they were alone.

Storm sat, running her hand over the teddy bear's faded fur.

Isaiah leaned against the desk. "I've missed you so much."

"I waited," Storm said softly.

"Waited?"

"That night. At the park." Her voice trembled. "I waited for hours. If you had come back… I think I would've said yes."

Silence.

Isaiah dragged a hand down his face. "But I didn't."

"No."

"Because I knew we were too young," he said quietly. "Too immature. I could see your pain—and instead of being there, I was focused on myself."

Storm's chest ached.

"That night made me realize I wasn't ready to love you the way you deserved."

A breath.

"But we did love each other, didn't we?" he asked gently.

"Yes," she whispered. "We did."

"And we let it go."

"Maybe we weren't meant to hold onto it back then."

"What about now?"

Storm swallowed. "We're different people now."

"How?"

She hesitated. "I'm engaged."

Isaiah went still.

The door creaked open.

"Isaiah, some of your father's friends are leaving," May said gently.

He nodded.

As he passed Storm, his eyes lingered.

This conversation wasn't over.

Chapter Sixty-Three

THE HOUSE WAS QUIET now.

The soft hum of the refrigerator filled the kitchen as Storm dried the last of the dishes. Exhaustion clung to her—not just in her body, but deep in her bones.

She set a plate into the drying rack when a soft creak of floorboards sounded behind her.

She didn't need to turn around.

Isaiah.

Just like old times.

She glanced over her shoulder. He leaned in the doorway, hands in his pockets, the top buttons of his dress shirt undone, sleeves rolled to his forearms. Relaxed—but guarded.

For a moment, neither of them spoke.

Then, without a word, he stepped forward, grabbed a towel, and started drying.

Storm blinked. A small, disbelieving smile touched her lips.

How many nights had they done this? Sneaking into the kitchen, whispering secrets, stealing cookies, laughing too hard and too quietly.

"You don't have to help," she murmured.

"I know."

He kept drying anyway—grinning.

They worked in silence until the last dish was put away.

"How long?" Isaiah asked.

"How long what?"

"How long have you been engaged?"

Storm's fingers tightened on the counter. "Since Sunday."

"Two days ago?"

She nodded.

"To whom?"

She hesitated. "Roman Carter."

Isaiah's jaw twitched. "I know the name."

"He owns *NY Fashion Magazine*."

Isaiah studied her. "And you love him?"

She forced herself to meet his eyes. "Yes."

He nodded—but something in his expression dimmed.

"You seeing anyone?" she asked.

"I'm not engaged."

"Don't do that."

"Do what?"

"Act like we weren't supposed to move on."

"I came to New York."

Storm's heart stuttered. "When?"

"Your last year at Marist. You were sitting on the steps. Jeans. Turtleneck. A girl with braids beside you."

"Dasha," Storm breathed.

"I watched you from a rental car."

"Why didn't you come to me?"

"I wanted to. I came to beg you to come back with me. But you looked happy. I couldn't ruin that."

Storm swallowed. "Were you in a black SUV?"

"Yeah."

"Dasha noticed it. Almost called the police."

He gave a soft, humorless laugh. "Guess I dodged that."

Silence stretched.

"I remember being your best friend," Isaiah said quietly. "It was the best time of my life."

"Stop," Storm whispered.

"What am I doing?"

"Going back to something we can't fix." She glanced at her watch. "It's late. I have to pack."

He reached for her hand.

Her breath caught.

"What happened to your wrist?" His voice sharpened.

"Nothing. An accident."

He studied her. "Storm—"

"I need to go."

"Stay," he said. "Leave Sunday."

"I can't."

"Why?"

"Roman is waiting for me."

"Meet me tomorrow," Isaiah said. "At the park."

"I can't."

"Please," he said quietly. "Just for a little while."

She should have said no.

She didn't.

"Okay."

Storm sat in her rented Lexus outside May's house. The porch light glowed faintly.

Her phone rested in her lap.

Roman, I won't be back until Sunday.

She didn't send it.

The phone lit up.

Roman.

"Hey," she said softly.

"Why haven't you called me?" His voice was clipped. "The funeral's been over."

"I went to the repast—"

"You were going to text me?"

"Roman—"

"Didn't feel like calling your fiancé?"

"I need to stay a little longer."

"How much longer?"

"Until Sunday."

"Sunday," he repeated.

"May asked me to stay," Storm lied. "She needs me."

Silence.

"And Isaiah?" Roman asked.

"He's leaving for Dallas in the morning," Storm added—another lie.

Another pause.

"Fine," Roman said finally. "If May wants you to stay, I won't fight it."

Relief flickered.

"But if you're not back Sunday," he added quietly, "I'll come and get you."

The words landed softly.

The threat did not.

Storm's grip tightened.

"I miss you," Roman said. "I want to start our life."

"I know."

"I talked to a therapist today," he added. "I won't ever hurt you again. I swear. I'm not my father."

Storm's chest tightened—hope and fear tangling in a way she didn't trust.

She closed her eyes.

"I love you," he said. "If you marry me, I'll be everything you deserve."

Everything you deserve.

Her wrist throbbed.

"You there, baby?"

"I'm here," she whispered.

Then the front door opened.

Storm looked up.

Isaiah stood on the porch, his gaze sweeping the yard—until it found her.

Even from a distance, she felt it.

"Baby?" Roman said.

"I'm tired," Storm said quickly. "Let's talk in the morning. I love you."

She ended the call.

Her eyes met Isaiah's one last time.

Then she pulled away from the curb and drove back to the hotel.

Straight into the storm.

Chapter Sixty-Four

STORM SAT CROSS-LEGGED ON the bed, the hotel room dimly lit by the bedside lamp. City lights flickered against the window, throwing fractured shadows across the walls. In her hand, she turned the engagement ring slowly, watching the diamond catch the light.

It was beautiful.

Flawless.

A promise of forever.

Her phone buzzed on the nightstand.

Dasha.

Storm hesitated only a second before answering. "Hey."

"Hey, yourself," Dasha said, gentle but alert. "How are you holding up?"

Storm exhaled. "It was hard, Dash. Seeing everyone again. Seeing him again."

"I figured. How was the funeral?"

"Emotional. Surreal." Storm closed her eyes. "It felt like I was walking through memories. Like time had folded in on itself. May, the house… Isaiah." She hesitated. "Especially Isaiah."

Dasha was quiet for a beat. "How did it feel? Seeing him?"

Storm bit her lip. "Like no time had passed. And like a lifetime had. Like we had nothing in common—yet everything."

Dasha sighed softly. "Storm…"

"I still have feelings for him." The words slipped out before she could stop them.

Dasha didn't sound surprised. "Of course you do."

"I don't want to."

"But you do."

Storm ran a hand through her hair. "Yeah."

A pause.

"What about Roman?" Dasha asked gently.

Storm's chest tightened. "He's seeing a therapist."

"That's good."

"He says he never wants to be like his father. He told me he'll never put his hands on me again."

Silence.

Not the comfortable kind.

Finally, Dasha said, "Storm… I don't doubt that he means it. But let me ask you something."

Storm closed her fingers around the ring. "What?"

"You told me once that trust is why things didn't work out with Isaiah. So tell me—how can you trust Roman?"

Storm's breath stalled.

"Can you ever fully trust that he won't hurt you again?" Dasha continued, her voice firm but loving. "Can you live with that fear under the surface of your marriage? Because this is what men say when they're scared of losing someone they've hurt. They promise. They cry. They swear it'll never happen again. Sometimes… it gets worse."

Storm didn't answer.

Because she couldn't.

And that was the truth.

"I feel like I should give him a chance," Storm whispered. "I didn't with Isaiah. I don't want to repeat that mistake."

Dasha exhaled sharply. "Do you hear yourself? You don't give a man who puts his hands on you—even once—another chance."

"Dasha—"

"Didn't you learn anything from what happened to your mother?"

Storm's stomach twisted. "That's not fair."

"What's not fair is watching my best friend explain away bruises like they're fixable. I love you. That's why I'm not being quiet."

Storm rubbed her face, exhaustion settling into her bones. The clock glowed beside her.

Almost ten.

"I need to go," she said softly. "I promised Isaiah I'd meet him."

Dasha sighed. "Fine. Go. But don't make me have to call him and tell him what's really happening."

Storm let out a tired laugh. "You'd need his number."

"Girl, please. I would stalk that man if I had to."

Storm smiled faintly.

"Go tell him the truth," Dasha said. "At least be honest with yourself."

"We'll see."

Storm ended the call.

The room felt too quiet.

Dasha's words echoed in her chest.

Didn't you learn anything from what happened to your mother?

Storm swallowed hard, staring at the ring in her palm.

Maybe she hadn't learned a single thing.

Chapter Sixty-Five

THE BRISK AIR NIPPED at Storm's ears as she made her way down the familiar path. Her heart pounded harder with each step—a rhythm that had nothing to do with the cold.

She stopped when she saw him.

Isaiah sat on the same weathered bench where they had once said goodbye. His long legs were stretched out, hands loosely clasped, his gaze fixed on the horizon.

He stood the moment their eyes met.

Without a word, Isaiah crossed the distance between them. He took her hand, wrapping his fingers around hers as if it were the most natural thing in the world. As if he had never stopped reaching for her.

"Come on," he said quietly.

He led her deeper into the park, past trees heavy with memory. When they finally stopped, Storm looked up—and froze.

Swings.

Brand-new, gleaming swings stood where there had once been nothing.

Isaiah slid his hands into his pockets, watching her. "You remember when you said this park always felt incomplete?"

Storm nodded, her throat tight.

"I put them in," he said. "A couple of years ago. The city wouldn't do it, so I did." He glanced at the empty swings. "It reminded me that without someone you love, everything feels like this place used to. Just space. A void."

Before she could respond, Isaiah stepped closer.

"There's something you're not telling me," he said gently. "I know you."

Her eyes dropped.

"Storm."

His voice pulled her back.

His gaze fell to her hand. "Where's your engagement ring?"

Her breath caught.

"You weren't wearing it yesterday either. Tell me why."

She swallowed. "Isaiah, I—"

"Please."

The words finally broke free. "He hurt me."

The world seemed to still.

Isaiah went rigid. His jaw tightened, his fists clenched at his sides—fury held tightly in check.

"That bruise on your wrist—was that him?"

Storm shook her head… then stopped.

"Yes," she said. "He did it."

Isaiah released a slow, controlled breath. "That wasn't the first time."

"No."

"You can't marry him."

Storm lifted her chin. "I didn't come here to be saved, Isaiah. I don't need a man to tell me how to live my life."

He nodded. "You're right. No one can save you. You have to save yourself." His voice softened. "But I can tell you this—you deserve better."

She folded her arms. "Better how?"

He stepped closer. "You deserve a love where the only touch you ever feel is a kiss, a caress, an embrace."

He lifted his hand.

His fingers brushed her cheek.

The contrast was devastating.

Gentle.

Reverent.

Safe.

Storm's breath stalled as his touch lingered—nothing like the grip that had left bruises.

Isaiah leaned in.

And then his lips met hers.

Storm melted into him, gripping the front of his coat as emotion surged through her. The kiss deepened—not desperate, not demanding—but full of years of love, loss, and longing.

When they finally pulled apart, Isaiah rested his forehead against hers.

"I still love you," he said quietly. "I always have."

Storm closed her eyes.

"Tell me," he whispered. "Tell me you still love me."

Tears burned.

"I love you," she said. "I never stopped."

Isaiah exhaled shakily, his fingers tightening around hers.

"Then don't marry him," he said. "Please."

Storm took a breath that felt like stepping into her own life again.

"I won't."

The moment the words left her lips, something shifted—like a door closing on the life she'd been trying to survive.

For the first time, Storm understood what real love was.

Not control.

Not fear.

Not bruises and apologies.

Real love felt like this.

Safe.

Chosen.

Free.

Chapter Sixty-Six

THE GRAND MARBLE FLOORS gleamed beneath cascading chandelier light in the vast hotel lobby. Elegant floral arrangements sat on sleek glass tables, their scent mingling with expensive cologne and freshly brewed coffee.

Guests drifted through—some pulling designer luggage, others sipping cocktails in the lounge—as Storm and Isaiah stepped through the revolving doors, hand in hand.

The weight of the past few days still lived in Storm's bones.

But for the first time, there was clarity.

She wasn't just walking away from Roman.

She was choosing herself.

Then a figure stepped forward from the shadows near the reception desk.

Roman.

He stood tall in a navy-blue suit, immaculate as ever. Not a thread out of place. But his shoulders were rigid. His expression too controlled.

His eyes dropped to Storm and Isaiah's joined hands.

"I guess I don't have to ask why you're not wearing your engagement ring."

Storm felt her stomach knot.

Isaiah's grip didn't loosen.

It tightened.

Storm didn't pull away.

"What are you doing here?" she asked.

Roman's jaw flexed. "You didn't call me this morning like you promised. That told me everything I needed to know."

Storm inhaled slowly.

Of course he came.

Roman Carter never waited. Never released control without trying to take it back.

He shot Isaiah a cold look.

"We need to talk," Roman said. "Alone."

Isaiah let out a low, humorless laugh. "That's not happening."

Roman ignored him. His gaze stayed locked on Storm.

"Come upstairs," he said softly. "Just you and me."

He reached for her.

Isaiah stepped between them.

"If you even think about touching her," Isaiah said quietly, deadly calm, "you're going to meet that floor up close."

Roman bristled. He wasn't used to being challenged—especially not publicly.

Storm placed a steadying hand on Isaiah's arm.

"Don't," she said gently.

Then she faced Roman.

"I'm not going upstairs with you," Storm said. "I'm not talking to you. There is nothing left to say."

His eyes darkened.

"Storm," he said softly—too softly. "You're making a mistake."

"No," she said. "The mistake was agreeing to marry you."

His lips pressed into a hard line.

Then he leaned closer, lowering his voice.

"I wouldn't have hurt you again. You know that. I love you."

Storm held his gaze.

"I believe you," she said. "I believe you think you wouldn't have. But here's what I finally understand—"

Her voice steadied.

"If you truly loved me, you never would have hurt me in the first place. Love doesn't hurt."

The silence that followed was heavy.

Final.

Roman's jaw tightened. Without another word, he turned and strode toward the exit.

He didn't look back.

Storm released a shaky breath she hadn't realized she'd been holding. Her legs felt weak—but she stayed standing, grounded in the choice she'd just made.

Isaiah waited until Roman disappeared through the revolving doors.

"You okay?"

Storm nodded, though her body still trembled.

Isaiah brushed his fingers gently along her cheek. "You were strong," he said softly. "That was all you."

She looked at him then—not as the boy she once loved.

But as the man who had always believed in her strength.

And this time, she knew the truth.

It wasn't love that saved her.

It was her courage.

Love simply stood beside her while she chose herself—and that made all the difference.

Epilogue

THE SOFTEST BREEZE WHISPERED through the trees, carrying with it the delicate scent of fresh blooms.

The park—the place where it had all begun for the two of them—was bathed in the golden light of a perfect spring afternoon.

It was to be a small wedding.

Intimate. Heartfelt. Everything Storm had always wanted.

Despite Isaiah's fame and her own success, they had chosen simplicity.

No grand ballrooms. No extravagant displays. Just them, their closest friends and family, and the place that had always meant something more than it appeared.

Storm stood at the edge of the aisle, her heart pounding as she took in the sight before her.

He was right there.

Isaiah stood beneath an arch wrapped in ivory roses and delicate greenery, waiting for her. He wore a tailored off-white suit, the crisp fabric accentuating his broad shoulders, his dark skin glowing beneath the afternoon sun. A silk tie in the softest shade of blue was the only touch of color, but he wore it with effortless elegance. His curls were slightly longer now, but it was his eyes—deep, warm, filled with a love so absolute—that made her breath catch.

May sat in the front row, a proud yet wistful smile on her face. She had been there since the beginning—through every tear, every triumph—and now, she was here to witness this moment.

Beside Storm, Dasha stood as her matron of honor, practically glowing. A knowing smile curved her lips—because, of course, Dasha had known everything before Storm had even admitted it to herself. But today, there was something else in her expression.

Love.

A glance at Liam Sinclair, seated a few rows back, confirmed it. The man who had once flirted shamelessly at a fashion show in California was now looking at Dasha as though she had personally climbed into the sky to hang the stars.

Storm would tease her about it later. She owed her for all those years of relentless teasing.

But for now, all Storm could focus on was this moment.

The life waiting just a few steps ahead.

She smoothed a hand over the fabric of her wedding gown, her fingers trailing over intricate floral lace. The strapless bodice hugged her frame, cinching at her waist before flowing into a mermaid silhouette. Sheer layers at the hem created a dreamy, weightless effect as she walked, while delicate white embroidery scattered along the tulle shimmered under the sun—as if the flowers themselves had been stitched from light.

She had designed this dress herself many months ago.

But only now, standing here, did she truly understand its meaning.

It was elegance. Strength. Resilience.

All woven into fabric.

Just like her.

She took a breath.

Then, she walked.

With each step, their eyes met and held.

When she finally reached him, his fingers brushed over hers—a silent reminder of all the years, all the moments, all the choices that had led them here.

"You're breathtaking," he whispered.

Storm smiled. "Isn't that why you're marrying me?"

A quiet laugh rumbled in Isaiah's chest, and just like that, the heaviness of everything—the past, the pain, all the what-ifs—softened into something new.

Something better.

The ceremony was simple.

Vows spoken not from rehearsed speeches, but from their hearts.

Words that meant something.

And when Isaiah kissed her—deep and slow, his hands firm around her waist—Storm knew.

This was the love she had been waiting for all along.

Not the kind of love that lived in the past.

But the kind that stood in front of her.

Beautiful. Certain. New.

A love without fear.

A love that had taken its time—and finally found its way home.

And she was grateful—not just for him, but for the woman she had become.

The reception was just as intimate, laughter and music filling the park as their family and friends surrounded them. But when it came time for their first official wedding photo, there was only one place they belonged.

The swings.

Storm sat on one, the layers of her dress cascading around her, her bare toes grazing the dirt beneath. Isaiah sat on the other, his jacket unbuttoned, his tie slightly loosened—looking every bit the man who had always felt most at home in simple, honest moments.

They reached across the space between them, their fingers lacing together.

From this moment forward, there would never be another empty swing.

Because together, they had finally found what had been missing.

And they would never let it go.

Support Resources

If you or someone you love is experiencing abuse, you are not alone, and help is available.

United States:

National Domestic Violence Hotline
1-800-799-SAFE (7233)
www.thehotline.org
Text: **START** to **88788**

If you are outside the United States:
Please consider contacting your local emergency services or a trusted domestic violence support organization in your country. Many international resources can be found through:
www.hotpeachpages.net

If you are in immediate danger, please call your local emergency number.

You deserve to feel safe. You deserve to be treated with respect, care, and dignity. Help is available, and reaching out is a sign of strength.

Author's Note

What Love Leaves Behind was born from a quiet question that stayed with me long after the first scene took shape: What happens to love when loss arrives without warning? And perhaps even more importantly—what remains after grief reshapes the life we thought we were living?

This story is not about perfect people or perfect outcomes. It is about ordinary individuals who are asked to carry extraordinary weight—grief that arrives suddenly, responsibility that feels overwhelming, and love that must find new ways to exist and endure. I wanted to explore how families are sometimes formed not through planning or intention, but through circumstance, courage, and choice.

At its heart, this novel is about resilience. Not the loud, triumphant kind, but the quieter strength that shows up in hospital corridors, late-night conversations, and moments when people choose to stay—even when staying feels impossible. It is about the ways we lean on one another when the ground beneath us shifts, and how healing often begins not with certainty, but with small acts of care.

I am especially drawn to the idea of chosen family—the truth that love does not always follow traditional lines. Sometimes it grows between friends, between strangers, or between people who never expected to need one another. These connections may not erase loss, but they can help us carry it.

If you found yourself lingering over certain moments, recognizing pieces of your own story, or feeling a quiet pull toward the characters' choices, I hope this book offered you both comfort and reflection. My deepest hope is that *What Love Leaves Behind* reminds you that while we cannot rewrite the past, we can choose how we move forward—and that love, in all its forms, has a remarkable way of leaving something meaningful behind.

Thank you for reading, and for allowing these characters to walk beside you for a while. Please don't forget to leave a review.

— **Marian L. Thomas**

Book Club Discussion Guide

These questions are intended to invite reflection, discussion, and personal connection. There are no right or wrong answers—only shared perspectives.

Discussion Questions

1. **Etta is drawn to Storm in a way she can't fully explain.** Do you believe in the idea of a deep, almost instinctive connection between people, even outside of biological relationships? What experiences or emotions do you think drive Etta's fierce desire to adopt Storm?
2. **James initially resists Etta's dream of adoption.** How did you interpret his hesitation? Did your feelings toward James shift as the story unfolded, and if so, what caused that change?
3. **Darren's grief is portrayed quietly but persistently.** How does the novel explore male grief and early fatherhood? In what ways did Darren's response to loss feel familiar—or unexpected—to you?
4. **Nurse May serves as a steady presence throughout the story.** What role does she play in the emotional journeys of both Etta

and Darren? How does her own past shape the way she shows up for others?

5. **The idea of "found family" runs throughout the novel.** How do Etta, Darren, and Storm each come to redefine what family means to them? Did this story challenge or affirm your own understanding of family?
6. **The letter discovered by Etta offers insight into Storm's mother.** How did this moment deepen your understanding of her choices and fears? What impact did it have on Etta's resolve to fight for Storm?
7. **Forgiveness—of self and others—plays an important role in the novel.** Which character's journey toward forgiveness felt the most difficult or meaningful to you, and why?
8. **The title, *What Love Leaves Behind*, can be interpreted in many ways.** What did the title mean to you at different points in the story? How did your understanding of it evolve by the end?
9. **Looking back on the novel as a whole,** which character's journey resonated with you most deeply, and what personal experiences or emotions made that connection meaningful?
10. **If you could ask the author one question** about the story, its characters, or what inspired it, what would you want to know?
11. **If you had to compare *What Love Leaves Behind* to two movies,** which would you choose, and what elements of the story make those comparisons feel right to you?

Suggested Wine Pairing

To complement the warmth, emotion, and reflective tone of *What Love Leaves Behind*, consider serving:

Pinot Noir – Soft, elegant, and expressive, with notes of red berries and subtle earthiness. This mirrors the novel's tenderness, emotional depth, and quiet resilience.

Non-alcoholic option: A **sparkling pomegranate or cranberry spritzer**, which offers brightness without overpowering conversation.

Book Club Menu Card:

https://tinyurl.com/bookclubmenucard

About the Author

Marian L. Thomas is the author of *What Love Leaves Behind*, a novel that explores grief, chosen family, resilience, and the quiet courage it takes to move forward after loss.

She is drawn to stories that center emotionally complex women, layered relationships, and the moments that change us—often in ways we don't expect. Her work focuses on the spaces where love, loss, and hope intersect, and on the strength women discover when life asks them to carry more than they thought they could.

Marian believes deeply in the power of storytelling to foster empathy, connection, and healing. Through her writing, she aims to create characters who feel real, choices that feel earned, and stories that stay with readers long after the final page.

What Love Leaves Behind is her latest novel.

To learn more about Marian's work and upcoming releases, visit: https://www.marianlthomas

Instagram: @marianlthomas09

Facebook: https://www.facebook.com/marian.l.thomas

TikTok: @authormarianlthomas

www.ingramcontent.com/pod-product-compliance
Lightning Source LLC
LaVergne TN
LVHW100515110826
845146LV00002B/646

* 9 7 9 8 9 8 9 3 9 7 9 3 8 *